Suttons Bay

Robert Underhill

Also by Robert Underhill

Strawberry Moon
Cathead Bay
Providence Times Three
Death of the Mystery Novel
Once Dead, Long Dead

Suttons Bay

Robert Underhill

Northport, Michigan

Suttons Bay
Copyright © 2013 by Robert Underhill
ISBN 10: 0-9798526-6-8
ISBN 13: 978-0-9798526-6-4

Library of Congress Control Number 2012937023
Underhill, Robert

Suttons Bay / Robert Underhill - 1st. ed.
p.cm
ISBN 13:978-0-9798526-6-4
    1. Crime - Fiction 2. Psychiatry - Fiction 3. Tarasoff rule 4.
Traverse City, Leelanau County - Fiction 1 - Title

Printed in the United States

Acknowlegements

Thanks to these friends for their generous help with this book: Jim Carpenter, Trudy Carpenter, Don & Kathy Frerichs, Phillip Mikesell, Kathleen Snedeker, Nancy Terfertiller and the Underhills, John, Michelle and Trudy.

For Griffin

"I'd make up some excuse to get him alone. Maybe open a couple of beers. Then, offhand I'd say, 'I understand you're screwing my wife.' I'd sip my beer and smile at him and wait. Brian would start to deny it, and then realizing I really did know, he'd try to play it real cool. 'So she told you,' he'd say. I'd shake my head. 'It was only a guess until you just confirmed it, asshole.' Then he'd be real pissed for allowing himself to be tricked like that. He'd snap back, 'Asshole? She's screwing me, so who's the asshole here? That's the reality my friend. Who's she opening those creamy thighs for?' Now he'd be laughing at me. I'd bring out my gun—the police special I told you I had—and say softly, 'No, this is reality,' and I'd shoot him in the balls. He'd be screaming in pain, so I'd wait `till he could hear me. 'The reality is you'd like to live, right?' He'd start begging for his life. 'Sorry,' I'd say, and shoot him in his fucking face."

I said nothing. I could think of nothing to say.

Harry Frey's chest heaved with emotion. He managed a sheepish smile and said, "Or something like that."

His vehemence had startled me. I tried my best not to show it, to be the neutral, unflappable therapist, but I knew I'd failed. I wasn't prepared for this. That's not completely true. I knew Marian Frey was having an affair with Brian Plante, a man Harry knew. I'd heard about it from another patient, and I realized there was always the chance Harry would find out too. But I'd never heard Harry like this . . . this violent.

I remained silent. When I did speak, the words would have to

1

be carefully chosen. I wondered how he had learned of the affair. The question must have shown on my face, because he said, "She's been acting oddly for a while. I'd wondered if something was going on, but then I'd dismiss the idea. Yesterday I learned the truth."

He paused and looked unseeing out the window, then at his hands, which he opened fully and then closed into fists. He sighed. I knew he didn't want to talk about it, but he couldn't help himself.

"It's so stupid. I feel like a character in a soap." He shrugged as if to say, hell let's get it over with. "Couple of weeks ago, I happened to comment—as we were driving by—on the new hotel on M22 just north of Tom's market. She said, 'Yes, the Windsor.' I know her so well and that's not the way she thinks. I mean she never knows the names of places she has no interest in. She'd be more likely to say, 'The new hotel with the green awning the color of my satin shoes across the street from the restaurant whose maître d' had a face lift in Mexico.' I'm also pretty sure she never looked at the sign before she spoke. The strangeness of her reply registered subconsciously but I didn't face its significance . . . until yesterday.

"My secretary usually brings me a sandwich from The Towne Plaza across the street from my office, but yesterday a friend wanted me to meet him at the Tuscan Grill north of town on M22. I'd just passed the new hotel when an approaching car caught my eye. It was Marian. I was surprised, because she'd told me at breakfast that she was meeting her bridge group in Northport at noon. She was going in the opposite direction."

He broke off, choked by sadness and anger.

I said, "Yes," more in acknowledgment of his feelings than to prod him on.

"It all came together like an equation that had been missing one number. Bam! I knew where she was going and whom she was meeting, even though I'd never consciously thought of the two of them

2

together before. I made a U-turn and pulled off onto the shoulder of the road and watched her park and go inside the hotel. Then, I drove into Tom's parking lot across the road where I had a view of the hotel door. She came out forty minutes later. Brian Plante came out five minutes after that. I wanted to run over him then and there—squash the bastard flat!"

Breathing heavily again, he shielded his eyes from my view.

"I'm sorry," I said.

He got control and looked up at me. "I haven't confronted her. Don't know what to say. Afraid of what I might do."

Harry Frey was a powerfully built man whose fists looked like they could break stone. He'd talked a lot during the past nine months about his childhood hatred of his abusive father and how he'd wanted to "beat him to a pulp" with those fists.

"You know I would really like to kill Plante. If I could get away . . . oh, shit." He buried his head in his hands.

Yes, I had to be very careful of what I said. I wanted to show empathy for his feelings, but I also wanted to maintain the kind of neutrality that makes it possible for a patient to say whatever he or she likes. In addition, I had to be careful not to reveal my prior knowledge of his wife's affair. That information, coming as it had from another patient, was confidential and therefore unethical to repeat even if appropriate. It would be easy to slip and make a mistake as Marian Frey had when she'd said, "Yes, the Windsor."

Another factor in my need for caution was that I'd been angered when I'd first learned about Marian and Plante. That anger— thank God I was aware of this—sprang from a personal source that had nothing to do with Marian Frey. So, I had to be wary now of coloring any comment about Marian with my own paints.

I let him talk and vent his rage toward the man he believed had ruined his life, only interrupting to clarifying his meaning from

3

time to time. I considered the likelihood of his carrying out his murderous thoughts and concluded there was none. At the end of the session, he appeared to have gained complete control of himself. I was congratulating myself on handling a difficult situation, when he turned at the door while leaving and said solemnly, "Thanks for listening to me, but I gotta tell you, if I ever catch the two of them together, I swear I'll kill them both." He closed the door firmly—not with a bang—but more like the rap of a gavel.

Harry Frey was my last patient before lunch, but I made no move to get up. I continued to sit and stare at the door. I had a sinking feeling a surgeon must have who can't stop a bleeder deep in an abdominal cavity. I quickly squelched this self-doubt, feeling it pass like a breeze that only disturbs the water's surface. I reassured myself about my assessment of the potential danger. Harry Frey was a very successful business man. His actions were governed by common sense and not raw emotion. The possibility of Harry acting on his feelings was really very remote. Harry, with all his bluster, was not a man to harm anyone. That happened to be a large part of his problem. He was so inhibited by fear of his own anger, which as a child he'd imagined to be powerfully destructive, that to have any angry feelings still led to paralysis rather than effective action.

I drew in a deep breath and let it out with a sigh, a sign, if I cared to notice, of the tension I was bent on denying. I got up and took my coat out of the closet. Putting it on, I glanced out of my office window that overlooks a bend in the Boardman River as it flows through downtown Traverse City. The river was unusually swollen and rapid after the heavy spring rains we'd had. The water's urgency matched my wish to get to my lunch date with my friend and fellow psychiatrist Derek Marsh and relate what had just happened, to be reassured about my judgement.

Outside, I stepped into one of those deceptive spring days.

The sun was bright but sudden cold winds swept across Grand Traverse Bay to shoot along Front Street. I turned up my collar and dug my hands deep into my coat pockets and began the three-block walk to Amical, thinking of Harry Frey with every step, ignoring the contents of the storefronts I passed, or the glances of people I met. Harry Frey: What effect would this new development have on the work in which he and I had been engaged? A current personal crisis bringing strong feelings with it can be useful. There was a lot about this situation with his wife that resonated with Harry's painful childhood experience, which could provoke old feelings to go along with those memories—feelings he had been able to effectively blunt in his therapy so far. The question was would the present crisis so capture his full attention that I'd have a problem getting him to look at, and make the connections with the past? When a child begins to run while passing a dark graveyard, there is no way he or she will slow down to a walk again until well past the place. I was afraid Harry Frey was already running.

2

Derek and I met for an early lunch every Wednesday—early, so we could get a desirable table. We rotated the venue among the downtown restaurants. Amical today, and I saw him seated at a rear table with the view of the river and bay. He was watching the swollen river churn by. As usual he was dressed for an audience with the queen.

"See anything interesting?" I said, taking the chair across from him.

"Just thinking that being a duck is hard work."

"You mean holding one's own against today's current?"

"Ah . . . right. You mean the ducks. For a moment there I thought you were commenting on the plight of contemporary Americans."

"Hey, I can understand your confusion," I said while unfolding my napkin, "since I usually begin our lunches with a profound philosophical observation."

Erin, the waitress, knowing our habits, brought a cup of coffee for each of us and interrupted our nonsense. "You can't go wrong with the lobster bisque today."

"Dare we argue?" I said.

When I made the decision to leave my position on the faculty at Wayne State's medical school and start a private psychiatric practice here, it was because of Derek's influence. He was a junior when I was a freshman in medical school, so we had little contact then. In residency training, however, he generously took on a mentor role with me. After he graduated he opened a practice in Birmingham, an upscale Detroit suburb, and married the daughter of a very rich holder of several automotive patents. This was still at the time when the American automotive world was powerful and the auto crowd the dominant social clique of southeastern Michigan. In short, he moved in a different circle than mine, but we still managed a dozen or so sets of tennis a year.

Derek hit a very rough patch six or seven years ago, when a couple of his patients charged him with sexual misconduct. He was totally cleared, but the social stigma proved to be so unsavory to his wife and her friends that she divorced him. Derek realized she was right about the social stain and decided to start anew in northern Michigan. Devastating as it was for him at the time, I believe the ordeal was the best thing that could have happened to him. He loves his life here, has a good professional reputation, has made many friends and has married a terrific woman. Donna is a cop, a Leelanau County Sheriff's deputy.

Erin brought our bowls of soup and we each agreed—with her standing over us—that it was possibly the best we'd ever tasted. When she left, I brought up the subject of Harry Frey.

"Remember a while back we discussed the problem of knowing something concerning a patient that he or she doesn't know about?"

"Sure. The example you mentioned had to do with knowing that the wife of one of your patients was having an affair."

"Right. And you reminded me that I would have an added problem with that situation, which, I've got to admit, I didn't want to be told about at the time."

Derek nodded slowly, and then realized why I was bringing the subject up today.

"He found out, right?"

Confidentiality is a sacred thing with us shrinks, but everyone has to have someone with whom he or she can discuss cases. Names, of course, are omitted and anything else which could identify the patient. Usually it is a case that puzzles, or when the wheels are threatening to come off the therapy.

"That's right," I answered, "He found out—but now there's more."

"More?"

"Just before I came here, he described in living color what he was going to do to the other guy. A pretty violent fantasy, castrating the guy before blowing him away—shooting him in the face."

"And you're worried that he will."

"No, no. I'm sure he was just giving vent to his feelings. This man has never been able to do anything when he's stepped on except apologize for getting in the way."

"Then why are you telling me about it before your third spoonful of bisque?"

He had caught me in a rationalization, but I persisted. "No, really. It's only because I'd told you about the situation earlier and, as I just said, you'd alerted me to the reason I might 'accidentally on purpose' slip up and tell him about his wife's affair."

I said this glibly. If only I could catch myself when I take on this tone, I'd save myself time and trouble, because it's a sure sign that I'm throwing up a smokescreen. The next best thing to having self-awareness is having a good friend who doesn't hesitate to point out the dodge.

"Sounds reasonable," he said nodding. "Too reasonable, in fact. What you just said was too neat, all the edges tucked in. I'm remembering what one of our professors used to say, 'Rely on your reading of what is not said instead of what is said.'" Derek then pushed an imaginary stack of chips to the center of the table. "I'm putting it all on 'He's worried that the patient will act on his words.'"

I chuckled. "OK, you win. There is a tiny bit of worry, but I also believe it is extremely unlikely he'd do anything."

"Maybe you're worried about the Tarasoff ruling."

"Tarasoff?" I was surprised, but of course I knew what he was talking about - the law that requires a therapist to warn the intended victim, if a patient speaks of his or her intention to do that person harm—especially if the intended harm is murder.

"No, no, I'm not worried about that," I insisted. "Never even thought of it. And anyway the law specifies a 'serious' threat and my patient's threat was only a fantasy."

Derek looked at me with a smug smile that said, "Who do you think you're kidding?"

"Eat your soup," I said.

He laughed, then I said, "You know you do that—try to promote gastric acidity. I'll bet you've got stock in Zantac."

"Peanuts. I've got all my considerable wealth poised to invest in the first really effective aphrodisiac."

"And about the Tarasoff law, can you imagine what the effect would be of calling up this guy's wife and her lover and warning them?"

"Good-bye treatment. But at least your patient couldn't sue you for breach of confidence. The law protects you in that case."

"Lucky me."

A dark figure was suddenly standing at our table. "The law protects you in what case?"

I looked up and had another gastric reaction. It was Gordon Pheney, or "Gorgon" as he's known among the psychiatric nurses at Munson Hospital. He saw himself as morality's gift to psychiatry. Without being invited, he took the empty chair next to me.

I noticed a malicious glimmer in Derek's eyes. "You'd be interested in this, Gordon, being Chairman of the Ethics Committee. Tom was just posing a hypothetical question—arising out of his reading—that concerns the action one should take when a patient, who has just discovered that his wife is having an affair, speaks in confidence to his therapist about his plan to kill said wife along with the guy who has fouled his nest."

Pheney straightened, obviously stimulated by this opportunity to render a moral judgment.

"There is no question here at all. The therapist must immediately notify the wife and her . . . ah, friend . . . and the police."

"What?" I croaked, incredulous. "Not the police, surely."

Gordon was offended by my failure to accept his pronouncement without question. Society has a tendency to empower persons like Gordon, individuals who imagine they possess special expertise while we, busy with our lives, and wanting to avoid unnecessary trouble, all too readily go along with their delusion.

"The bit about the police," Derek put forward in an even tone, "Some might think that would be going rather far. Don't you think that the treatment alliance would be strained beyond repair?"

Gordon had been stung by my reaction and Derek's point. He became reckless in replying. "You guys think you know everything. It so happens that the state statute MCL 330.1946 spells out exactly what a psychiatrist must do. He or she must notify the intended victim and the police. This stuff you're so concerned about, bullshit like 'therapeutic alliance', is all about endlessly looking for reasons instead of dealing with the here and now. Thank God you've had your day. This passive liberal psycho-crap is finally where it belongs, flushed. Flushed! Call the police. The guy will be put where he can't hurt anyone and given Haldol. That's real treatment—the kind that gets results." He brought his fist down on the table hard enough to cause my spoon to jump out of the bowl.

I said, "You know, Gordon, you're beautiful when you're angry."

Yes, I knew I'd gone too far, but the devil made me do it. Gordon vaulted out of his chair and stalked away without looking back, his body language continuing to reject us all the way to the door.

"It will be ages before he forgives you for that," Derek said.

"You're right, I went too far, but look at it this way. I probably did old Gordon a favor. He got a self-righteous chance to put us wimps in our place."

I'd had enough of Gordon Pheney and changed the subject. "Have you and Donna got plans for the weekend?"

"Not that I know of. I need to clean up the vegetable garden. Get ready for planting. How about you?"

"Mainly, I'm going to work at finishing my unpacking in my new place. Get settled finally."

"Donna and I are anxious to see that new place. Actually to be truthful, we're really interested in seeing Crawford Croft's old place. There is something unwholesomely secret about the way you've been holding back on an invitation."

Derek was right; a couple of occasions had passed where it would have been normal to invite them over, but I wanted the famous artist's former pad to be presented at its best.

"Secretive? Yeah maybe, but in the way a woman is secretive about her preparations to seduce you."

Derek laughed. "Can't imagine why this came to mind—maybe the word 'seduction'—but weren't you planning to ask Audrey Shaw for a date?"

"Oh that," I replied with feigned nonchalance. "It happens that I have a date with her tonight."

I couldn't maintain the pose; a broad smile took over my face. Derek was well aware of my interest in Dr. Audrey Shaw. I'd become immediately taken with the beautiful and talented woman the moment I first saw her. She'd moved here last summer from Chicago where she'd been on Northwestern's psychiatric faculty. Derek and I wondered at her decision to move to the relatively pastoral setting of Traverse City, since the word was out that she was upward-bound in national psychiatric politics - in other words a high powered, big city kind of girl. Then we discovered that she was writing a book with her

11

former mentor, the renowned Dr. Laslo Bach, who had retired to a new home on Lake Michigan just north of the village of Leland. So I expected that her term of residence here would last as long as it would take to finish and publish the book. That forecast now seemed to be quite wrong, since she had thrown herself into serious involvement in our community, securing a place on the local symphony board and assuming the chairmanship of an ambitious fund raising campaign for the Leelanau Conservancy. Although my interest advanced from "taken with" to "infatuated", I was stymied in advancing my interest, because I'd heard at the time she'd first moved here that she was seriously involved with a guy back in Chicago. Turns out that was not the case, and her inviting manner with me should have told me so. It took months for that erroneous information to be corrected for I am one of those who is the last to be told rumors and gossip. I seem only to come by that kind of personal information by accident. Consequently I was long overdue asking her out. She'd declined that first time pleading a prior professional obligation. Her tone had been one of true regret and her manner said, "Please try again." So, I did.

"Terrific," Derek said. "She really said yes?"

"Don't sound so surprised. I shower daily and . . . "

"I'm kidding. She'd be a fool to say no and she's certainly not that."

Erin brought the check and took away our cards.

"But getting back to your problem," Derek said when we were out on the sidewalk, "I'm afraid you're in a bind."

"How's that?"

"About the guy who threatened to kill his wife and her lover. You are in a bind. The same one we're all in if that's any consolation. Our best clinical judgment may turn out to be wrong. You're sure a patient will do one thing and he or she goes and does another. Unfortunately, those who then get to judge you will be using a different yardstick."

"Hey, very reassuring! Go to lunch with a friend for a little relaxation and conversation, then leave and jump off a bridge."

"I'll always be there for you, friend," he said putting his hand on my shoulder. "I'll stand at that bridge and say, 'There jumped a man. When jumps such another?'"

"Now that is reassuring. By the way, which of our professors was it who said that bit about listening to the thing that is not said?"

He pondered the question a moment. "Ah . . . Come to think of it, my older brother said that. It was when I'd asked him how to talk to girls."

3

Back at the office, I struggled through the afternoon appointments, thoughts of Harry Frey tugging at the edge of any attempt to concentrate on my other patients. I was relieved when time came to lock the door and drive home—my new home.

When I moved to Traverse City two years ago, I rented an apartment on Midtown Drive and immediately began looking for a small house on one of the wonderfully shaded streets near downtown. Not many came on the market and I was about to settle for less than I'd hoped for, when Crawford Croft died. I managed to buy his home. "Managed" is the operative word. I just managed to come up with the down payment, and my having the opportunity at all to acquire it was another example of management, or, to be accurate, skullduggery. My attorney, Stanley Kramer, was the executor of Croft's estate and should have handled the settling of it in an open and impartial way. Instead, I got a call from him telling me that he had submitted a bid on my behalf for the property and the bid had been accepted. Yes, I could have raised a question, but instead I went to view what I'd bought—what the bank and I had just bought.

Croft, as everyone knows, was an internationally famous artist and certainly this area's all-time most famous citizen. The building he owned is a two-story former warehouse overlooking the harbor on Grand Traverse Bay just across the city limits in Leelanau County. The date July 4, 1911 is carved above the front door. Croft fashioned the upper floor of the building into his living quarters and used the first floor as his studio. Later, when his canvases took on museum-grade proportions, he moved the studio to another building and rented the

14

lower floor to a wine wholesaler, who, I'm happy to say, was still there providing a tenant to help pay the mortgage.

I guess we all owed a lot to old Crawford. He was the artist most responsible for leading the art world out of the quagmire of post-modernism toward a new statement of the possibility of a rational society. I'd read that in a catalog at the only exhibition of his work I'd seen. Whatever that all meant, as I surveyed my new digs for the first time, I believed it. The same catalog called him, "the greatest American artist in the last half of the twentieth century." This has caused me to feel a reverence for my new home, as if I were the privileged owner of Freud's couch.

I managed to put Harry Frey and his threat out of mind by concentrating on the remaining unfinished work of unpacking books and putting them on the loft's unique assortment of shelves—ten books here, twenty there—with the idea of getting Audrey back here after our dinner date. Bringing her here was not about what you may be thinking. That idea was way ahead on another square of the board. I was hoping her sure fascination with Croft's digs would rub off on me.

OK, you've spotted a measure of insecurity. This originates in two sources. The first is that I'm very serious about wanting her to like me. All of the dates I've had since my divorce have been "friendly outings", devoid of any emotional investment on my part. This hasn't been a conscious intention, but it's a fact. Perhaps I've been protecting myself from a kind of hurt that I'd found out I didn't handle too well during my divorce. What I feel about Audrey is different—seriously different. Part of that difference, I've realized, was a growing readiness to look again for a life partner. The second reason for my insecurity— she is a very formidable person. Beautiful: she's straight-on gorgeous, large eyes the color of rich Dutch cocoa, and engaging mannerisms like tipping her head down and looking at you with those eyes upturned, creating a feeling of shared intimacy. Smart: I heard she'd gotten a BA with honors from an Ivy League school at eighteen and was AOA at Harvard Med. Athletic: the story is she was a member of the U.S. team at the 2002 winter Olympic games in Salt Lake City. I hadn't heard what event. Ambitious: there was nothing overbearing about her attitude, nevertheless you knew she was on a mission, like the friend who has dedicated him or herself to the goal of running in the Boston Marathon. Your friendship remains unchanged, but part of their mind is always focused on the run: diet, hours on the road and advice in runners' magazines. I figured there was no way she wouldn't become president of both the American Psychiatric and the American Psychoanalytic Association, and that's only on the way toward whatever her next goal would be.

And, what about me? I'm afraid my credentials are pretty pedestrian by comparison: good grades, but no honors, tennis enjoyed with my friends, but no trophies. Ambition? I have none beyond trying my best to help my patients. Oh yes, my looks. I have been admitted to all public events, most private parties . . . and some beds.

I finished showering and shaving and slouched into the soft leather chair Croft had placed at a window overlooking the harbor, a glass of Johnnie Black in my hand and the Ray Brown trio playing off to my left. Adding encouragement for the night ahead was a slogan carved into the window's lintel—hence impossible to ignore—that read, "It's all up to you, Bud."

Audrey's interest was sure to be tweaked not only by Croft's having lived here, but also because the place is unique. He designed the interior to dictate the experience one must have. This window, for instance, was placed at the end of a declining, funnel-shaped enclosure several inches lower than my direct view, causing me to have to look down on the harbor scene below. Instead of viewing a panorama of sky, the hills of Old Mission Peninsula and the sailboats out in the bay, he was making me focus on the detail of the action on the dock and

16

around Biddle's Grotto, the rustic, seafood restaurant at the dock's end. The restaurant had turned on the string of colored lights that runs around the eaves and I could see the shapes and shadows of the people working inside. Two guys wearing aprons came out onto a side deck off the kitchen to take a cigarette break. A waitress arriving for the night shift laughed and returned some playful remarks they'd made to her. The big view, the panorama, was from my loft's roof terrace, but here in the chair, it was life around the docks. Up there it was the global scale, here the human scale. The human scale must have been what I needed, because watching the easy way those down there interacted, reminded me that my plans for the evening were among life's natural pursuits.

I'm not a beginner. Like I said, I've been married and divorced. In fact, it was that experience that complicated my knowing about Marian Frey's affair. Cora and I had met in medical school, I was a senior, she a freshman. We fell very much in love. I went into psychiatry and she into surgery. We spent long hours apart, our clinical rotations taking us in different directions. She met a fellow surgery resident who was there at hand and paid her the attention she was missing from me. They got involved. I found out. She wasn't remorseful enough . . . I felt. That's the outline.

"Damn!" I said out loud. "I forgot the wine."

This morning, when I'd checked to see what I had on hand for this evening should Audrey agree to return here, I discovered the cupboard was bare. Antonio Salpino, my tenant downstairs, had supplied Croft with wine at wholesale and offered me the same courtesy. I'd stopped by this morning on my way to the office to give Mr. Salpino ("Call me Tony") a list to cover all possible requests. I'd forgotten to pick up the damn wine! I rushed to a window that overlooked the parking lot and saw what I'd feared—it was empty. Tony and his crew had gone home. Damn! Now I'd have to go shopping on my way to pick her up. I'd planned to open a bottle of Mawby's Sandpainting, but now it wouldn't be cold.

I hurriedly finished dressing, remembered to take the note with Audrey's address in Suttons Bay and opened the door to the stairway. There on the threshold was a cardboard box. I flipped back the flaps—my complete order and a note. "Tom, thought you might need this tonight. Good luck. Tony." He must have knocked while I was in the shower. The carton was full, but it felt light carrying it to the kitchen where I put the champagne and a bottle of chardonnay in the refrigerator. My heart was light, I was ready; I had Crawford Croft and Tony Salpino in my corner.

A while back I was driving on County Road 643 just north of Cedar looking for the address of an estate sale, which listed one of Bill Perkins' great twig rockers. I'd come to a driveway with a sign, "Zillertal." No address or anything about an estate sale, but judging by the last address I'd passed, Zillertal figured to be the place I was looking for, so I drove in. The long, climbing and wooded driveway ended in a parking lot beside a large white, frame house. A broad view of Lake Leelanau faced me when I got out of my car. Again, now over the door to a glass enclosed porch, the sign, "Zillertal." The door opened before I got to it. A smiling, young woman wearing an apron said, "We open at 6:30."

With estate sale still on my mind, I must have had a very puzzled expression. "Open?" I repeated.

Reading my confusion she added, "You don't know that this is a restaurant—right?"

"A restaurant? No, I didn't."

"We've only been open a couple of months. If you can make it, come back at 6:30, it's very good. Austrian food," she said with a German accent.

"You're Austrian?"

She laughed at my slow comprehension. "Yes, my grandparents

own the restaurant. I make the desserts. I'm Gaby."

"Terrific. I'll be back tonight."

I went on to find the right address and buy the chair, but I then doubled back that evening to have one of the best meals of my life. I thought it likely that Audrey hadn't been here yet, so I counted on it as another ace up my sleeve.

I drove the fifteen miles north to Suttons Bay and parked in front of Audrey's apartment building in one of the angled spaces. As she'd instructed me, I walked up to the first of the four building entrances and pushed the button for her apartment number. My heart rate knew more about my hopes for the evening than I'd let myself admit, which was a problem, considering the calm, confident person I wanted to project. She buzzed me in and I climbed to the second floor. She had one of the units at the back that overlooked the marina.

Approaching her door, no trace of my morning apprehension about Harry Frey remained.

The door was flung open.

"Hi, come on in. I'll be just a minute."

I was viewing a different Audrey. Instead of a business suit, she was wearing black slacks, black sweater and a silver down vest. Instead of the professional restraint her usually tightly pulled back hair implied, it was now loose, shoulder-length, swinging free, bouncing as she skipped down the steps ahead of me.

Walking towards the car she said, "If we're going to Martha's we could walk."

"Martha's is an excellent idea, but I have another place in mind tonight."

In the car, she sat on her left leg, turning in the seat to face me.

"So where are you taking me?"

The question struck deeply right into basic male/female stuff, not "Where are we going?", but "taking me", as in "Take me!" It took

19

conscious effort to concentrate on backing out of the parking space. As I shifted my Miata into first, I realized I hadn't bothered to check for traffic before I backed out.

"Ah, well that's a secret," I said.

She laughed. "Turn myself over to you; no questions asked? I can do that."

I was getting dizzy. I mustn't let my imagination run wild here. I scanned my brain for bland topics.

I turned left off Suttons Bay's main street onto the highway toward the village of Lake Leelanau and said, "Nice apartment you . . ."

"I know where we're going," she said. "Bella Fortuna!"

"Another excellent idea, but another time."

"I give up," she laughed.

"I was saying that you have a nice apartment right there on the marina."

"Yes, as you say. In the summer, the deck serves like a front porch in a small town. I can sit, sip a drink and watch all the action around the marina."

My thoughts looked for a way to continue an easy conversation about summer and boats, when she took the reins and switched to shop talk, starting with observations on the politics of the local psychiatric community, and then becoming focused on the national organization, speculating on who would likely head up this committee or that. At that moment, aroused by her nearness, these issues were as relevant to me as who would win the mayoral election in Schenectady. I interrupted her a couple of times by commenting on something we were passing on our drive, which she politely acknowledged, then returned to her subject.

"Do you know Frank Soble well?" she asked.

"Yes, but not well."

"I offered to help him edit the Medical Society's newsletter. He initially sounded interested, but he never contacted me. What do you think that means?"

"Is that so?" A safe answer. I didn't say that I thought the newsletter was Frank's own little fiefdom and that he wouldn't welcome sharing it with anyone.

"I had experience running a newspaper as an undergraduate. I think I have some ideas for the newsletter that the membership would like."

I was sure she had, and I was also sure Frank thought so too. I saw an opportunity to shift the subject.

"What college paper was that?"

"The Daily Herald, Brown's student paper."

"You were a journalism major?"

"No. I was premed. I joined the paper to meet people, interview important people who came to campus."

No moss growing on this lady. "You're from the East?"

"My parents were living in Washington when it came time to start college."

"And medical school?"

"Harvard."

"Why Harvard?"

She laughed, "Because it was there."

For an ambitious student, it was the hill to climb, but unlike Edmond Hillary, who couldn't top Everest, I figured she had many other peaks in mind.

We had reached the driveway to Zillertal. "And psychiatric residency?" I asked.

"Stanford. I had decided I wanted to live on the west coast. As you may know, I also graduated from the San Francisco Psychoanalytic Institute."

Yes, I did know. We got out of my car and she admired the

view and we made small talk about the restaurant as we climbed the stairs to the entrance.

"Gut eefning. I'm happy to see you are returned so soon," the grey-haired proprietress greeted me. "And gut eefning to you my dear."

Trudy Weitzl led us to a table by the window. I watched Audrey's eyes sweep the hunting lodge-like décor, noting the many small deer antlers mounted on one wall. On each mounting plaque was written the date the deer was shot. I'd been told on my previous visit that they were antiques from Austria, the European deer being a smaller species than our white tails.

Trudy and a tall Sikh named Sanji handled the ten tables, while Josef, her husband, and an apprentice cooked. The granddaughter, Gaby, as I'd been told, did the desserts. Together, they made what had to be a difficult act seem as effortless as Clayton Johnson catching a pass.

"Grey Goose on the rocks," Audrey responded to Trudy's question.

"I'll have the same." Not usual for me, but . . .

The moment Trudy turned away, Audrey said, "So, can I recommend you to Ben Moss for the Program Committee?"

It was the committee of the national organization she was talking about. She had sprung this idea on me during the drive here. It was clear she'd thought it through already. As I understood it, being appointed to this committee was not just a matter of making your interest known. It was considered a plum by the high rollers. If she thought, as she apparently did, that she could give the word and it would happen, then another rumor I'd heard about her was true; she was Moss's pet and he was grooming her to succeed him as chairperson.

We were at different places in our professional lives. I was five years older than she. I had come to terms with the fact that I really preferred working one-on-one with my patients. Period. I loathed committee meetings and organizational politics. I was telling myself that she was still young; she'd mellow, catch a few brass rings and then tire of the merry-go-round. After having put in a full day in her office, she'd find herself having to go back out on a cold winter night to a committee meeting and she'd envy me sitting by our fireplace reading a good book.

"That's a prestigious committee," I ventured. "Doesn't one usually make a more modest start?"

"If tenderloin tastes better, why order flank steak?"

Now, that was very quotable. She was not being cautious with me—a good sign.

"Let me think about it. I've just moved into a new place and have a lot to do to get settled in and . . ."

"You don't want to be on the committee, do you?"

How to respond? I didn't want her to lose interest in me. I tried humor.

"OK, you've unmasked one of my tragic flaws, I'm not a committee man."

She didn't laugh. "Why do you think that is?"

I made as if to ponder. "Genetic?"

"You puzzle me, Tom Morgan. There are many things about you that suggest that you are a normal, upwardly mobile creature like the rest of us, but then unexpected abnormalities show up."

"Really?" I gasped and studied my hands for evidence.

She laughed and drank some of the vodka Sanji had brought. "All right, but you're missing out on a great opportunity."

Sure, I thought, opportunity to travel across the country to listen to endless debates about things in which I had no interest. But, I could also hear a promise in her proposal. She liked me—with some modifications. It occurred to me that this was a critical moment in our relationship and therefore maybe in my future life. Would I be written off if I continued to seem alien to her interests? It would be next to impossible to regain the status I enjoyed at this moment. But, if I went along, wouldn't I be betraying myself? Definitely . . . but I wanted her too much.

"On second thought, I'd like it if you spoke to Moss on my behalf."

"Great." She took a lusty swallow of the vodka. "You won't be sorry." There was unmistakable promise in her tone now. I could feel our relationship move up to a new level. Like climbing on the back of a friend's Harley, I was unsure about the outcome, but I was aboard for the ride.

Trudy brought a sweet squash soup with cranberry relish. She poured a Dry Creek Valley Zinfandel.

"We have a mutual problem," Audrey said.

I did the raised eyebrows.

"The Freys," she said and looked for my reaction.

"Ah, the Freys," I agreed. I had thought earlier about the possibility that she'd bring this subject up. You see, Audrey was the person who'd referred Harry Frey to me. She was treating Harry's wife, Marian, and had told her that it sounded as if her husband also needed to be in treatment. Marian heard this to mean that Harry was the one with the problem and promptly put it to him that her therapist thought that if he didn't agree to therapy, the marriage was as good as dead. Harry hurried right over to my office. Because of the source of the referral, I have to admit, the success of Harry's treatment had an additional importance for me.

According to Gordon Pheney, I should have told—warned— Marian about Harry's threat to kill her and Plante. If so, shouldn't I also have told her therapist? Now here's where it got very complicated. If I told Audrey of Harry's threat, I would not only be breaching a confidence with my patient, I would also be tossing a stinking problem

24

into Audrey's treatment of Marian. She would become obliged to tell her patient. If it turned out to be a false alarm—as I was sure it was—Audrey would not appreciate the needless and destructive disruption of Marian's therapy. At the very least I'd look like a stupid alarmist. If, on the other hand, Harry did do some dumb aggressive thing and Audrey came to know that I'd had knowledge of the possibility here tonight and hadn't warned her . . . well.

"I have to tell you something about the Freys," I said. "I assume she's told you about her involvement with Brian Plante." I looked to her for confirmation.

She nodded. "Yes."

"Well her husband found out yesterday - saw them going into a hotel."

"Ouch." She shook her head, "When she first spoke of her interest in Brian Plante, I questioned her action in a way that left no doubt that I thought she was looking for trouble. What did Harry say?"

"What he said was very dramatic, but what he felt was sadness."

"Dramatic?"

"He said he'd kill them if he discovered them together, but . . ."

"Shit!"

"But he wasn't serious. It was more like, "I'll kill her if she runs out of gas again.""

She thought about this a moment and said, "You're sure?"

"As sure as one can be about what someone else will do."

"There's the Tarasoff thing, you know."

"Yeah, but wouldn't a warning really screw things up for no cogent reason?"

"You can say that again," she agreed.

I decided not to tell her about Harry's description of how he'd shoot Plante. She'd hear that as very serious, no matter how I qualified it.

"Is Harry planning to confront her?" she asked.

"He didn't say."

"Trouble ahead - marriage trouble I mean."

"I'll know more tomorrow; I see him at my Suttons Bay office at eleven."

"I'd appreciate . . . ah, guidance . . . after you see him."

I nodded as Sanji removed our soup bowls and Trudy served rabbit loin with braised endive, spatzle and lingonberries.

We ate in silence for a while. Sanji came by and refilled our glasses. Audrey began to study the room.

"Probably most who dine here would think those are some pretty pitiful antlers mounted on that wall," she said. "They are roe deer, the small deer one hunts in Austria and thereabouts. I can see the date on the nearest one, 1732. No doubt that one was shot on some nobleman's estate. Back then, the common guy had to poach. We did that," she laughed. "Not poached, but hunted on a nobleman's estate – east of Vienna – Baron von Schornstein."

I was taken aback. The most remote picture I could imagine was this thoroughly feminine creature shouldering a rifle.

"You hunted?"

She smiled at my surprise. "Yes, a lot – my father and I. He was an army colonel and we traveled a lot and hunted where ever we went and whatever there was to hunt. I loved it."

I grew pensive. What would this mean about our relationship? I was not a hunter. I hadn't fired a gun since I was an early teen when we shot at tin cans with a 22.

"What are you thinking?" she asked.

"I was thinking that I couldn't remember hearing many psychoanalysts talk about hunting."

Her laugh was explosive. "You're right. One would be more likely to hear the Vestal Virgins talk about orgies."

"And I can't remember a single president of the APA who was a hunter."

"No, and you never will, because this confession stays right hear at this table. Right?"

"Right." I was very pleased. She had just let me know - included me in a secret – about two very intimate facts about herself: she was an avid hunter and she had confirmed an ambition to become president of the APA.

"How about other members of your family? Did you hunt together?"

"I am an only child, and no, my mother hated the idea of hunting. It was something Dad and I shared. He, of course, taught me all the lore and skills. He had excellent credentials. He won an Olympic bronze in the winter pentathlon. It shocked the Europeans, who had a lock on the event. You see it includes cross-country skiing, shooting, downhill skiing, fencing and horseback riding. We Yanks weren't strong in any of those at the time."

"How'd he pull that off?"

"He was a good downhill skier and rider, but he'd never fenced until he took some lessons a month before the games. So those scores cancelled each other out. Then the two cross-country favorites came down with the flu."

"Way to go!"

She was enjoying the telling of the story and my excitement. "Still, he wouldn't have made it to the podium if it weren't for his shooting, which was almost perfect, the highest score ever recorded up to that time."

I fell back in my chair, flooded with the feeling of victory, just as if I'd been there that day.

"I wasn't there, of course," she said, a little disappointment in her voice. "I may have been a glint in my father's eye, however, because

27

my parents had met by then. Anyway, I finally benefited by all he taught me about . . . well, about everything he could do well."

My glance went to the mounted antlers. "You've shot some of these, then?"

"Oh yes. And if you hear any local deer hunters scoffing at their size, remind them that these deer make smaller targets and they're quicker than white tails."

"I'll remember."

Trudy put a dish of apple-fig latke in front of each of us and also a glass of dessert wine, compliments of her husband, who had been told how much we seemed to be enjoying our meal.

The date, to this point, was to my mind a roaring success and the evening was young.

I awoke in the leather window chair. After I'd taken Audrey back to her apartment, I'd returned and sat in the chair trying to make sense of the evening, and I'd fallen asleep. I opened my eyes to see activity out on one of the docks through a fine misty rain. I got up to take a leak, then grabbed a blanket and returned to the chair.

I'd been dead sure when we left the restaurant that we'd come here, have a glass of the Mawby champaign and then hop into bed. Instead, she'd wanted a tour of Croft's house. She was especially interested in a piece of sculpture that came with the place and compared it with his other work, etc, etc. . . . etc. She passed on the bubbly and had another vodka. Once we'd settled on the sofa, Moss's committee and the various points of view of the members became her topic. She was again surprised and disappointed to discover how far I was from being current on the subject. I hurriedly reassured her of how diligently I was going to apply myself to catching up. This restored harmony. To help things along, I invited Wynton and his dad to join us. She dispensed a few very warm kisses, and responded to my exploratory caresses .

. . and then remembering that she had been forced to make an early appointment with a patient the next morning, she was on her feet. Before I could comprehend what was happening, she was already at the door.

It hadn't been my plan for the evening to turn toward the sexual, but her intimacy had surprised me, and this was spring and this young man's thoughts had not been turning toward baseball. Perhaps she had sensed that I was surrendering to the season and her early departure was intended to re-establish the appropriate stage for our relationship, seeing that the host was beyond maintaining it through the rest of the champagne and a few more kisses.

What the hell, all in all I gave our first date high marks.

4

Thursday was one of the two days each week I use my Suttons Bay office. Like many physicians in this sparsely populated corner of the state, I must resort to the marketing ploy of proximity—make myself available. I sublet from a travel agent, John Patrick, who was happy to rent out some unused space. Compared to my T.C. office, it was cramped. But with the vertical blinds pulled open there was a view eastward over the water of Suttons Bay, creating an illusion of space. I only worked until noon here, seeing just four patients, then it was back to T.C. to a clinic run by the hospital. Harry Frey had the last appointment. He had been in the back of my mind all morning: had he confronted his wife, and what had happened if he had? And behind these questions was the main question; had I misjudged his potential for violence? No, I told myself once again; he would be here in a few minutes full of his usual self-doubt, apologizing for his outburst in my office during yesterday's session. Then why was I tense?

Wait a minute. My reaction to this situation was way overblown. Actually, there was no situation. Had the malpractice bug bitten me? I'd seen physicians I knew succumb to its dreaded bite, going against their better judgment and many times against their patients' best interest just to cover their own asses. I soberly considered the question. No, malpractice wasn't my concern. Like it or not, I had to admit that my uneasiness emanated from uncertainty. Could I really be so sure what Harry would do?

My ten-fifteen patient was Mrs. Fleming, not someone to see when one's attention was deflected. She had been an adopted child and watched people closely for signs of flagging interest, a sure sign to her of impending abandonment. With this keenly in mind, I managed to put thoughts of Harry Frey on hold until she left.

Usually Harry was a few compulsive minutes early, but not today. I glanced through a magazine that lay on the desk, really just turning pages, reading nothing. I looked at my watch. It was twelve minutes past eleven. I opened the door to the waiting room just in case I hadn't heard him enter it. No Harry Frey. I returned to my chair and stared out the window, restlessly drumming my fingers on the desk.

At eleven fifteen, I decided he wasn't coming. As I sat waiting, my mind shifted to Audrey and last night. I'd learned much about who she was: her experiences, her outlook and her sense of humor. I'd liked what she'd shown me. There was good chemistry - except for her interest in politics and maybe that was my fault. Maybe it was a sport I'd also enjoy if I allowed myself. I didn't know how hunting would fit into our future, but if she didn't demand that I join the NRA, I was cool with it.

I had an urge to talk to her. I'd agreed last night to look up a journal article for her and I'd taken the time this morning to do that before I left home. It gave me an excuse to call her now. I had her cell number, her only phone, in my phone, so I dialed it. It rang several times and I was about to hang up when she answered breathlessly.

I said as a chatty opening, "I hope I didn't interrupt something."

"Treadmill," she panted. "Got home from seeing a patient a while ago and jumped out of my clothes and onto my treadmill to catch a few miles."

I couldn't think of anything witty to say about treadmills. Part of my brain was occupied picturing her jogging in the nude. After too long a pause, I told her I'd looked up the article she'd wa' think she'd forgotten all about it, but did a good job of preten' remembered.

"I'm happy you called. I wanted to tell you tha'

evening very much."

Any leftover annoyance with her sudden departure melted away. "We enjoyed the evening also, Croft's ghost and I. I hope you'll pay us another visit soon."

"Alone with two men?"

"Actually there'll be three of us; I'm picking up my cat, Kato, today. He's been staying with a former neighbor until the turmoil of moving settled down."

"I hope he'll find the place as interesting as I did. Oh, I just remembered, you were going to give me a status report on Mr. Frey after you'd seen him."

"Right, only Mr. Frey happens to be late for his appointment. We're talking on his time as a matter of fact."

"I'd still like an update when you see him."

"Sure."

I would've liked to have returned to the pleasant small talk before she'd asked about Frey, but I could pick up a note of her wanting to get back to her jogging or showering. I rounded the exit off fairly effectively and hung up feeling good. I hummed "Isn't It Romantic?" as I got my coat from the closet.

The phone rang and I answered it hoping Audrey had thought of something sweet she wanted to add.

"Doctor Morgan?"

It was Harry Frey and there was terror in his voice.

"Mr. Frey, what's the matter?"

"Doctor . . ."

I could hear him crying.

"Mr. Frey, what's happened?"

"They're both dead."

"What do you mean? Who?"

"Marian . . . Marian and Brian."

My God, he'd done it! Done what he . . .

"How? How did they die?"

"Shot . . . I . . ."

"Mr. Frey, where are you?"

"At home," he sobbed softly.

"Are you alone?"

"Yes."

"Have you told anyone else?"

"No. Only called you."

I knew where his home was, just six or so minutes away on the road that runs around the small bay that gives the village its name.

"Stay right there. I'll be there in a few minutes."

Every bad feeling ran through me at once. Some was concern for Harry Frey, but a good part, I'm not pleased to have to say, was for myself. I'd made a gross error. Two people were dead because of my mistake and the whole world would know this. I had to put that out of mind and concentrate on the best thing to do at the moment. The police should be called. Should I wait until I saw him to call them? Should I try to contact Donna, Derek's wife? I needed her to be involved; she was a sergeant with the County Sheriff's Patrol. I'd wait until I was nearing Harry's house to call. I wanted some time to speak to him alone.

I ran from the building to my car and looked up Derek's name on my cell phone's contact list before starting the engine. I shot out of the side street onto St. Joseph Street turning south causing an approaching car to do a nose-stand. I found myself behind a car with an Illinois plate driving slowly, a man and woman peering with total interest at each storefront they passed. A steady stream of cars oncoming lane - probably heading to the Indian casino nortꞌ - made it impossible to pass. I reached my emotional redꞌ on my horn. I could see the driver's startled and puzꞌ rearview mirror. He moved his car over a few reflex inches away from the mad man behind him. I shot past and accelerated for a quarter mile, and then swung hard onto Stony Point Road. I pressed the button on the phone. I desperately wanted Derek to answer and hoped by some miracle Donna was nearer to Suttons Bay than their home, a good forty-minute drive away. Derek answered.

"Derek, it's Tom. Is Donna at home?"

"No, why?"

"I need to talk to her and I don't have time now to explain. Is there somewhere I can reach her?"

"She took Frieda to our vet's."

"Where is it?"

"On 204 near Sheriff's Headquarters. Leelanau Veterinarian Care. I can give you her cell number."

Thank God! I knew the animal hospital he meant and it was only ten minutes from the Frey house driving at the speed I'm sure Donna would drive.

"What's up, Tom?" Derek asked.

"Tell you later. Gotta make that call."

At the entrance to Harry Frey's driveway, I stopped and dialed the number Derek had given me. Donna answered.

"Donna this is Tom Morgan. I need your help."

"Sure Tom. What's happening?"

"A patient of mine named Harry Frey just shot and killed his wife. I'm on my way to his house right now. I'm going to call 911 . . . I wanted you to know, ah . . . to be part of the uh . . . "

"I understand. Where is the house?"

"It's on Smith Road, the continuation of South Shore Road across the bay from Suttons Bay" I looked at the sign at the end of the driveway and read off the number.

"How do you spell his name?" she asked calmly. I recognized

34

her attempt to quell the panic she heard in my voice.

"F-r-e-y."

"You don't need to call 911. I'll take care of it. And don't go into the house until a deputy gets there. I should be there in ten minutes."

"Thanks." I felt I should say more, but she had already hung up.

Harry's house, at the end of a long drive, was built on the slope of an orchard-covered hill that ran down to the bay. The trees were just coming into blossom, normally a joyful sight, but not today. I was only vaguely aware of the wall of white blossoms on each side of the driveway. My thoughts were focused on what lay ahead. I had never seen the house and my mental image taken from Harry's comments in our sessions was unlike what I now saw, a long, single-story building that seemed to be backing into the hill that rose behind it.

A car was parked near the front walk. I pulled up, jumped out and ran to the door and opened it. At that same moment I heard the sound of tires on the gravel driveway. The police had arrived, no doubt a deputy on patrol nearby. I had only a moment to talk to Harry alone. I walked quickly into the foyer, calling his name. I heard a response to my left and looked and saw him standing at the end of a long hallway.

I ran to him. "Where is she?"

He pointed to a doorway a few feet farther along the hall. I brushed past him, aware of the biting odor of burnt gunpowder. Before the police would be able to detain me, I was compelled to see the woman who was dead because of me. Marian Frey lay on the large bed, nude except for a wide, gold choker. Bright blood covered her ample breasts. In the left breast, I could see a single bullet hole. Her long, rich red hair was spread freely across the pillow.

Sitting on the floor, legs extended toward me, back against the foot of the bed was the nude body of a man. His genitals were a bloody, mutilated mess. What had been his face—now a gory, featureless cavity—made it impossible to recognize him . . . but I knew who he had to be.

5

"Put your hands on top of your head," commanded a voice behind me. His voice, tense, carried his own fear of a dangerous situation. He patted me down with one hand. I knew his other hand held a gun and I did not move a muscle.

"You do this?" He said sharply, staying behind me.

"No. I'm the one who called the . . . called Sergeant Marsh. I'm Doctor Thomas Morgan."

I hoped the "doctor" rendered me less criminal. I heard another person enter the room.

"It's alright, David," I heard Donna say to the deputy, "I know this man."

She came forward and knelt beside the body of Brian Plante and felt for a carotid pulse, mere routine, since it was obvious he was very dead. The same went for Marian, yet Donna repeated the task. She was out of uniform, wearing jeans and a sweatshirt.

Harry had done exactly what he'd said he'd do if he caught his wife and Plante together.

Donna stood up and came close. "Is that your patient in the hall, Tom?"

"Yes."

"He told you he shot them?" she asked quietly.

"Yes, he called me at my Suttons Bay office and then I called you."

"Tom, I'd like you to sit in one of the other rooms and wait for me to finish here. I'll need to ask you a few questions."

I was happy to leave that room. I was experiencing that gutted feeling that comes with a sudden elevator drop. Ahead, down the hall, I saw Harry sitting in a straight-back chair, bent forward and holding his head in his hands. Donna must have stepped into the hall behind me and signaled to the deputy standing next to Harry, because the guy motioned to me, pointing toward the doorway of a room across the hall from where Harry sat.

He said, "Have a seat in that room, sir," and then he walked a few feet away to talk to a newly arrived deputy.

I took a few steps to where Harry sat. I leaned down and asked, "Have you spoken to any of the police?"

He looked up surprised, as if he'd forgotten I was here.

"Ah, no. No one has talked to me."

"Don't. Don't say anything to anyone. What is your lawyer's . . ."

"Please go into that room," the deputy said again, pointing to the room where he'd told me to wait.

I bent closer to Harry's ear. "Don't say anything, not a word until I get an attorney for you. They'll ask you questions, what you did and so on. Say only that you won't talk until you first talk to an attorney. Understand?"

He understood and nodded.

The deputy came over and pulled me away with a measured force and guided me into the room that was furnished as a study. He stood over me until I was seated in a leather armchair. At first he closed the door and then he probably thought it wise to be able to check on me, so he reopened it a few inches. Others started to arrive and a general hubbub followed. I got my phone out of my coat pocket and dialed the number of my attorney, Stanley Kramer. Stanley's secretary answered.

"Mrs. Booth, this is Dr. Morgan. I need to talk to Stanley right away. It's an urgent matter that can't wait."

She must have heard the fear and urgency in my voice, because

Stanley came on the line immediately.

"Tom, What's up?"

"Big trouble, Stan. A patient of mine just murdered his wife and her lover . . . Brian Plante. He needs a good lawyer fast."

I thought that I too was going to need legal help just as fast.

"Brian Plante! No shit."

"Yeah. I told my patient to say nothing to anyone until he had a lawyer."

"When did this happen? How did you manage to speak to him?"

I ran through a complete description of everything that had happened since Frey called me.

He was silent for a moment, absorbing what I'd told him, and then said, "Holden Cutler is our man. I'll see if I can reach him. Call me later." He hung up.

Several times different people opened the door wider and gave me an inquisitive look. I felt very uncomfortable docilely sitting there, especially since my adrenal glands had just pumped a quart of adrenaline into my bloodstream. What I'd just seen in that bedroom, I'd never seen before. Sure, I'd witnessed serious trauma during my medical training days, but that was in the context of an emergency room, not a bedroom—not a patient's bedroom! And with all the terrible mutilations I'd seen, I'd never seen a man's genitals blown apart. The thought of it made me queasy.

Only then did I begin to notice the details of the room I was in. Even in my distracted state, I discerned something discordant. The chair I was in couldn't be more stereotypically male. Every traditional male sanctuary featured a few, from London clubs to the U.S. Senate lounge. Yet the floor lamp next to it was topped with a frilly shade. Only a medal-bedecked dictator, or a cigar smoking Hollywood studio chief properly belonged behind the immense mahogany desk, yet it was lit by a lamp on which a porcelain shepherdess sat at the feet of a frail shepherd who had certainly never seen many days work among sheep.

And this had been Harry's complaint about his marriage; Marian never permitted him any interest on which she didn't impose her imprint.

Someone had just greeted a new arrival outside the study door with, "Simple case. He comes home and finds this guy humping his wife and boom-boom. The gun was in his pocket—registered to him— but he's not talking. His psychiatrist . . ." He paused and must have motioned toward the study door. ". . . told him to keep his mouth shut."

Yeah, I thought to myself, it was a simple case, but still a clever lawyer might convince a jury of . . . of what? Temporary insanity? Not if they knew about Harry's threat. The threat meant premeditation and the prosecution would certainly make that the centerpiece of their argument. Still the lawyer might point to the threat as a sign of Harry's fragile emotional state, causing him to be vulnerable to the trauma of discovering Marian with Plante and thus – temporarily insane.

I got up and opened the door a bit so I could see Harry. They were handcuffing him in preparation to taking him to jail.

I yelled out, "Mr. Frey, we're getting you a lawyer; hang in there!"

I'd never said, "Hang in there!" to a patient before, but it seemed right. I called Stanley Kramer's office again. I was told he was on the phone, so I told Mrs. Booth that they had just taken Harry to Sheriff's headquarters.

I was too restless to sit. Why didn't Donna come to talk to me? What could be keeping her this long? I wanted to walk out into the hall and look for her. Not a good idea. I went, instead, to the bookshelves. Here too was evidence of their marital pattern, half a dozen books about Harry's passion, vintage cars, while the rest of the books on the three shelves were romances: Krantz, Steel and Bradford. I took one of the car books off the shelf and began flipping pages in a futile attempt to prevent the bedroom scene from reasserting itself in my mind. Each picture on the book's pages was overridden with the repulsive image of Plante's carcass. Brian Plante, the man whom I'd seen in newspapers and magazines, be they from the sport page, where he'd just skippered his boat to a win in the Mackinac yacht race, or from the society pages, where he'd given a party for a major studio film crew shooting in the area. He'd smiled out from those pages with a complacency that crowded arrogance. In spite of my gut feeling that in person he was an obnoxious prick, I was strangely disturbed by his fate. Active one minute, inert the next, like movie film breaking in a projector. Then, as if a camera were panning upward, I again saw Marian in my mind. Only a moment before her death she'd been fully caught up in the intense sensations of lovemaking. Now, unmoving, she stared steadily at the ceiling with a concerned look as if she'd just discovered a crack in the plaster.

"I'm sorry I kept you waiting, Tom," Donna said coming into the room, "I was making sure everything was being done right, if you know what I mean—so that the evidence will stand up in court."

She motioned toward the armchair, "Let's sit and go over everything you know."

I became relaxed in her presence as I had the many times she and Derek and I had been together. If ever there was a good cop, that's whom I experienced at this moment. At the same instant, as I began to tell her what I knew, it came to me that I now faced a daunting dilemma. I had told confidential information to Derek in his special relationship as a consultant, a relationship that required him to hold the information told him in strict confidence. But now, that information had become an important fact in a double murder. Could I still expect him to remain silent? Was he even legally required to reveal

41

what he knew? After all, the doctor/patient privilege didn't extend to information told to a friend even if he was hearing that information in the capacity of a consultant. And what about the fact that his wife was a deputy sheriff? If I didn't at this moment tell Donna about the detailed threat Harry had made, Derek would think I wanted him to withhold significant knowledge about a double murder—putting him in a bind. I had to tell Donna all I knew, choosing a breach of confidence with my patient over putting Derek in the situation of withholding evidence. I told Donna the whole story, but I wasn't sure I'd done the right thing.

I added, "I would have bet the farm on it being so much bombast, hot air—steam. And once blown off, I was sure he'd gotten his anger off his chest, at least as far as his turning it into violence toward his wife."

"You are aware of the law . . ."

"Yes, of course, but I didn't think he'd seriously meant what he'd said."

"You say his outburst was unlike him."

"Yes."

"He was behaving abnormally in your office then. Mightn't he behave just as abnormally if he caught the two together?"

Jesus, I thought, she'd make a good prosecuting attorney. "But, you see, he had calmed down before he left the office." I remembered then, but didn't say that Harry had left my office quietly saying he'd kill his wife and Plante, if he found them together.

Donna nodded her understanding of the situation I'd been in, and shrugged as if to say, "The best laid plans . . ." She continued, "The gun is his, by the way. We checked the registry. His prints are sure to be on it. It was in his pocket."

None of this surprised me.

"Tell me again about his phone call to you today."

"Well, he was late for his eleven o'clock appointment. At eleven fifteen I made a personal call that took perhaps two or three minutes and when I hung up, the phone rang. It was Frey. He told me straight out what had happened. I told him I was coming to his house, then I called Derek and found out where you were and called you."

"That was eleven-thirty-one. According to the temperature readings of the bodies a tech just took, it figures they'd been dead less than an hour."

I ran the times through a mental calculation. At the very time he should have entered my office for his appointment, Harry was pulling the trigger three times—maybe more, judging from the look of Brian Plante's face.

"You know," she said, "All that you've told me will have to be in my report. A lot of doctors I've questioned in the past would have claimed doctor/patient privileged communication."

"I'm aware of that. You see, I'd already told Derek about Frey's threat. I told him at lunch right after my appointment with Frey yesterday. I didn't mention Frey's name, of course, but now it's pretty obvious whom I meant. I can't yoke Derek with a dilemma of having to decide whether he should remain silent for my sake, or come forward with evidence about a murder."

The approving smile that formed on her beautiful face was gratifying, but was it worth what telling the truth might turn out to cost me - me and Harry Frey?

"Tom, we've recently added a Detective Bureau to our department. It's headed by its only member . . . so far, Lt. Panetta—Primo Panetta."

"Primo?"

"Yeah, I know. He's second generation Italian and they tell me that in his parents' generation the name isn't that uncommon; it means first born.

"Anyway, in the past, my being the first sergeant on the crime scene would have meant I'd be in charge of the case, but I got word a few minutes ago from Sheriff Davis that it will be our new man this time. He's on his way here now. I'll tell him what you've told me, and ask him to see you first if he has more questions, so you can leave here as soon as possible."

She stood up and came to me and gave my shoulders a little hug, not what one usually expects from a sheriff's deputy.

"I'm sorry this has happened to you, Tom. I'll see you soon."

So I had to wait. To calm myself, I took a history of European auto racing from the shelf and began reading. I'd gotten up to the 1930's before the door opened and a man about my own age came in, swept a straight-back chair from against the wall and in one motion plunked it down with its back almost against my knees. He sat straddling it and leaned his forearms on the top rung. First impressions: clean shaven, but with such a heavy beard that his cheeks were blue-grey, curly black hair and brown eyes, not warm milk chocolate, but the kind with the high cocoa content. His attitude did not reach overly hard for friendly.

"I'm Lieutenant Panetta. Sergeant Marsh has given me a brief description of your part in this." He went on to tell me that I must come to Sheriff's Headquarters the next morning at nine o'clock, but I wasn't really listening. I was stuck on his phrase "your part in this." I had no "part" in these murders!

"You're a psychiatrist, right?"

"That's right."

"Is this Frey guy a nut case?"

The question startled me. I'd never had anyone refer to one of my patients as a "nut case."

"Lieutenant, I can't discuss a patient with you. That, as I'm sure you must know, is privileged communication. I can't answer your question."

Unlike my answer to Donna, I now reflexly retreated behind "privileged communication" when he said "nut case."

"Let me phrase it this way, doc. Did he say anything that caused you to suspect . . ." He noted my expression. "Privileged communication, right? So anything you know about this guy is gonna be privileged?"

We were off to a bad start. I tried to soften my replay. "Lieutenant, I want to cooperate with the police, but I also can't allow myself to be guilty of a breach of confidence. I'd be committing an illegal act to answer your question." A stupid thing to say, when I'd already told Donna, but I was into a pissing contest with him.

He seemed to consider whether or not he'd be wasting his time to ask me anything else. He abruptly stood and made his exit, leaving his chair where he'd put it right in front of me.

Driving back to my loft, I felt as battered as the state budget. Just a couple of days ago I was a happy bachelor, able to believe myself to be a solid professional, respected by colleagues and patients, desirable to a decent number of the women whom I found desirable, comfortable income and a great new house. On top of the world one might say. Well, I still had the house—if I could keep up the payments. Which made me think of my tenant. I hoped Tony Salpino had no plans to move his wine wholesaling operation to a larger space. Earlier, when I'd first toured his space, I'd been pleased to see his abundant inventory. Suddenly, I was thinking of it as cramped. As I was well aware from my practice, the interpretation of facts depends on one's point of view— the euphoric new property owner versus the worried mortgage holder.

Arriving at my place and noticing Tony's Cherokee parked in the lot, I couldn't wait until I had an answer. A cold wind, coming in gusts across Grand Traverse Bay from the north nearly yanked the car door from my grasp when I opened it. I got out, and leaning into the wind, ran to the door of Salpino & Son.

There I met Gretchen, the office manager, on her way out.

"Ah, Dr. Morgan; I guess you want to talk to Tony."

"That's right, if he's free for a moment."

"He's in the back." She stepped to the door of the warehouse area and called out, "Tony, Dr. Morgan is here. Wants to talk to you."

His voice answered from the depths. "Send him back."

She smiled and stepped aside from the door.

I started walking back past rows of wine cases stacked to the ceiling.

"I'm back here in Alsace, Tom."

He was on a rolling ladder in the last aisle.

"So this is Alsace. I've always wanted to go there," I managed to quip although I was far from being in a joking mood.

"We're having a big customer over for dinner, gonna impress him."

He climbed down from the ladder with four green bottles in his arms. He handed them to me to hold, while he pushed the ladder to the end of the aisle.

"Rieslings."

"Want your customer to carry this wine in his store?"

"Nah. Not at all. This guy owns the PriceKing drug chain. Nothin' there over eighteen a bottle. These go four times that. Just want to convince him Salpino and Son's got class."

I handed him the bottles and he handed one back. "Got this down for you."

I was taken aback by his generosity. I'd never been given an eighty-dollar bottle of wine before.

"Thanks, Tony, and thanks for covering my forgetfulness yesterday."

"What are friends for? I hope they did good for you last night."

I didn't want to get into a locker room talk about whether or not I'd scored with Peggy Sue after the prom. I went to the subject that had brought me to his door.

"You've got a lot of merchandise in this space." I didn't want to put ideas in his head, but then again if the space was too cramped, he'd already have thought of it. "Is it adequate for your business?"

"You mean my whole operation? Hell no. I only keep the good stuff here. The stuff I like to be near. You didn't know about my other warehouse? No, no. I got fifteen thousand square feet on Hammond Road, across from UPS. I got all the volume stuff there. Three guys there plus my son, Dino, who runs it. This place here is my home; it's where I'm surrounded by the best the world makes. I like it here by the harbor and close to downtown."

I was relieved and my face must have shown it. He added, gripping my arm, "I plan to stay here as long as I'm welcome."

"I'm happy with that, " I replied.

I now had a different attitude toward the crowded stacks we passed. It had become a wine cellar . . . tended by my own sommelier.

Having relieved my anxiety about this concern, my thoughts returned to my more pressing problem, the murders, and my upcoming questioning by Lt. Panetta. I had a foot on the first tread of the back stairs to my loft, when I made the connection between Panetta and Salpino, two Italian names. The relevance was weak I knew, like asking a New Yorker if he knew a friend of yours who lived there. Need overruled reason.

I returned to the warehouse where Tony was putting the three bottles of wine for his customer's dinner into a stout paper shopping bag.

"Tony, one more thing. I met a guy today named Primo Panetta. I wonder if you happen to know him."

"Primo Panetta? Primo Panetta from Detroit?"

I shrugged my answer of having no idea.

"Hey, how many Primo Panettas can there be? How do you know Primo?"

"He just joined the Leelanau County Sheriff's bunch—a detective."

"Yeah, that's him." He was smiling and shaking his head as one might upon encountering an unlikely coincidence. "Yeah, I know Primo. He and my youngest brother hung out together. As a matter of fact for a while he practically became part of our family—trouble in his home. I didn't know him well. I was going to Wayne State, living with a friend down near the campus—living in a whorehouse actually, but that's another story. I'd see Primo when I was home some weekends. He was a troubled kid, a kid with an attitude, but I tried to understand. Know what I mean? I was surprised when I heard he'd become a cop. Go figure."

"Can you tell me about him? I have an interview with him tomorrow."

"Interview?"

"A patient of mine murdered his wife . . ."

"Primo's wife?"

"No, no, his own wife. Murdered his wife and also a guy named Brian Plante. You'll hear all about it on the evening news. The lieutenant wants to ask me some questions."

"Jeez, Tom, I'm sorry. That's terrible. And Brian Plante! Our very own celebrity: baseball owner, yacht racer. You're damn right it'll be on the news—everywhere." He stopped caught by a thought. "This ain't gonna be good for you is it, Tom?"

I was grateful for his thought. "No, I'm pretty sure it won't be good for me."

"That's a shame. So Primo's in charge of the investigation." He paused, then said, "What can I tell you about him? He's a complicated guy. Smart guy. Like I said, he went through a bad patch when he was a teenager and that experience seemed to gel into having a chip on his shoulder. Like I said, I tried to make allowance for his situation, but I still got pissed off with him. Course, I had no need to tolerate him; my life was elsewhere. I don't even know if he and my brother are still friends."

What he did remember wasn't reassuring to me and Tony recognized this.

"Tom, I wish I knew more. I wish I could tell you he's an OK guy and he'll give you no pain, but I can't."

We stood looking at each other, I making myself swallow his unsavory assessment, he wishing he'd had a more hopeful one. I lifted the green wine bottle in a kind of salute.

"Thanks again, Tony."

6

I went upstairs to my loft with my bottle of Alsatian Riesling and heartburn. Two Pepto-Bismol tablets and two fingers of Johnny Black seemed appropriate for covering all the bases. It was at a time like this that a man really needed to be comforted by a wife. Well, I had no wife, but I did have Stanley Kramer. At three hundred dollars an hour, at least he was on my side. This time Mrs. Booth put me through.

Without giving me a chance to say anything - the usual form when someone calls you - he began, "I got Cutler. He's on his way to Sheriff's Headquarters right now. I had no trouble getting him to take the case when he heard that Plante was one of the victims. Cutler is the best there is, but like all the best criminal defenders, he's a hot dog— lives to be seen and heard. If they had a sense of humor at all those guys would have been stand-up comics. By the way, he was very happy you told your patient to keep his mouth shut."

I wanted to say that I hadn't exactly put it that way, but why waste the effort. It was good news that he'd gotten Cutler; both Harry Frey and I needed him. I had read about his many successes defending people that I thought should have ended up doing time. Instead, these scum now sat in their Scottsdale Jacuzzis drinking champagne with the life savings of trusting investors. How easily we shake hands with the devil, when it's to our advantage.

"There's another matter I need to talk with you about, but not on the phone."

I'd decided that if I'd told Donna about Frey's threat, I'd better tell my attorney also.

"Can it wait until tomorrow?"

"Sure."

"I'll see you at ten o'clock."

"Can't. I see patients until noon."

His momentary silence said he didn't like it. He was the one who told others when he'd meet them. "I can make it at eleven-thirty: I leave at noon," he said.

It meant I'd have to reschedule an appointment with a patient, a thing I didn't like to do on short notice, but I was the one asking for help and I understood that Stanley had to have his way. It must have been that way in the sandbox too.

I said, "OK, eleven-thirty it is," as I heard him hang up.

I swallowed some scotch and dialed Audrey's number. I dreaded this call. She answered, this time not out of breath. I pictured her cool and composed.

I took a deep breath mentally. "Hi, it's Tom Morgan again, only this time I have some very bad news."

"What is it, Tom?" Her voice was soft and sympathetic.

"Harry Frey, ah . . . This morning Harry Frey shot and killed Marian and Brian Plante."

I heard a sharp intake of breath. "Harry killed them? You mean murdered them?"

"Yes, I'm afraid so. I was at the house. I saw the bodies."

"That's terrible. How could that happen? How were they killed?"

"He shot them. He discovered them together."

"Good God! When did it happen?"

"It had happened just before he called me and that was immediately after we talked. So, around eleven fifteen."

"You mean while we were talking he was shooting them?"

"I guess that's about right." She was having that reaction we tend to have upon hearing of a catastrophic event, trying to place it in

51

the context of our own lives.

"I remember looking at the clock when I hung up and deciding I'd had enough treadmill. My God." She paused, letting the shock level out in her mind.

"How did it happen?"

"He must have come home unexpectedly and caught them together. He was supposed to be at a therapy session with me, but he didn't keep the appointment - must have gone home instead."

I thought to myself, that the regular appointment Harry always had on Thursday must have made Marian and Plante think they were safe to meet at Marian's house.

If I didn't include Audrey in those who knew about the detail of Harry's fantasy about shooting Plante and she learned of it later . . . she'd be very, very pissed with me.

"There's this other thing. I didn't say anything last night, because at the time I regarded it as a bit of Harry's bombast. In my session with him yesterday he described in detail the way he'd shoot Plant, and . . . "

"And that's the way he did it?" she finished my sentence.

"Yeah."

She was silent so in my own mind, I supplied her response. "You were sitting across from me at dinner and you didn't tell me?"

Instead she said, "Hey, it was your judgement that he wasn't serious and you were no doubt right. It became a different thing, however, when he actually saw them together. It's not surprising that he'd then do what he'd already thought of doing."

Her empathic response was a surprise and a relief.

"You said you went to the Freys' house? Why was that?"

"I called the police right after he called and then rushed right over there. The police just released me."

"Did you tell the police about the details of Harry's threat?"

I felt like a kid being quizzed by his mother, acceding to guilt bit by bit.

"Well . . . I'm not sure. I mean I told Derek's wife, Donna. She's a Leelanau deputy, and the guy in charge of the case, a detective, told me Donna had briefed him about the information I'd given her. But as he questioned me, it didn't seem like he knew about Frey's threat. Knowing the disclosure of the threat would be a problem for me, maybe she decided to keep it to herself."

"Tom, I've got to make a call to the hospital, but I believe we should sit down together right away and talk and think all of this through."

"Fine. How about dinner tonight?"

"I can't. Laslo wants to work on the book this evening. Can you meet me in half an hour at Wines and Vines? It's in that big barn structure on M22 south of The Leelanau Hunt Club."

"I know the place."

"Good. I'll see you there, OK?"

I opened my mouth to repeat, OK, but she was gone. I didn't care, because I was flooded with relief; I had told her the whole truth and she hadn't become angry. She even wanted to get together.

I'd already called the clinic at Munson Hospital and told them I wouldn't be in today. There was no way I could give the proper attention to patients. I shed the shirt, tie and jacket, my office uniform, and took a shower, letting the hot water pour over my head as I stood still, willing the awful reality of the day to wash away.

At three-forty, I parked and walked into the restaurant. The room was narrow with booths running down one side, the décor quiet, comfortable. Audrey was seated in the first booth, facing me as I entered. She gave me a welcoming smile and I felt a surge of pleasure. Only one other booth, the most distant from the door, was occupied.

She reached for my hand across the table. "I appreciate your calling me, Tom. I really do. This is a terrible thing for all of us, especially, of course, the Freys. Hell, even for Brian Plante although I never liked what I'd heard about the conceited bastard. He was married wasn't he? I think I remember a newspaper picture of him and a wife."

"I don't know."

Her expression segued into a deep empathy. "I've been thinking that you might think I fault you for not telling me immediately the violent details of Frey's thinking. I want you to know that I don't. In your position I believe I'd have done the same. When your judgment told you he was just venting his anger, the idea of calling Marian and Plante telling them that her husband had threatened to kill them, would be ridiculous."

Her words were salve for my anxiety even though I could identify in myself that ever ready wish we have to embrace what we want to hear. True or false, I felt better.

"Why I thought we should talk," she continued, "is that I'm concerned that if we don't anticipate what can develop and be ready for it . . . well, we'd better think this through and be on the same page."

I nodded as the waiter came and gave us menus and took our orders for wine, a glass of Gill's Pier Royce for Audrey and Verterra's Pinot Grigio for me.

"How long had you known about Marian and Plante?" she asked.

"Umm, perhaps a month. Another patient of mine, who knew both of them by sight, said she'd seen them kissing in a car parked in the alley behind the State Theater. I presume Marian told you in a therapy session."

"Yes. He'd hit on her and she was eager. I tried to slow down the stampede to no avail."

"Did you know they were meeting at the Frey house today?"

"No, I didn't. After Marian understood that I wasn't cheering her on, she only told me things after the fact. I hadn't heard of their ever meeting at the Frey house."

"To tell the truth, Audrey, in the hours after the shock of seeing both their bodies and acknowledging the fact that my patient did it, I've become seriously concerned about the fall out regarding the Tarasoff Rule. I don't think I'm being an alarmist anticipating potentially heavy lawsuits. For starters, if there is a Mrs. Plante, she could claim that the untimely death of her husband could have been prevented had I acted as the law demands. She could claim that she'll lose millions because of my negligence, my incompetence."

"Do you usually flagellate yourself like this? Do you happen to own a scourge?" She was smiling, teasing. "I understand your concern, but seriously the law states you yourself must hear the threat as real." She squeezed my hand. "You worry too much. Now having said that, there is, however, a concern I have."

She looked to me for my attention—she had it. "This notion is only just now forming in my mind, so I might not be able to express it well. There are two parts. First, you said you told Derek's wife about the threat Harry made, but you didn't tell the detective. My concern is that the Marshes are going to feel you expect their silence. That's a burden, especially since she's a law officer. They are your good friends. Can you afford to jeopardize that relationship? The second part is that when a person withholds information that later is uncovered, that person will be thought of as a chronic liar and his or her story is doubted from then on. You can't afford that where the detective's concerned. Wouldn't it be better to tell him everything you know, emphasizing that you were sure Frey wasn't serious? The important thing is to have the detective believe you're telling the truth."

I considered what she'd just said. First, I was impressed with the cogency of her argument. She'd said she might not be able to express her thinking well. Sounded very clear to me. She was dead right. I had to tell what's his name, the detective, all that Harry had said . . . and the sooner the better.

I said, "Are you really hungry? Why don't we go to my place and later we can have some pizza delivered?"

Her spontaneous laughter followed my suggestion. She reached across and stroked my face. "There has been too much ugliness today. I don't want that to spoil anything."

I knew she was right again—in theory. I couldn't agree physically, but that something, which I credited as my saner self, said to back off. I picked up the menu.

7

I'd gone home after a passionate goodbye kiss enhanced by Audrey's unspoken promise to keep the fire banked until a later time. I drifted around my loft for the rest of the evening, finally getting to bed past midnight for a fitful sleep.

In the morning I put the kettle on and sleepily went down the front stairs to get my Record-Eagle. The headline jolted me awake. In huge block lettering, "BRIAN PLANTE MURDERED." I hurriedly closed the door as if the city were watching to see my reaction. Back upstairs, I sat at the kitchen table and read the article. It said that according to Detective Lieutenant Panetta of the Leelanau Sheriff's Department, Harry Frey, who had confessed to the crime had been charged with double murder. He was to be arraigned on Monday and was to be represented by the nationally known criminal attorney, Holden Cutler. There was no mention of me, or that Harry had been seeing a psychiatrist. I was surprised. I expected Panetta would have had pleasure feeding that morsel to the press.

Panetta had told me yesterday to come to headquarters at nine this morning. Not knowing how long this interview would take, I'd cancelled my morning patients. I'd tell him about Harry's threat as Audrey had advised. And if I had time, I'd visit Harry in the jail. I called to check on the visiting hours and was told that regular hours were on Tuesday from one until eight. I asked if his physician or attorney could visit a prisoner at other times and was asked who the prisoner in question was.

"His name is Harry Frey and I am Dr. Thomas Morgan."

"There is a note here that Judge Hackett issued an order last night that Mr. Frey is not to be permitted any visitors."

What was that all about? "Are you sure? I'm his psychiatrist and I'm sure I should be allowed . . ."

"Sorry sir, the order is very clear, no visitors," the woman deputy replied courteously.

"There must be someone you could call . . ."

"The order comes from the judge. I suggest you call his office."

"Would you do me a favor and tell Mr. Frey that Dr. Morgan called and will visit him at the earliest time I can?"

She hesitated a moment and then said, "Sure" in a way that meant our conversation was at an end.

I was at loose ends after this, wandering around the loft and finally pouring scotch at least eight hours ahead of normal opening time at chez Morgan.

The phone rang. I knew it had to be Audrey calling to lift my spirits.

"Tom, it's Tony. I wanted to let you know that I ran into Primo Panetta at mass this morning. After we talked about the catchin' up kinda stuff, I told him I'd heard about the shooting. Told him you were a friend of mine—my man. He said, 'Is that so?' in a way to let me know he'd heard me. Know what I mean? Thought you'd like to know."

"Thanks Tony. Thanks a lot."

"What are friends for? Take care."

I hung up feeling a lift from an unexpected source, even though I wasn't sure what being Tony's "man" would get me. I plopped down in the window chair and closed my eyes. They snapped open again with the unbidden thought; had I unconsciously denied the danger to Marian Frey, the wayward wife, because I still wanted my own wayward wife punished? A sobering thought. No, no, not true, not true, I thought, shaking my head vigorously. The emphatic nature of the negation caught my attention. He protests too much! I had seen the meaning of that kind of vehement denial too many times in therapy to let myself walk away. I thought about it. I'd still say Harry's threat hadn't been serious, but at the same time, I had to admit that my feelings about Cora were still unresolved. Coincidently, she'd joined a surgical group here in Traverse City. And although I saw her around Munson Hospital where we're both on the staff, we never spoke.

At nine, I presented myself at the receptionist's window at the Sheriff's Office and pressed a button. A minute later a deputy arrived to ask my business.

I told him I was there to keep an appointment with Lt. Panetta. She looked surprised, as if she didn't know Panetta was there.

"I'll check."

She put her mic on mute and made a call, and then another, and then another.

"OK, I've located him. Come with me," she said buzzing the door lock.

The deputy led me back to an inner hallway, passing several closed doors. A door opened and I saw Panetta wave me in while talking on the phone. He motioned to a chair. His side of the conversation was a series of "Rights" followed by, "When did I become a saint, for God's sake?" Then he hung up.

As soon as he reoriented himself to focus on me, I launched into the complete description of the threat Frey had made in my office.

"Yeah, I know. Sergeant Marsh told me."

"Donna told you?"

"Yeah. Before I talked to you yesterday."

So, he'd kept that to himself to see how much I'd volunteer.

"I also asked you if he was a nut case."

It was very distasteful to me to answer, but I said, "There was nothing he ever told me that led me, or would have led any therapist, to foresee this violence."

He gave a short snort of a laugh, "No other therapist either, eh?" This was said with a rhythm that should have been followed with a stinging knock out punch, but he withheld it. Maybe because Tony had said I was "his man."

"Did you know he had a gun?"

"He had told me that- yes."

"He missed an appointment with you yesterday morning and then called to say that he had shot his wife, right?"

"Yes."

"The appointment was at . . .?"

"Eleven o'clock."

"He called you at . . .?"

He knew all this, but I complied. "It must have been around eleven twenty."

He must have concluded I knew nothing more, and after his words with Tony Salpino, decided to not maul me like a cat would a mouse, because he then abruptly said we were finished and—although I believed the words were alien to him—thanked me for coming in. Lieutenant Panetta didn't fit the profile of other Leelanau deputies I'd met. He was another species altogether compared to Donna Marsh. Would Sheriff Davis mold him into a team member? I wondered.

I stood outside the sheriff's headquarters wondering what Panetta thought he had gained that he hadn't already known. One hundred yards away stood the Government Center Building where this Judge Hackett, who was denying my access to Harry Frey, had his office. I decided to talk to him and explain that mine was a special case.

This was my hopeful mood as I entered the building. Although new, the interior was gloomy and somber. Before I walked the length of the hall to Hackett's office, my hopeful mood had deflated.

I knocked on the door bearing the judge's name and cautiously opened it. There was no one sitting at the secretary's desk that faced the door.

"In here," came a voice from an adjacent room.

A slim, perky, young woman with closely cropped red hair sat at a desk stacked with law books writing on a yellow legal pad and smoking. A notice at the building's entrance declared this to be a "smoke-free facility." She glanced at me and continued to write. Apparently there were to be no wasted words.

"I'm looking for Judge Hackett."

"Not here."

I thought first and edited before I asked, "When?"

No words this time, only a shrug which was good for, "Who knows when the old goat will be back. He's having a long lunch with Matilda down the hall."

It was fun in a way. "I'm Dr. Thomas Morgan. A patient of mi . . ."

"Harry Frey."

"Ah . . . yes, and I want to talk to him. Judge . . ." I waited and wasn't disappointed.

"Hackett."

We were a team. "Has left orders that Mr. Frey isn't to have visitors, and . . . "

"You want that order set aside in your case."

"Uh huh."

She looked at me for the first time and smiled. It was a friendly smile that said she knew more about my plight than I did myself.

"I'm Pat Furst, Hackett's law clerk—until June. You really didn't think he'd do it, did you?"

"Judge Hackett?"

She smiled an acknowledgment that I'd scored. "Harry Frey."

There was such a disarming directness about the woman that

61

it seemed unnatural that we weren't having this conversation in bed.

"I was sure he wouldn't harm anyone."

"Maybe he didn't," she said tapping her cigarette on the edge of an ashtray.

"Are you my fairy godmother?"

She enjoyed that.

"Wouldn't that be great?" I mused, "Unfortunately he's confessed."

"Your request poses an interesting question," she said. "Which should take precedence, the health of the accused or his legal defense? It wouldn't be interesting to Hackett, however. Unless someone is in need of a straitjacket, he considers psychiatry to be useless."

She looked at me wondering if I understood my position. She added, "It's Cutler. He talked to Hackett and Hackett thinks they are . . . buddies."

"Then Cutler must have contacted the judge immediately after he first talked to Harry Frey. Why doesn't he want Frey to have visitors?"

"I don't know. Maybe Hackett doesn't either. All it would take is an arm squeeze by a celebrity for Hackett to see him as a buddy - and Holden Cutler is a celeb to Hackett."

"And you think Hackett will continue to do Cutler's bidding against any request of mine?"

"Hands down."

My eyes out of habit looked at her hands for a ring.

She noticed and smiled.

Our conversation having begun on such familiar terms, I'd not thought of her frankness as strange—until now.

"Thanks for your honesty. I'm curious though; should you be so up front with me?"

"Should has nothing to do with it, I'm made that way."

"Then how about dinner tonight. I badly need to talk to someone made like you."

I stopped on the way back into the city at Aroma's coffee shop and got a cappuccino from Laura, the manager. My cell phone buzzed as I got into my car again. It was Stanley Kramer and he was angry.

"Why didn't you tell me that this guy had told you in detail just how he was going to shoot Brian Plante? You set me up to look like a fool as your lawyer."

I wondered how Stanley had found that out. But that was beside the point.

"I was going to tell you when I saw you today, Stanley. When I called you right after the murder the urgent issue was finding a lawyer for Harry Frey."

"Don't you think if you called a friend to ask him to take on a patient for treatment it would be fair to inform your friend at the same time that the person was a hopeless case? Because that is exactly what Cutler found out from his new client after he'd agreed to take the case. He found out he'd accepted a case that he could have no hope of winning. I got a call from him a few minutes ago and he let me have an earful."

"I'm sorry, Stanley. I didn't anticipate this happening. How did Cutler find out about the threat?"

"Frey told him. Like I said, Cutler wouldn't have taken the case if he'd known what Frey had said in your office. Now he feels obliged to defend him and believe me your not having told me will come back to haunt you – haunt us – because Cutler has decided to make Frey's threat the center-point of his defense. He's going to claim Frey was temporarily insane after discovering his wife's affair and then told you of his plan to kill her and Plante. Cutler is going to point to the Tarasoff law and claim there would have been no murder if you had acted as the law demands. In other words, he plans to save his client by destroying you."

I thought about the situation from Cutler's point of view. The issue was pre-meditation. Without Harry's threats he'd be defending a man who'd caught a guy in bed with his wife. Angry rage, impulsive action, no premeditation eliminates first-degree murder. The threats meant first-degree and a life sentence unless Cutler could bend the jury's sentiment toward blaming me.

There was good news embedded within Stanley's rant; Harry Frey had told Cutler about the threat and Cutler would tell everyone in sight. My breach of confidence by telling Derek and Donna would have no impact on Harry's fate.

"My purpose in making an appointment was to tell you about Frey's threat, so I don't need to see you now," I said.

"We need to talk. How about noon tomorrow. I'll have more time."

After seeing my last patient for the day, I drove to my former neighbor's condo and picked up my cat, Kato, and brought him to his new home. He proceeded straightway to inspect the place like a security team sweeping a room for hidden microphones, especially evaluating odors I was unaware of. It's fair to say he was unimpressed with Croft's design and my choice for his new home.

8

NON ILLIGITIMUS CARBORUNDUM! These three words were printed on a piece of note paper and wedged into the crack in my front door. Pat Furst and I had come back to my loft after dinner at Biddle's and there it was.

I knew what it meant and who had left it. The first big exam in medical school was in anatomy. We were all scared shitless. All of our fears about being able to make it through medical school became concentrated on that day. Our weekly psychiatry lecture was scheduled the hour before the exam. The professor came into the lecture room and without saying a word, went to the blackboard and wrote those three words. He turned to us and said, "Don't let the bastards grind you down!" And knowing that our thoughts were totally on the coming exam, he added, "Class dismissed."

It was nostalgically funny to read those words now, but at the time it had been a lifesaver. We'd walked confidently into the exam room, no longer the cowering troop the anatomy department had expected.

Derek had had the same psychiatry professor two years earlier and he was trying to recreate the same effect for me today.

Pat got a kick out of this when I explained the note.

We'd had a lively conversation during the excellent dinner at Biddle's, partly influenced by the high level of energy that always flowed there. We'd discovered we shared many interests and views. It turned out that I was in error thinking she had developed an interest in my problem when we'd first met that afternoon. She had actually taken a keen interest when she'd read my name in the morning paper. Coincidentally, she had already heard about me from the young woman she was staying with, someone I'd had occasion to help after she'd experienced a very traumatic incident at her job.

Sitting opposite her in my living room, I was faced again with that seemingly unsolvable mystery of what ingredients are necessary for one to fall in love. Pat was a very attractive person physically and in personality and very easy to be with, and yet no fireworks. I think it was the same for her, but even if there were such a potential in her feelings about me, she let me know by subtle means that she liked me; she would like to be my friend, but at this time in her life and career nothing more was going to happen. Fine, the same went for me, because I already had someone in mind to fill that role.

I'd learned over the meal that Pat had graduated from U of M Law School in January and was going to begin a clerkship to a U.S. District judge in Ann Arbor in June. In the meantime, with time to kill, she had accepted an invitation to come north to visit and stay with a childhood friend in Suttons Bay. She had immediately contacted Judge Hackett and suggested she work as an unpaid law clerk, wanting to gather every bit of experience from all levels of the law. Hackett had jumped at the idea of being able to casually drop word to one and all that he had a law clerk, even if of short tenure. I knew that great prestige went with being a clerk to a high-ranking judge—only the very top graduating students are chosen. By the same token, it is prestigious to be a judge for whom someone wants to clerk. I heard later that he'd been boasting that Michigan's top grad was clerking for him.

I proposed opening my bottle of Alsatian wine. This time it was turned down for coffee. I put the kettle on and we settled into two living room armchairs. To kick off conversation, I asked her how she had come to choose law and Pat told me her story.

Her parents, her older sister and she lived in a comfortable

Dallas neighborhood until she was fourteen. Two years earlier, her father, who was a builder, got a contract to build a very large home in Southlake, a Dallas suburb. The projected cost was over a million, but it went higher and higher as the guy kept making additions and changes. He was paying cash, no mortgage for him; this was just pocket change. The problem was, he was slow to put his hand into that pocket. Her father should have stopped further construction until he was paid, but he didn't want bad feelings, and he reassured himself he would get paid—eventually. The guy seemed to run with the moneyed crowd and Pat's father looked forward to building many more of their homes.

"You can guess the rest. The place was finished, the guy moved in and said he would not pay the huge amount still owed to Dad. He claimed the building wasn't according to plans and he was never consulted about the changes."

"Your father must have sued the bastard."

"He did that all right, but . . ."

"Don't tell me your father didn't win his case?"

"Afraid so. Dad's lawyer did a lousy job. Totally incompetent. Of course, I couldn't appreciate just how incompetent at that time. All I knew is that my father had lost a lot of money. He made good on what he owed his subcontractors and ended up with very little. We had to sell our house and move to a low income neighborhood where we could afford a home."

"You had to leave your school for a new one?"

"Yes, and that really hurt. My mother kept our spirits up, however, so my sister and I made an adjustment without too much loss of hair."

"And, you decided to become the good lawyer your father didn't have," I said.

"That was an easy slam dunk, Doc, too simple to award you more than one point."

I shrugged. "Simple, yes, but it's the kind of story that lies at the base of most of our heroic efforts."

It came to me that my present problem might be seen by her as another opportunity to right that old wrong her father had suffered if she thought I was getting a raw deal. It would explain her readiness to go behind Hackett's back.

I noticed her begin a movement toward her purse, then interrupt it to settle back in her chair.

"If you'd like to smoke, it's OK with me."

"Thanks, but I quit."

"Oh?"

She knew I'd seen her smoking in the afternoon.

"It happened sometime between two o'clock and seven."

"Have you . . . "

"Quit before? No, but I've been thinking about it for a while."

"Good luck, then."

"Luck has nothing to do with it," she smiled. "If you really want to quit, you quit."

"My congratulations in that case."

When I took her home, she lightly kissed me on the cheek and said that I now had a mole in the halls of justice. I laughed, but I knew that for her to be caught leaking information to me would be no laughing matter.

I returned to my place with resurgent confidence. I opened the door to the sound of the phone ringing. I sprinted to it and took a moment to control my breathing for a normal, "Hello."

"Doctor Morgan?" a deep, man's voice asked. Uncertainty modulated it.

"Yes, this is Doctor Morgan."

"My name is Tom Morgan also . . . I'm your father."

What? I didn't know how to respond. The guy must have made

a mistake, must have thought he had another Tom Morgan on the line.

"You've made a mistake, I'm afraid. I'm not the Doctor Morgan you want."

"Ah . . . I'm sure I have the right number."

"You're mistaken, because I have no father."

"You were born in Ann Arbor. Your mother's name was Thelma and her mother was Gayle Moran who lived in Croswell, Michigan."

That was all true. How did he have this information? He wasn't my father—of that I was certain. My father had died when I was a child. I became suspicious that this was some kind of con.

It was as if he were reading my mind. "This is no trick," he said. "I know your mother told you I'd been killed in an auto accident, but that wasn't true. The truth is . . . well, different. I'd like for us to meet, so I can explain everything."

I was really off balance. I had to regroup. "You know some things about me; tell me something about yourself."

"You're still suspicious—and you should be. But if this is some kind of gag or trick, I would probably have done my homework and have a slew of facts ready to snow you with. Why don't you pick the topic?"

"OK, let me see." I searched my memory for things my mother had told me about my father. There wasn't much. My mother had made it clear to me that she didn't welcome questions about him. I knew he'd come from the East to attend the University of Michigan, but he'd had to drop out when I was born. "OK, what was your college fraternity?"

"Lambda Chi."

'Where was your family's vacation cottage and what was its name?" I felt a little silly, as if this guy had got me to play a game with him.

"Camp. They call them camps up in Maine. Because the building was on a hill, the family called it Morgan's Mountain. That was shortened to The Mountain."

I was either totally conned or convinced. I was afraid to come down solidly on either choice. One element of my reaction to all this, and one I didn't understand, was anger toward this man, anger, not merely irritation at having one more confusing problem heaped upon the plenitude already there.

"What's this all about?" I said.

"Simple really. A father wants to meet his son."

9

After that call, I had a very restless night. I got up, put the kettle on, and began filling Kato's bowl. He stood back very self-possessed, appraising my functioning as if he were a headwaiter at a Michelin three-star restaurant judging a trainee's setting of a table. When I finished, he stood for a moment, looked at the bowl, looked up at me and then slowly walked over to the bowl and began to eat. The trial period was over; he'd decided to stay with me.

The morning paper featured a telephone interview with Holden Cutler in which Cutler said Harry Frey was pleading innocent due to temporary insanity. He told the interviewer that Mr. Frey had been in an extremely unstable emotional state since discovering that his wife was having an affair. Cutler went on to say that his client had been seeing a psychiatrist, Dr. Thomas Morgan. Mr. Frey had told the doctor of his discovery of his wife's affair and declared that he would kill his wife and Brian Plante if he caught them together. Cutler was then quoted, "This unfortunate tragedy could have been prevented if his doctor had taken the proper and legally demanded action to warn the victims of their danger and to hospitalize his patient."

There must be worse ways to start a morning—none came to mind. Thinking about the others who would also be reading about the incompetence of Dr. Thomas Morgan while munching their breakfast toast started a ragged pain in my gut. A new, palpable dread had joined the ones I already had. What would my patients' reactions be to this newspaper article? Earlier, I'd been focused on lawsuits, because I'd been talking to my attorney. Now I knew each patient would hear the news and take it differently. Based on what I knew about them, I began to anticipate what I'd face this morning when I had four appointments scheduled.

My first patient was a woman who thought her family was drifting away from her, no longer finding her of value. She was a timid person who couldn't control her need to impose cautionary restrictions on those she cared for. She began the session with comments about the weather. This was unlike her. Her usual opening concerned how her good intentions had been, yet again, unfairly misunderstood. I thought she was avoiding mention of the newspaper article. I had to be careful not to let my own concerns guide my interpretation. And, I knew she was primed to hear anything I said as one more instance of her being unfairly misunderstood.

I observed to her that she had never begun one of our sessions with thoughts about the weather, and I wondered if there might be something else on her mind that she was reluctant to talk about. She was silent. Which way was her reaction to my question going to go? Would it be heard as criticism or would it hit the mark?

She began, "I think it's terrible the way the newspapers are only interested in stirring up trouble—taking things out of context. They only care about selling papers. They don't care who gets hurt."

I prompted with a neutral, "Yes?"

"A psychiatrist can only try his best to help."

She had welcomed me into her camp, those who tried their best, only to be misunderstood and vilified for their honest efforts. She was offering a truce. She would support me if I would agree that her troubles stemmed from the failure of others to appreciate her. An even trade, I would be held blameless and in return I would give up my attempts to understand her in any way other than the one she wished to cling to—a tempting offer given my mood.

She wasn't going to be happy when I turned down the offer. The trick would be to do it in a way that permitted her to leave the session with a little more awareness of what she wished to repeat here with me, rather than believing she'd suffered one more rejection.

The next hour I heard about how I'd dropped the ball. It was from a man who held very ambivalent feelings toward his father and following upon that, any men he perceived as being in a superior position to himself. Most of the time he was obsequious, keeping hidden the wish to strike out at those he envied. He saved his attacks for moments when he identified vulnerability in another man.

His father had been a ruthless mental bully and my patient had been doing his best to pass on the favor to his two sons until his wife packed them up and moved out. He wanted her and the boys back, but she maintained a firm position that she would only consider it if he got himself into treatment. A gun to the head is not the best motivation for the kind of treatment I do, but there was also his own hope for a normal emotional life. The problem was that he was fixed on the idea that he had to first slaughter his abusive father. He was like the injured and disabled athlete, who thinks he'll never feel like a whole person again unless able to reenter his sport and win. But along with his wish to kill his father was his fear that he'd only show his hand and his father would kill him instead.

The way it played out in treatment was a continual testing of me, probing with hostile statements and then quickly retreating behind the shield of denied intent. I had a hunch that the newspaper article might be too fat a chance to attack and finish me off for him to resist. Important for him was to discover that he could deliver his coup de grace without my retaliating—or dying.

He began by quipping, "Congratulations on becoming famous."

Before I could frame a question asking what he meant, he hurried to, "I read a magazine article about how one should go about picking a therapist. There was a list of questions that should be asked at the first interview. As you know I never did that. My wife got your

73

name from that dippy Fran Ferguson. I saw her at a party a couple of weeks ago. She gets crazier all the time. I heard that she's seeing a psychiatrist herself. I think he's doing her more harm than good."

So, I was obviously the psychiatrist in the tale. Wouldn't Fran Ferguson have recommend the man that she herself was seeing? And, this doctor did a patient more harm than good, a patient who wouldn't be stuck with an incompetent therapist if only he'd read the magazine article and been able to ask the right questions.

Well, he hadn't dared a serious coup de grace, but he presented me with the opportunity to deliver my own fatal blow by reacting stupidly—a battlefield wound that might do its work through festering. I had to work carefully, as if picking bone splinters out of a brain, to lead him to an open acknowledgment, however tiny, of his hostile intent, while at the same time leaving him with the reality that I'd neither retaliated nor bled.

"I see. You say your wife got my name from Fran Ferguson. Where do you think she might have gotten my name?"

"How the hell should I know?"

And so it went.

My third patient was a no-show.

Only my last patient, a young man whose anti-psychotic medications I monitored on a monthly basis, was unaffected by the news of the murders. It had no significance in his highly introverted world. He simply had no interest—a welcome relief.

Work, which was usually stimulating and energizing, left me exhausted. I'd had to work to keep my own personal sense of fault separate from the individual spin each patient put on the news.

The phone had rung four times while I was seeing my last patient. I didn't have a secretary, as was the practice with many of us psychiatrists, and I let the machine take the calls while I'm with a patient. I now played back the messages. The first was from the man who hadn't shown up. He said he was not feeling well. Had it been a true virus, or had the news been more than he wanted to deal with? The second call was from a new patient who said she'd have to break her appointment Monday - "Something has come up." - but would call again to reschedule. I stopped the machine and thought about this. She had spoken hurriedly, as if she wanted to get her call over with. I doubted that I'd hear from her again.

I started the machine again. Audrey's voice broke into my gloomy mood. "I just read the paper. That attorney's statement is outrageous. Try not to take it seriously. These guys will say anything to win a case. Give me a call when you're through at the office."

I discovered another one of her many skills was that of cheerleader. Her statement may have been an exaggeration, but it let me know I had an ally.

The final call was a complete surprise. It was from Cora, my ex-wife. "Tom, I read about your patient in the paper this morning. I know this lawyer is riding roughshod over you for his client's sake, but I know it's painful for you. If I can help in any way, let me know."

It had been six years since our divorce and this was the first time she'd contacted me since we'd passed each other in the hall outside the courtroom. She'd put her hand on my arm then and said, "Good luck." The sound of her voice just now grabbed at me inside. It was nice of her to call, but I couldn't think of any way she could help and besides, I'd never ask.

I called Audrey and she fed my need for more support. I asked her to go to dinner with me, but again she had a meeting with Laslo Bach. He was on the point of panic, because the publisher was applying pressure. She also had a book group meeting the following night, but she'd pass it up so we could get together.

I didn't come before Laso and the book, but I'd edged out the book group. I walked down Front Street toward my attorney's office with more spring in my step.

10

Mrs. Booth opened the inner door to Stanley's office as timidly as the mother of a teenage son does his bedroom door. He was on the phone. He waved me to a chair, but continued the conversation. He was wearing a colorful power tie to set off a well-tailored dark suit. Stanley's end of the conversation consisted of grunts punctuated with groans. I sat ten minutes, hoping the time would be billed to the person on the phone and not me—maybe we'd split it. Finally he hung up and told Mrs. Booth to hold all his calls, then reconsidered and told her to put Schaub through if he called.

He offered me a semi-limp grip of his manicured hand across the desk. What the hell, I couldn't help liking Stanley. Anyway, my disgruntlement probably sprang from my dislike of being dependent on him.

"I've been giving this a lot of thought, Tom. You have a problem—actually several problems. You . . ."

"Could be in deep shit."

"Yes, extensive excrement."

I had an image of myself in a small boat nearing the brink of Niagara Falls. I was safe and dry at the moment, but I could hear sure disaster ahead. Defending a lawsuit, even if won, meant money shredding.

"Tell me about my troubles."

"Well, to begin with, Cutler doesn't come cheap. He might well suggest to Mr. Frey that one way to finance his defense is a malpractice suit against you. Do you think he can get expert witnesses to testify that you should have hospitalized him?"

"What do you think?" I said sarcastically. I could see now that engaging Cutler for Harry was double-edged, and I could hear him honing that second edge to take a slice off me.

"Then of course, there is the lawsuit for damages that Plante's bereaved ex-wife might file. They were divorced six months ago. I've sent for a copy of the divorce decree. The question is, was he paying alimony and how much. I would guess, yes and a lot. If the decree states that the alimony terminates at his death . . . Well, the newspaper said he was a very healthy fifty-five. Say he could have lived to ninety with the standard of medical care he could afford; that's thirty-five years of alimony."

He stopped and observed me for a moment. I must have been pale, expecting another blow.

"By the way, Plante had two daughters: they too have viable claims."

Again he appeared to evaluate my condition like a referee pondering whether or not to halt a fight.

"And finally, there is the question of whether or not the Leelanau County District Attorney wants to charge you with violation of the Tarasoff law."

"I have a hunch you've formed an opinion about that."

Stanley may have seen himself in the role of a referee, but I felt more like a person who was being told little by little that he had untreatable cancer. "We found a shadow . . . this is usually a tumor . . . a malignant tumor."

"I believe that because of the celebrity status of one of the victims, the D.A. will have to go for it. If you're convicted it could mean losing your medical license," he added.

I hadn't considered this. It chilled me.

He leaned back in his swivel chair and placed his fingertips together carefully. The fourth fingers hadn't juxtaposed exactly, so he concentrated on adjusting them.

"The Tarasoff case involved a University of California coed named Tatiana Tarasoff and another student at the Berkeley campus named Poddar," he began.

"Stanley, I know about the Tarasoff case. Every psychiatrist is familiar with the story," I sat with irritation caused by his insensitive observation about my future in medicine.

"Poddar had met Tatiana at a folk dancing class. He fell for her, but when he discovered that she didn't share his feelings, he became despondent and made an appointment at the University Health Clinic. There he was evaluated by a psychiatrist, who referred him to a staff psychologist for psychotherapy."

"Yeah, as I said, I know. He told the therapist he was going to kill the girl when she returned to school from the Christmas holiday," I said, hoping to cut the recitation short.

"The psychologist, Dr. Lawrence Moore, consulted two staff psychiatrists, who agreed with him that Poddar should be hospitalized. The campus police were summoned, and they took Poddar into custody."

This was going to be the most costly lecture of my life.

"Upon questioning Poddar," he continued, "The police officers decided on their own that he was rational and released him. When Tatiana returned to campus, Poddar killed her as he'd said he would. Her parents sued Dr. Moore and the university, because they failed to warn their daughter of the danger she was in. They won and on appeal, the Supreme Court of California ruled in their favor. That is the Tarasoff law. It has since been adopted in nearly all the states—most relevantly, Michigan."

"Thank you, Stanley. What you failed to mention is that it has to be a serious threat."

We sat looking at each other, my anxiety mounting, because it had just occurred to me that Stanley thought I was guilty of negligence.

He hadn't finished. Again he realigned his fingertips. "There was another ruling that followed ten years later, Thompson versus Alameda County if I recall correctly, which stated that there must be an identifiable victim. If the patient says, 'I hate the world and I'm going to kill someone', a psychiatrist is not obligated to warn anyone, since there is no specific person to warn."

I figured he was just showing off how much he knew.

"But, that wrinkle in the law is irrelevant in this case," he continued, "because in this case there were specific persons to warn."

"Jesus, Stanley, whose side are you on?"

He smiled an indulgent smile. He was the cool calm professional and I was a hysterical client. "The experts are likely to say you should have erred on the side of safety."

"If I erred, Stanley, it was on the side of safety for the therapy. Calling Marian Frey and Plante would have destroyed my patient's therapy."

"A point, Tom, but I'm afraid a jury will consider the treatment to have been of lesser importance than the lives of your patient's wife and her lover."

"Not very damn supportive this morning are we, Stanley?"

He was right of course; the jury wouldn't give a damn about the therapy. I thought to myself how many times it would have been way less stressful for me to have hospitalized a person expressing suicidal thoughts rather than signaling that I had confidence in his or her ability to continue the work to master their depression by sticking to our usual schedule. I could hear the prosecutor's voice, "Not relevant Your Honor."

Stanley opened a drawer and took out a folder. "We have to line up our own . . . experts. Can you give me some names? People with celebrity status would be best, of course."

Mrs. Booth interrupted. "Mr. Schaub is on line two, Mr. Kramer."

Stanley looked up from the folder. "Tell him I'll call him back."

Hey, Stanley's a great guy.

Back on the street, I felt like Job, happy one minute and trashed the next—a penniless Job to boot. I found myself crossing streets on the wait signal and standing on the curb when the little walking man was urging me on. I noticed the capital "H" on a road sign, meaning that Munson Medical Center lay in that direction. My body made a definite move toward it. It was Cora's offer of help that drew me. Crazy what you'll attempt to grab onto when you're drowning. There was nothing she could do. Maybe lend me money to pay my legal fees. Pediatric surgeons earned a helluva lot more than psychiatrists, but I'd bet our combined savings wouldn't pay an attorney's fees for just my defense on a Tarasoff charge.

11

Last night the man claiming to be my father had told me that he wanted us to meet soon. He'd amended that to, "Immediately." He explained that he was terminally ill with cancer and wanted us to meet and talk while, "I'll still be capable of full sentences." My head was spinning, but the same auxiliary mental system that directs you to crawl along the floor to the stairs in a fire - even though the rest of your mind is screaming, "Run! Get me out of here!" - kicked in. I did a rapid assessment of the situation and concluded I had to do what he suggested; I had to fly to Chicago as soon as possible. I told him I couldn't come today, but would try to make the arrangements to make the trip the following day - Sunday. He told me to take care of what I'd have to do here and he'd see to the travel arrangements.

I had immediately called Derek. This was a time when a psychiatrist needed to talk to a psychiatrist. Half an hour later I drove through the dense pine forest that surrounds his log home west of T.C. He and Frieda, his lab, greeted me and led the way to his living room where Derek poured each of us a glass of port. Donna, whose shift started early the next morning, had already gone to bed.

Derek wanted to know word for word the conversation I'd had with the man calling himself Thomas Morgan. When I'd finished, he said, "Sounds genuine to me. What a bolt from the blue!"

"Driving over here I searched my memory for any story like it I might have heard before. Maybe in a novel by Dumas. The thing is, if I'm convinced he's the real thing after I meet him, what am I going to say to him?"

"I couldn't possibly advise you, old friend. I don't know what

I'd say either. You're going to have to play it by ear. A problem is the time factor he implied. One could say that you should proceed with caution, let the situation become clearer before committing yourself, but, with his implied imminent . . . demise . . ."

We talked on, my repeating my mother's story about my father and Derek, who had met my mother, confirming having heard it from me before.

"Now in retrospect, I'm able to discern that your mother never brought a mention of your father into any conversation I was party to. Even on a casual, social level the name of the deceased spouse enters the surviving spouse's conversation. That's normal; after all, the dead partner had played such a central role in that person's life. I probably put the absence of her mentioning your father down to his having died so many years in the past. Now—if, indeed, this guy turns out to be your father—your mother's behavior becomes very strange. Otherwise, I never saw anything abnormal about her."

During the short, impromptu telephone quiz I'd come up with to test the alleged Thomas Morgan, I'd used up about all that I'd ever known about him. My mother never talked about him and it was clear to me, even as young as I was, that asking questions about him was not a way to win her love, and hers was the only love available. She told me he had died in a car crash in Chicago shortly after having abandoned her and me. I must have been three at that time and I adapted myself quickly to her wish to treat the subject of my father as an unpleasant interlude in her life, best forgotten. She was generally an optimistic person, looking ahead rather than dwelling upon mistakes in the past. I believe I understood her reticence about my father to be consistent with this. I also accepted her hinted assessment of my father's character, or lack of it.

That was about the level of understanding Derek and I achieved before I left him to return home last night. I had experienced comforting from friends three times yesterday. In neither case did Audrey or Derek or Cora solve a problem, but they left me feeling I wasn't alone.

My voice mail informed me, when I got home from Derek's, that the flight arrangements had been made. I was to go to Traverse City's charter air service, Air Services, at 12:50 p.m. tomorrow, Sunday, and a plane would be waiting for me.

I called Audrey and left a message that I'd be going to Chicago the next day and wasn't sure when I'd get back so there was no reason for her to miss her book group.

Air Services office and hangar were located on Airport Access Road, the road to the old airport terminal. I had noticed the building many times going to the former terminal, but had had no occasion to go there. I parked near the first door on the north end of the building and gathered up my small bag. A hall led back to a comfortable, well-appointed waiting area and a counter where a friendly, attractive woman greeted me. I told her who I was and she introduced herself as Cindy and told me my plane was waiting. I looked out the glass doors beyond the waiting room where a corporate jet waited just a few feet away on the concrete apron. I had never flown in anything like this before. I asked and was told it was a Cessna CJ1.

"All that plane for little old me?"

She understood my reaction and smiled. "A jet was ordered. We have a slightly smaller one, but it wasn't available today. The pilots will be ready in a few minutes if you'd like to sit down." She motioned toward the leather seating.

I saw some other planes in a hangar through a glass door at the end of another hallway and a little boy's curiosity made me take a look. Four planes, all white and of differing size, sat on an immaculate, white floor that one could not only eat off of, but on which one could also perform open-heart surgery. Cindy came and got me, saying the pilots were ready to take off. The copilot met me inside the cabin and introduced himself and the pilot, who looked back from his seat in the cockpit and waved. They both looked young enough to have just finished a tour of duty in Afganistan. I declined to have anything to eat or drink once we were in the air and sat back to experience my first private jet ride.

It was 12:50 central time when the plane landed at Chicago Executive Airport south of Wheeling, a less busy and much more convenient airfield than O'Hare to Chicago's northern suburbs. We had been in the air forty-five minutes.

There have been moments in my life when I'd wished I could cancel whatever was scheduled to happen and just turn and run. I never have. I've always marched forward. But when the plane came to a stop on the tarmac and the copilot came out of the cockpit and approached me, I wanted to tell him to get the plane back up in the air. A sixteenth-century churchman about to keep a lunch date with Copernicus must have felt the same, anticipating that his world was about to be turned upside down.

I was to be picked up by a man my alleged father called "Henry, my man Friday." I searched the faces of the men standing at the arrival gate. I was looking for someone described as short, built like a breakwater and wearing a U of M cap.

I spotted him walking toward me, his hand out. "Pleased to meet you, Doctor. I'm Henry Thorp."

He immediately took off the cap, saying, "I grew up in Columbus—Ohio State fan. Your dad, telling you I'd be wearing this damn thing is just the latest round in our on-going battle. He won this one." He smiled broadly. "I'll think of something to get even."

A traffic light stopped us as we left the airport. He turned to look at me. "This has gotta be one helluva thing for you."

There was such an honest straightforward quality to his

statement that I answered in kind. "I'd say I'm plain scared."

The light changed and we moved on. "Yeah, he's been a damn fool, not contacting you before. I've been really pissed off with him and I've let him know. Oh, I understand how he feels. He'd already avoided it so long and so it was always easier to delay a little longer. Time ran out on him."

"He said on the phone last night that he had terminal cancer."

"A melanoma. Too many hours on the golf course without a hat. Vain bastard. He's got a head of hair like yours only it's white. He claimed it was too thick for the sun to penetrate."

We rode in silence for some miles and then he said in an off-hand manner, "Your mother told you your father had been killed in an accident."

It was a statement, but it was also a question.

"That's right."

"She said that he'd abandoned the two of you."

I made no reply, so he shot me a glance and I supplied the affirmation he expected.

"Did she say why he'd left you?"

"No." It was like facing an attorney with good timing, like tapping a hoop at the right place and with the right timing to keep it rolling.

"And you didn't ask, I take it."

This kind of interrogation by a stranger had gone too far, yet his manner—like a tough, rough-times-burnished old rancher, implying that there was no time for waltzing and bullshit—made it OK.

"No, I didn't ask her."

"So, the whole story, as you know it, was that he had abandoned you and then he was killed in an accident—period." He said this with empathy, not the incredulous, sarcastic tone that same attorney would have used to address the jury.

"Isn't that interesting. I mean the way the mind works." His tone contained only the awe we feel when confronted by that which is surprising in nature.

"What do you mean?" I asked.

"I mean, you became a psychiatrist, a person who asks people a lot of difficult questions about themselves." He paused, searching for the right words. "I mean, you couldn't ask your mother the obvious questions and you've . . . perhaps consequently spent your career asking others just these same kind of questions . . . the ones you couldn't ask your mother . . . or yourself."

I was shocked, as if he'd hit me in the gut—as if I'd been stripped. He'd summarized my professional life as a little boy probing for the truth in others, because he couldn't face the truth in himself. My reaction told me there was at least some validity to what he'd said. I looked at this stranger for a sign that he was self-satisfied with his observation. It wasn't there, he had made it in the same spirit that one might point out to a friend that he resembled his brother.

We drove on into a wealthy suburb, the homes gaining in grandeur with each block. I relaxed a bit and said, "OK, you tell me the answers to those questions."

Henry smiled. "I'd better let your father tell it. One thing you can be sure of, it'll be the truth."

He turned into a brick paved driveway. The size of the trees that lined it said that people had been living here for a very long time. At the drive's end stood the kind of house you'd expect. The charter jet was no rash, desperate expenditure.

Henry got out, waited for me and then led the way to the front door.

12

From the entrance foyer, we entered a long room with a massive fireplace. Several groupings of furniture were arranged in such a way that there remained plenty of open floor space scattered with oriental rugs. It was a room for a cocktail party of easily forty guests, leaving comfortable openings for the caterer's people to pass among them with their trays of drinks and appetizers. Not a decorator's creation this room, but an eccentric collection of individual purchases, each no doubt with its own story. A short hall lined with books led to a sunroom bright with the morning light.

A man obviously suffering from the depletion and pain of a life-sapping illness rose unsteadily from a wicker chair. He looked more debilitated than I had expected. Putting aside the alteration caused by his illness, it was evident that he was a man sure of himself and one used to seeing this self-evaluation reflected in the opinions of others. He was shorter than I. His hair, while thick like mine was totally white. His eyes were gray, also like mine. His other features were enough like those I see every morning in my mirror to remove any doubt from my mind that I was facing my father.

He held out his hand to me, a twinkle in his eyes. "Dr. Morgan, I presume."

"Sir," I returned.

"Have a seat," he said nodding to the chair that faced his and turned to Henry Thorp. "Henry, I think I can take it from here; thanks for the help."

He lowered himself part way, then surrendered to gravity with a sigh. "Two things not worth talking about: what you should have done and how our bodies fall apart. The first is pure fiction and the last is too trite to be a topic for conversation."

He'd said this humorously, now he looked at me eye to eye.

"I'm your father, Thomas Christopher Morgan. The Christopher is for Wren; your grandfather was an architect. I know you bought Crawford Croft's place. It would have pleased him. I don't know if you know this, likely not, but you have a large family back east. You'll have to check that out on your own now."

With a rueful smile he said, "I'm sorry for coming on like that. I'm just filling the air with words to delay saying simply that I know I was a failure as a father and I'm profoundly sorry."

I was dumbfounded. I couldn't think of anything to follow this. What could I say? "Hey, no problem, forget it." I watched him move around in his chair, apparently seeking relief from pain that he'd already said he wasn't going to speak about.

More comfortable now, his face and manner relaxed a bit. "I know this has to be overwhelming for you and I wish there had been another way to do this, but ... there wasn't."

A middle-aged woman wearing an apron appeared in the doorway to an adjacent room.

"Excuse me Mr. Morgan, but is there anything you want before I start preparing lunch?"

'Oh, of course! I should have offered you a drink, Tom. Thank God Victoria monitors my manners. Tom, this is Mrs. Victoria Morales. Victoria, this is my son, Tom. Dr. Thomas Morgan."

"I'm happy to meet you Doctor." Her expression added, "at last."

"I'm happy to meet you, Mrs. Morales."

"I'll have a Bowmore, as usual, Victoria. What'll you have, Tom?"

I didn't know Bowmore, but I figured it must be a single

something—Scotch or Irish. "The same would be fine for me, please."

"Neat or with water?" he asked.

"Neat is good."

When she had gone, he put his hand on a spiral notebook that lay on a table by his chair. "I've spent a lot of time these past six months writing a kind of memoir about my family—your family—myself and how I met your mother . . . all that. It's not a finished product and now it never will be. When I started it, I had no reason to think there was a deadline. I'd like you to take it to read . . . or not."

Victoria returned with a tray on which stood a half-full bottle of Scotch and two glasses. He poured a triple shot in each glass and handed me one.

Smiling he said, "Cheers!" and then began soberly, "I'll start at the end of the story. I've been planning to contact you for years, but I've always put it off, telling myself that after all this time I had no right to barge into your life and present you with facts you might rather not know." He took a swallow of the Scotch. "I'm doing it now, because I've been diagnosed with metastatic melanoma and they are telling me my time is short—very short. Only discovered it two weeks ago. My barber discovered it on my scalp. Not very big, but the MRI showed that it had spread widely. I'd noticed fullness on the right side of my abdomen, but I'd ignored it, put it down to too many calories. Turns out it's my liver. Full of cancer."

I glanced at his head as he talked, but saw no sign of recent surgery. I guessed it had been a punch biopsy with no further excision since . . .

He stopped and thought about what he'd just said. He obviously was still finding it unbelievable. He shook his head as if to shake those thoughts away. "Well anyway, since, aside from a few bequests, you are my only heir and would be hearing soon from my lawyers anyway, I decided to call you. I wanted us to meet."

I felt like I was passively riding in a car through the House of Horrors at an amusement park. One startling thing after another was springing out at me, not the least troubling of which was the idea that my mother, whom I'd trusted implicitly, had lied to me. And this lie was a whopper.

Victoria again appeared carrying a tray and began setting the lunch out on a table against one wall of the room. Having finished, she came over to him and helped him walk to his place at the table. She poured each of us a glass of wine and then left the room. I noticed, however, that while busying herself in the next room, she glanced from time to time with concern at my father.

I cut and took a bite of the quesadilla on my plate. It was delicious and I was hungry. I became aware that he was not eating, just watching me.

"Sorry, I was only thinking of how to summarize those early years. I wasn't happy with your mother."

I felt a stirring of anger. Was he about to criticize my mother when she wasn't here to defend herself?

He saw this. "I'm not interested in bad mouthing your mother. I couldn't anyway. I thought she was a . . . good mother. I just want to explain how I felt, so you'd understand."

I relaxed, sipped at the wine.

"We were entirely different types of people," he continued. "But one overlooks that at that age. You just fall in love or whatever it is. I was studying towards an electrical engineering degree at the university when I met her. In short order, she got pregnant—with you, and we got married—remember this was some forty years ago. I dropped out of school to get a job to support us—a common story back then. I could have, instead, borrowed money from my parents back east, but getting a job seemed the manly responsible thing to do. I thought I'd be out of school a semester or two, save money and get back on course

91

again. Of course, it didn't work that way. On the money I could earn as an apprentice electrician, we couldn't save. And then, there was a recession and getting any job was tough. When you were three, I was offered a job with a large construction outfit that had taken on a big job in downtown Chicago. The pay was going to be better than I could get locally. It meant I'd be away for three months. I got there, liked the people I was working with, liked Chicago, and faced up to the fact that I was happier away from your mother. But I didn't seriously think of splitting up—there was you. "

"And then a strange thing happened." His face was drawn, partly I was sure from the illness-engendered fatigue, but it was remembering this "strange thing" that brought about the sudden change. He raised his wine glass to drink, but then put it back down.

"For a while I'd noticed something different in your mother, when we talked on the phone. She began questioning me in a way she apparently thought was subtle about whom I was seeing, where I'd been the night before and so on. Her voice was very tense. I'd remained in touch with your uncle, Tim. He and I had roomed together our freshman year. In fact it had been through him that your mother and I met. I called him and told him about my concern and asked what he thought. He hadn't seen her for over a month, but said he'd make a point of visiting her. He called me back confirming that she was acting strange, seemed suspicious, wary. He said he'd find a reason to make a follow up visit."

My father looked at me as if he were not sure I'd understand what he was about to say.

"Then she did the damnedest thing. When Tim went to our house a few days later he discovered that she'd told you that I'd been killed in a car accident." My father looked to me again for confirmation that what he'd just told me was crazy. "My first thought when Tim told me was, that's crazy: how can she say that; doesn't she realize I could just walk in and tell you it wasn't true? Tim said it was clear that she'd had what he termed a 'nervous breakdown'. He had an appointment scheduled for her to be seen by a psychiatrist and wanted me to sit tight until he learned more."

He looked down at the plate of food he hadn't touched, shaking his head. "Oh yes, Tim said her change in mood was the weirdest thing. She was no longer tense. She even appeared mildly elated. Anyway, I waited. I wanted to call and ask to talk to you, but the psychiatrist advised against it. After talking to your mother, he understood that she had been terribly afraid that I would abandon her. She believed I was angry with her because your birth caused me to have to quit school. She was sure that my taking the job in Chicago was an excuse to get away. The odd, tense behavior your uncle had observed was a sign of an impending psychosis. She was breaking down - as I understood it - under the chronic emotional stress her fear of abandonment had caused. She then went on to form a totally irrational, psychotic solution to her fear: I had not abandoned her. Instead, I had been killed."

He moved a little in his chair in obvious pain, then continued, "I'd never heard anything like this before. I had no knowledge of insanity. It was gobbledygook, but I had sense enough to realize I was out of my depth, so I decided I'd stand on the sidelines and wait a bit."

His story had cast my whole childhood in a different reality. In part, I wanted to tell him to stop—that I couldn't digest any more— that I couldn't even begin to absorb what he'd already claimed, but I submitted to his need to explain himself.

"This doctor presented your mother's case at a meeting of the university's psychiatric department. The consensus was that it was advisable not to disturb your mother's delusion that had 'stabilized' her from slipping into a deeper, maybe irrevocable psychosis. With support from her family and medication, it could be expected that with time she'd give up the delusion. There were a lot of 'ifs' and 'maybes' in their recommendations, and don't forget this was not their lives they were speculating about, but I knelt to their authority. Weeks became months, my job in Chicago was finished. Tim reported that you seemed to have assimilated my "death" well and were thriving. It's a crazy story!

"I'm aware that my hope in telling you all this is to make excuses for myself and argue that I was doing what the experts advised, and say that I really was a good father in an impossible position, but it isn't true--at least not totally. I liked my life in Chicago. I'd made friends. I was happier without your mother. I wanted a divorce and to get custody of you. While the doctors were talking about eventual recovery with the proper this and the proper that, in my heart, I didn't believe it would ever happen. Looking back, I recognized that she'd shown signs of mental problems since we'd met. At the same time, I could see that taking her to court to get a divorce and custody might push her off the deep edge for good. I was ready to listen to Tim tell me that you were just fine. I convinced myself that having a dead father might be better than having one who'd won custody at the cost of condemning your mother to the hell of insanity."

He sighed. "I convinced myself I had to make a life for myself here in Chicago. One of the guys I'd worked with suggested we start our own contracting business. He'd saved up some money and I borrowed from my parents. Building was booming and it turned out to be the ideal time for us. We grew. We grew until we were the largest electrical contractor in the state. From the very beginning, I'd been sending money for your and your mother's support. Tim handled it. I know you thought the money came from him. He'd been put in a very difficult spot by the way things had spun out. He didn't want to be in that role, but that had become the program—one he'd been part of initiating. I hope you can appreciate how important he's been for you your whole life."

I was shaken to the core with what he'd said so far. If it were true, why didn't I recognize that my mother had a problem so blatant that it would permit this kind of massive delusion? I recognized that she had few friends outside of my uncle, but I thought she was just shy and preferred to be by herself to read and work in her garden. I was busy with my own friends and she seemed happy enough. But, again, if this tale was true, I was blind to the point of . . . I'd think about it later.

"I've been with you in the wings for important events." he went on, "Like your graduation from high school, undergrad and medical school. I was in a parked car watching you and your bride come out of the church. Later at the reception, when Tim signaled to me that your mother was occupied and the coast was clear, I even shook your hand and congratulated you."

Good God! I began searching my memory for his face. Impossible, of course, there had been so much hand shaking and backslapping that day.

"I also met a woman here in Chicago whom I loved very much. Virginia understood my position and didn't mind our not getting married. She had no wish for children. Our friends thought we were married, but she'd wanted to keep her maiden name. When your mother died four years ago, we did tie the knot. Tragically, Virginia also died a year ago in a car accident."

He looked uncomfortable with what he'd just related about his bliss with another woman. Covering this, he hurried on, "You're in a jam because of that patient of yours who killed his wife and Brian Plante. Don't look surprised; I read the paper. I talked to my lawyer and he talked to his friends. They think you are in a serious spot. I only say this to let you know I've done my homework. Before I say anything else, I want to pass along what I've learned over the years. You may believe I'm making like Polonius, but that's OK. It's this: never appear to be weak. You have a strong hand, but you're willing to cut a deal, because it will save you time and you have more important things to do." He laughed out loud. "On the way to the scaffold let the executioner know you've better things to do, so you'll cut a deal."

We sat looking at each other. I wondered if my disappointment showed. I didn't know what to say. Was this the advice he'd been saving up for me: learn to bluff well. Was the lesson from both of my parents that the truth came last?

He went on, "The other thing I wanted you to know is that I know Brian Plante. I've been involved with projects where he's been one of the investors. From what I've heard, if your patient hadn't killed him, someone else would have — another angry husband. If I can collect enough of these stories it may point to justifiable homicide. Best yet, we might identify another credible suspect."

"Sounds good," I said. He didn't know or had forgotten that Harry had confessed.

Establishing that the homicide was justified could possibly help Harry Frey, but it would not help me at all. Even if Cutler were encouraged to change his tactics in Harry's defense, the fact remained that I knew about the threat that Harry had made - and carried through - and I didn't warn the victims. I was about to say this when his eager expression made me pause. He sincerely wanted to help me. He wanted to make amends, build that kite with me that he'd failed to do.

"Yes, but won't it be too much with your illness?"

"No problem. I'll get to work on it this evening. My life for the past twenty-five years has been networking."

I looked at my watch. "It's time I should be getting back to the airport. Thanks very much, by the way, for the special ride. It's definitely the only way to fly," I said with irony.

He got to his feet. "I like what I've seen of my son. I only hope . . ." He started to cough, his frail body racked with the effort. Victoria materialized in an instant.

"Son, I'm going to take a nap, but I'll be on the phone this evening. I'll be in touch."

I said goodbye to Henry Thorp at the airport, asking him to contact me if my father's condition deteriorated quickly. Henry presented a stoic exterior; inside that, I discerned a sympathetic friend. There was no mystery why my father valued his company.

I took my seat in the plane, noting that I was quickly adapting to this form of travel. As we taxied I called the answering machine at my office. There were three new messages. The first was from a young man who said that Dr. Shaw had referred him to me for treatment. He left his number at work and home. It was good to hear that someone wanted to see me in spite of the publicity, but what pleased me most was that Audrey had made the referral.

The second message surprised me. The man said he was Leelanau County Sheriff Davis. He asked to be contacted as soon as I was able, and left his number at Sheriff's Headquarters. Why would he want to talk to me - and on a Sunday?

The third message was a cymbal crash. A middle-aged woman with a nasty, angry voice ranted about psychiatrists messing with good people's minds and turning them into killers. She ended with a threat that my "time was coming." A stunner, like getting clotheslined in the dark. Where did all that anger come from? I knew it wasn't personal— she didn't know me—and that the woman had problems, but it sure felt personal and very unsettling. Unsettling also, because I knew there were a lot of unbalanced fanatics out there. And, in Michigan, if the legislators have their way, they could all carry guns—anywhere.

I called the number the sheriff had left and was told by the receptionist that the sheriff wasn't available at the moment and would I like his voice mail. I left the message that I was just flying out of Chicago and would call him when I got to Traverse City.

The flight back home was a needed respite. My father, of course, was on my mind. Suddenly I had a father, back from the dead and soon to be dead again.

The copilot came back to my seat and asked if I'd like something. Again I declined, but I noticed his interruption of my thoughts had irritated me. Why? What had I been thinking about? Two words came to mind—four years. With those words the anger flowed freely. My mother had been dead for four years. There could have been no excuse not to contact me after she'd died. He'd said that he didn't want to disturb the status quo in my mother's condition and her relationship with me. Bull shit! He didn't want to change anything in his life, his life with his new wife. But, she'd been dead for a year already. What about after that? He'd waited until he was terminally ill to tidy things up, to assuage his guilt! The gall to sit there and offer me his wisdom of a lifetime, and what wisdom at that: learn to bluff well!

My level of anger tripped a reminder alarm that had by this time become hard-wired in me: try to look at the situation from the other guy's perspective. The same professor who had armed us students with the slogan, non illigitimus carborundum, had pointed out that everyone is doing the best he or she can at every moment, given the circumstances as they perceived them. I'd rebelled against such an idea when I'd first heard it, but over the years I've come to see that it is true . . . in every case.

Still, he was a lousy father. Did that mean I should withhold a dying man's wish to make amends? I didn't think so. And . . . to be honest, I was glad I had a father . . . if only for a short time.

I thought again about the wisdom my father thought was so valuable, always appear to have a strong hand, but be willing to cut a deal. I thought about it as it might apply to my current problems until we landed and taxied to a stop. I concluded there was nothing I could fool anyone about.

13

I thanked Mike, the pilot, for the great ride and walked to my car in the parking area. As I walked I called Sheriff Davis again.

"Doctor Morgan, thank you for returning my call. My call has to do with one of our prisoners. I'm told that Harry Frey is a patient of yours. Is that right?"

"Yes, that's right."

"He still is?"

"Yes, I consider him a patient. Why, may I ask?"

"Doctor, I believe it would be in his best interest if he were able to talk to you. I mean here at the jail."

But, what about the order banning visitors, I wondered. Surely the sheriff would know about that. Was he purposely violating the order? "Ah, I see. Do you mean, perhaps, in the interest of his health?"

"Yes, that's what I mean. If you're able to, now would be a good time."

What was this all about? I thought it best not to pursue that question. I would find out soon enough.

"I'm just leaving the airport, so I should be there in half an hour."

"I'll be here."

I parked and entered the building as I had two days ago. The receptionist looked up as I approached the window, and buzzed the door open as I said "Doctor." I was expected. She led the way back to the office with Davis's name on the door.

It was the first time I'd met the man. I'd seen his picture in the paper, the usual official portrait, but one couldn't appreciate the guy's total mass from a picture. He'd been an All Big Ten tackle at Michigan State. I'd seen him play in The Big House, but then he was standing next to guys about as large. I remember wishing he'd been wearing maize and blue.

He rose from his desk chair and came forward to greet me, shaking my hand, or something like a handshake, because his hand was too large for me to grip.

"Thank you for coming, Doctor," he said as he guided me out of his office and down a long hall. "I am concerned about my inmate, Harry Frey. I believe he is depressed and in need of professional evaluation."

He said this in a perfunctory manner, as if speaking a required formula like reading a detainee his legal rights. He also maintained a gait that was faster than mine, so I could never catch up to ask more about his request that I come there.

When we got to the jail section of the building, we had to wait a moment for a deputy to open the door, so I approached the question that had been on my mind ever since he'd asked me on the phone to come to see Harry. "Sheriff Davis, I understood there is a court order against Mr. Frey having visitors."

"That's true. You are, as I said, here solely in a professional capacity."

Again, I had the feeling he was speaking pro forma. This wasn't the real Hoss Davis I was talking to.

He gave the deputy instructions to have Harry brought to an interrogation room to talk with me.

"When you're through, Doctor, I'd appreciate your remarks on a form that Deputy Wolf will give you. He will show you how to get out to the parking area, and thanks again."

Very strange I thought. I was shown into a room where Harry arrived after several minutes.

"Dr. Morgan," he said, surprised. "Thanks for coming. I told the sheriff I wanted to talk to you. I told him I was very depressed, but I didn't know if he'd contact you."

"You asked to see me?"

"Yeah, I had to explain."

I carried a chair around the table and placed it next to the chair he'd taken.

"Explain what?"

"Explain what Cutler is up to."

That surprised me. "What Cutler is up to," made me think of some covert, sneaky act. My expression asked for an explanation.

"I have to start at the beginning. It's the only way to help you understand his thinking and it's very important to me that you do understand. From the moment the police arrived at my house, I could see that they thought I had committed the murders. My impulse was to say there was a mistake, and I would have if you hadn't so forcefully cautioned me to say nothing at all until I was with an attorney. As soon as I could think somewhat calmly about the situation, I could understand how the cops were so sure. It was my gun, I had a perfect motive and the strong smell of gunpowder meant the killing took place shortly before I found the bodies."

What had he just said?

"You found the bodies? Do you mean they were already dead when you found them?"

"Yes, of course. You mean that you thought I shot them?"

"But, you told me on the phone that you had."

"I don't remember what I said on the phone, but I couldn't have said I killed them, because . . . well, because I didn't."

"You didn't? Jesus, I told a deputy that you'd confessed."

"I see. Well, that explains the detective in charge telling Cutler that I'd confessed."

I tried to remember the exact words he'd used, but I could no longer be sure.

"I could have sworn that's what you told me. I'm sorry."

He thought about this for a moment. "Yeah, I understand. If you'd heard me say I did it, then naturally you'd report that."

He was silent. I thought he must have been digesting the fact that his own psychiatrist had contributed to everyone's belief that he was a killer.

"As it turns out," he said at last, "this idea that I'd confessed strengthens Cutler's defense. In his opinion, having confessed my sins, as it were, makes those sins more forgivable, and forgiveness is the cornerstone of his defense. You see, he believes we don't have a snowball's chance of winning a plea of not guilty. The evidence is too strong against me. He believes - and he's had a lot of experience with juries - that our best chance is to plead guilty as a result of temporary insanity. That conviction will get me committed to a psychiatric hospital, from which I could be discharged in a few years once the docs feel comfortable that I'm not innately insane. I was only a guy who went nuts for a moment when he discovered his wife with another man.

"Whereas, if we claim I'm innocent - which is the truth - Cutler believes I'll likely lose and get a life prison sentence. And since it was a double murder and one victim was a big shot in the community, it would be life without parole."

"I don't understand. Can an attorney say in court that his client is guilty when he knows otherwise?"

"Yeah, I know it sounds strange at first, but a lawyer is not required to believe what his client claims, he must only do the best he can to defend him. And I am convinced Cutler has read the situation correctly, because not only was the gun that fired the shots mine and only my prints were on it, but it was also kept in a drawer

102

in my study where only I - and Marian of course - knew where it was kept. The timing too is against me. There is no evidence of anyone else having been there as I was at the time they died. And then there is my 'confession'. Even if you took the stand and said that you misheard what I'd said on the phone, there would be doubt in the jurors' minds - perhaps your memory was adjusting itself to your wish to help me."

"Mr. . . Harry. I'm not able . . . well, this is all so surprising . . . Please start at the very beginning of what went on that day."

"OK." He paused while he organized the story in his mind. "Let's see. I started driving from my office in the city out to your office to keep our eleven o'clock appointment. I was very embarrassed about my behavior during our session the day before and the farther I drove the more I felt that I didn't want to have to talk about it with you. When I was nearing Suttons Bay - South Shore Drive - I made the sudden decision to turn off and drive home instead. But, the road was barricaded, because of an annual 10K race that follows South Shore Drive for a few miles. A cop told me that the last runners were just about to finish, so I waited until the road was opened and I then drove on home. What I'd planned to do was grab a yogurt and then drive back to T.C., since I had more work to do at the office. I parked in front and went in the front door. As I entered, I thought I heard Marian in the kitchen and started back that way. She wasn't there. Walking over to the refrigerator I saw a couple of scraps of paper on the floor - one was a register receipt from Hansen's Market that Marian must have dropped. As I stooped to pick them up - my head nearer the floor where the odor was stronger - I became aware of the smell of burnt gunpowder. I followed the intensity of the odor to the bedroom hallway and on down to our bedroom. I stood for a few moments paralysed in the doorway when I saw their bodies. It was obvious that they were both dead. It was a horrible sight and I guess I looked away and my eye fell on the pistol lying on the floor. It looked like mine. This really surprised me and I went and picked it up to make sure. It was mine all right. It came to me at that moment that I had to do something, call someone. I knew you were at your office waiting for me, so I put the gun in my jacket pocket and went to the study and used that phone to call you."

He gazed at me as if mesmerized by the scene he had just described. "That's the story," he said.

I was thinking of the strong smell of gunpowder that I'd experienced when I first arrived at his place and the fresh, liquid blood on both corpses. In other words, evidence that the shooting had happened only minutes before. The first thing one thinks of when a person is suspected of a crime is alibi. But Harry Frey could have no alibi, because he was there in the house alone at essentially the same time as the killings took place.

"There was no other car at your house?"

"None in front. I didn't go around back, but if there had been a car it would have still been there when the police arrived."

And there was a car, I'd learned; Marian's car was in the garage.

"What about on the road? Did you meet a car when you drove home after the barricade was lifted?"

"No. And here's a fact the police may not have thought of: I couldn't have met another car as I drove home, because the road had been closed at both ends for an hour."

He studied me to see if I understood the point he was making about how all evidence was against him.

"Here's the thing, Doctor. I can't endure a life sentence. I would have to kill myself. We all know what happens to people like me in prison. I'd be raped. I'd fight back and would probably end up with a "shank" between the ribs. So, you see, I have to go along with Cutler's plan. The problem for me with that is what it will do to you. He will lean heavily upon the idea that you should have warned Marian and

104

Plante about the threat I made in your office. I told him about that. Cutler will make sure everyone knows what I'd said, because he intends to turn blame for the murders on you - your fault that the murders happened. He said it is the psychology of a jury today to blame the professional, because the jurors tend to identify with the poor guy who suffered as a result of incompetence. I know you acted as you should have. You were right, I didn't harm anyone. But Cutler will convince the jury Marian and Plante are dead because of you.

"I hate that Doctor, but I've given this a lot of thought and I've concluded I have no choice. It will be hard on you, but you won't be going to prison for life."

Like that mountain climber who cut a fellow climber's life-line, he was telling me he had to sacrifice me in order to save himself. Of course, he was giving me the option of revealing to the world the story he'd just related, but he had laid out the consequences of my doing so—he would go to prison and die at the hands of other inmates or by his own hand. I don't know if he was counting on it, but there was no way that I could let myself become responsible for his getting a life sentence - and its consequences.

"Did you tell the sheriff any of this when you asked to talk to me?"

"Not all of it, but I did say that I was innocent and I needed to tell you that."

"And he didn't ask you to explain?"

"Sure. Sure he did, but Cutler said I wasn't to talk about it and . . . I'd already said more than Cutler said I should . . . so I didn't tell the sheriff more. I said my lawyer said I wasn't to say anything."

I thought about what he said. Had Davis believed him?

"So no one knows the details of your story except Cutler and me?"

"That's right--and the real killer."

What he'd just said stunned me. Of course, if he didn't do it, someone else did.

"My God yes. Do you have any . . . "

"None. And believe me I've thought hard about that. It would solve my problem. One of the hardest things about accepting Cutler's advice, in addition to the fallout you may suffer, is the fact that Marian's killer is not being sought. I said that to Cutler and he pointed out that even if I shouted from the roof tops that I was innocent, the real killer would not be sought, because the police are satisfied that the case is solved. That's something I plan on doing on my own."

"What do you mean?"

"Finding the real killer. I'll hire a private detective agency. I can't do so now because there's the chance that it would jeopardize Cutler's defense if it became known that I was searching for the killer. That's too bad, because a crime is harder to solve the older it gets, but just as soon as the trial is over, no matter the verdict, I'll launch my investigation."

I had a better appreciation of Cutler's problem. He had a client who had described to his psychiatrist just the day before how he would kill someone, the guy had no alibi and the murder weapon was found in his pocket with only his fingerprints on it. Cutler could go for a plea of not guilty and take his chances. But if he did, he would loose the dramatic effect of playing what he saw before him as a trump card—ME. If he went for the insanity defense right at the outset, he could point the public finger of blame at me, the arrogant shrink, who plays God with other people's lives. Very fucking creative Holden old boy. I saw that it would be his aim to make me appear to be the most negligent, uncaring son-of-a-bitch of all time.

Just then it came to me what I'd been doing the night after I'd heard Harry make those threats. I had actually enjoyed a dinner with the therapist of one of the victims. Cutler could elicit her testimony to reveal that I hadn't cared enough to warn her of the real danger to her patient. I'd be dead meat when he finished with me.

I talked with Harry a little longer, shifting to an attempt to reassure him. I very much wanted to believe him; it meant I hadn't been wrong in my assessment of his threats. But as for the direction his attorney was taking . . . I was confused and very worried about how I'd end up.

I pressed the button to signal the guard that I was ready to leave. A deputy came to take Harry back to his cell and Deputy Wolf gave me the evaluation form the sheriff had mentioned, which I guessed was for Judge Hackett's eyes. I checked off the boxes next to ten questions and added the comment that I thought the consultation had been timely and that I advised a follow-up visit.

Instead of giving the deputy the form and leaving as the sheriff had suggested, I told the deputy that I needed to give the form directly to his boss, because some details needed to be explained. He gave me directions on how to retrace my steps to Davis's office. He must also have alerted the sheriff I was coming, because he was standing in his office doorway waiting for me.

"There was something you wanted to explain, Doctor?"

He stepped aside for me to pass and motioned for me to enter, then closed the door.

"You know what Harry Frey just told me, isn't that right?"

"Ah, I respect the fact that it was a privileged communication between a patient and his doctor," Hoss answered quietly.

I brushed that aside. "I think you must believe him, or why would you go against a court order forbidding visitors, an order Holden Cutler buttered up Judge Hackett to make in order to prevent Mr. Frey from slipping and making the mistake of saying he was innocent and thereby blowing the insanity plea out of the water."

His smile said I was on target. When he put words to the smile, it was to say, "If I believed everything I hear in this place, Doctor, I'd become one of your patients."

He said that while getting up and going to the door which he opened.

"Thanks for coming down, Doctor Morgan."

Part way out the door I stopped. "Sheriff, what was the time of death?"

He looked surprised. "Why, just a few minutes before we got there, of course. The blood was only beginning to clot and the core temperatures of the bodies had only dropped a degree or so."

Again with a smile as if kidding me, he added, "I thought you of all people would have noticed that."

I had my phone out of my pocket and Audrey's number dialed before I got to my car.

"Tom," she said sounding pleased. "What was he like?"

Harry Frey and his blockbuster revelation was all that was on my mind and her question, "What was he like?" didn't make sense.

"Your father: was he really your father?"

"Oh. I'm sorry. I was thinking of something else. Yes, miracle of miracles. There's a lot to tell you about, but another subject is more pressing. I'd like to meet you to talk about it. It concerns Harry Frey."

"Sure. When?"

"As soon as possible."

"I see. How about if we meet at your place. We won't be disturbed."

"Good. I'll be there in half an hour."

Five minutes after I got home Audrey walked through the door saying, "I'm so anxious to hear what he was like. And why he never contacted you before."

"There's a lot to tell, but first I've got to get your input about

Harry Frey."

I took her coat and hung it on a hook, got us two glasses of wine and guided her with a tender hand on her back to the living room couch. We sat and I half turned to face her.

"First, I'm going to ask you to not repeat what I'm about to tell you. I know that asking that without your knowing more is asking a lot, but I think you'll understand once I've told you."

She studied my face, a serious and expectant expression on hers. "OK."

"Harry Frey told me he didn't shoot Plante and Marian. He said he came home and found them dead."

Audrey's expression was of total confusion. "But he told you that he'd . . .He admitted that he did it."

"That's what I thought. Now he says he didn't say that and I can't remember his exact words."

"But Tom, think about this calmly. You are very practiced in hearing what people tell you. You couldn't be mistaken about something like this."

I shrugged. "Here's the thing; his attorney, Cutler, in spite of Harry having told him he was innocent is planning to plead guilty due to temporary insanity. He has directed Harry to tell no one about his story of innocence. Apparently he believes this way Harry has a better chance of avoiding a first-degree murder conviction and a life sentence."

Audrey appeared dumbfounded. "But, can he do this, plead guilty when his client says he's innocent?"

"I doubt if attorneys make a habit of this. I've certainly never heard of it, but I imagine the law says he can proceed with any defense he deems best for his client."

She sat and thought about the idea. "If it's true, his innocence solves your problem."

"How's that?"

"Right now, you're being blamed for not warning Marian and Plante of Harry's threat. If Harry didn't do it, then where's the blame?"

"You're right, but there's a problem. Harry told Cutler what he'd said in my office and Cutler realized that when that threat was known - as it soon was after I'd told Lieutenant Panetta - he'd never be able to win a not guilty plea. No jury would believe it was a coincidence that Plante was shot in the exact way Harry had described. So, Cutler decided he should go with the insanity argument. So, you see, even though I believe Harry, I can't reveal that he says he's not guilty, because that would jeopardize the insanity defense. I know that if he went to a psychiatric facility the docs would declare him sane in a couple of years at most and he'd go free – half-way house and then probation."

Audrey was nodding slowly. "The part about being released . . . that's correct."

Still nodding she added, "On the one hand you remain silent about your patient's claim of innocence and thereby save him from a life behind bars. On the other hand you tell the world Harry said both wife and lover were dead when he came home and you do the best thing for your reputation and your net worth."

"Thank you," I said with a chuckle. "I wasn't able to distill it so clearly."

We each took a swallow of wine.

"So," I asked, "Which choice should I take?"

"I know what I selfishly want for you . . . and me. I want everyone to know you acted correctly when you chose not to warn Marian and Brian Plante. But . . . I don't think that will be your choice."

She reached out and squeezed my hand. "Don't worry, I give you my word I won't tell anyone that Harry claims he's innocent."

Her loyalty felt very reassuring.

"There's this, Harry also said he slipped up and told the sheriff he was innocent. I confronted Davis, but he acted like he didn't know anything. He gave no indication that he believed Harry or that he was planning to act on Harry's claim."

Audrey thought about this. "I imagine most people claim innocence. Now tell me about your Dad."

I gave her a full account of my trip to Chicago. When I'd finished, she said, "I'm bothered by one point; why did he wait so long to make contact?"

I shrugged. My thoughts were shifting to being next to her. I moved closer and we kissed passionately, then she said, "Why don't you come over to my place and I'll make us something to eat."

I didn't welcome the break at the moment, but there was a note of promise in her voice.

"Sounds good. Is there something I can bring?"

"A bottle of this same wine . . . and your toothbrush."

I floated around my apartment for the next ten minutes, all other thoughts now pushed aside except that of my toothbrush. The phone interrupted my euphoria.

"Tom, it's Derek. I'm curious about your trip to Chicago."

"There's much to tell, but I need your help with a more immediate issue."

"Sounds serious."

"It is . . . very serious."

"No problem. When do you want to talk?"

"If I drive out to your place now, are you free to talk?"

"Sure, and Donna just came in the door, so she's here too."

"I can't tell Donna this. It has to be between you and me. I have a dinner date with Audrey, but I have time to swing by your house first."

"OK, I'll see you in what, fifteen minutes?"

"More like half an hour. I've got to take a quick shower."

I hung up the phone, wondering for an instant if I was doing the right thing telling Derek. Not telling him felt like a breach of our relationship. He was my best friend and keeping this kind of thing from him negated the whole meaning of "best friend." True, telling him would present him with the problem of not telling his wife, a cop. Yet, I knew Derek's attitude would be the same as Tony Salpino's downstairs, "What are friends for?"

He opened the door as I came up the walk to his home and we walked to the kitchen where Donna had begun the preparations for their dinner. She gave me a greeting kiss and hug.

Derek said playfully that we two had "man stuff" to talk about and led me to his study and closed the door.

"There's a problem," I said. "What I want to tell you is something you shouldn't repeat to anyone, even Donna. I can understand if you don't want to be put in that position."

Derek raised his eyebrows. "It must be serious or you wouldn't have driven out here." He leaned back in his chair. "All right," he said. "Let's hear it."

I laid out Harry's story and my dilemma.

"And you believe him, believe he found them dead when he came home?"

"Yes, I do. But I'm aware that my judgment isn't infallible."

"Does anyone else know this?"

"I did tell Audrey, but she swore not to repeat it."

"One thing you didn't say; if Frey didn't do it, someone else did. A murderer would be walking around with no one particularly caring about it."

"Frey is acutely aware of that. He says he plans to hire private detectives as soon as the trial is over and his doing so won't confuse the jurors."

"Confuse the jurors?"

"Yeah, One can't plead temporary insanity for killing one's wife and at the same time hire an investigator to look for the murderer. "

"Right." Derek shrugged and said, "If he's telling the truth, discovering who that someone is provides a solution to both your and Frey's problem."

"Yes, of course, but when I talked to the sheriff—and he had heard Frey's claim of innocence—I didn't sense he was considering other suspects."

"You talked to Hoss?"

"Hoss?"

"The sheriff's nickname. He picked it up long ago, because he's huge like the character on the old TV series, Bonanza.

"It just now occurred to me, old friend, that your telling me what Frey told you puts me in your position. If I breathe a word of it to a certain cop I happen to be sleeping with, it will undermine Cutler's defense and perhaps the only avenue open to your patient to avoid a life sentence."

"Yes, well I told you if you listened to what I had to say, you'd have a problem."

"Hmm. Still, I wish we could tell her just to get her input."

I could see his point, but this option was off the table.

"Got an idea. Sit tight."

Derek got up and went to the kitchen where I heard him talking to Donna.

"She's coming in a minute. Putting potatoes on to boil. I'm going to ask her a hypothetical question."

She came in and sat on an ottoman, looking brightly to each of us in turn. "What's up?"

"We'd like to have your reaction to a hypothetical question, dearest one."

"Dearest one? I'd better be careful here."

"The question: What if Harry Frey were not guilty? For instance, what if he came home and found his wife and lover already dead?"

"Is there a question there worthy of parting me from my potatoes?"

"Well, what's your answer dearest one?"

"This must be a trick, but OK; if he came home and found dead bodies, then he wouldn't be guilty and I wouldn't be cooking dinner, because I'd be on extended duty trying to catch the murderer or murderers. Is that what you had in mind?"

"And how would you go about that?"

Donna assumed a mischievous smile. "I've wondered what 'man stuff' was. So this is it?"

"Actually this is serious. If you were trying to identify the killer, how would you proceed?"

She pretended to wipe the smile off her face.

"The basic elements of an investigation are . . ." Here she threw a glance at Derek. "As I recall you yourself lectured me on the subject in this very room." She paused, inviting his recall of the day, several years ago, when they'd first met.

"Ah yes," Derek said smiling, "I remember it well."

"You said at that time that the basic elements are: opportunity, means and motive. I would first identify those who had at least one of those attributes and try to discover if they had the others as well. Along the way, I'd hope like hell that I'd get a break, such as one of the perpetrators getting cold feet and blabbing."

"Is that the way your department approached this case?" Derek asked.

"Yes—in a condensed way. First, I have not been concerned with the investigation. Lieutenant Panetta is in charge. But, here's the way it was: we had a man with the murder weapon in his pocket, only his prints on the gun and only he and his wife knew where it was kept. He was the only one with the opportunity to have committed the act, and had adequate motive. In addition we knew that he had announced his intention to commit the murder in the exact manner it was done. To top this all off, he confessed to the crime."

I joined in with, "You say he was the only one with opportunity."

"Tom, you are the best witness to that fact. You saw that the blood was fresh. The rectal temperatures taken immediately after I arrived were only a degree below normal. You drove to his house as soon as he called you and you met no cars leaving his place. So, who else could there be?"

Donna stood. "Was there something else? I hear the timer in the kitchen."

I had that elevator drop feeling again of the bottom falling out. Falling away was the hope that Derek had moments before held out—that the real killer could be found.

Derek regrouped, exhorting me to be positive. "You feel strongly your patient was telling the truth. So someone else is the killer."

"There's a fact that I haven't had time to tell you. Harry said the road that passes his driveway had been closed for an hour before he came home. It had been closed for a 10K run. He had to wait a few minutes before it was opened again. In other words, no car could have driven away from the Frey house without coming to the blockade and after that, Harry would have passed the car on the road leading from his house. He saw no car. And, what about the blood not having begun to clot?"

"Maybe they were taking anti-coagulants."

I laughed, "Both of them?"

"Tom, listen to me! You said you believed Frey. Have confidence in your clinical judgment. If he didn't do it then someone else did. We can't go to the police and insist on a wider investigation for the reasons Donna just enumerated, plus Frey has told you not to jeopardize his defence. We can, however, do just what Frey says he eventually plans to do - undertake the investigation ourselves. There would be no need to say anything to anyone about Frey being innocent; we would only be investigating."

"How would we go about it? Motive, opportunity and means sounds simple, but I wouldn't know how to begin."

"To tell you the truth neither would I. We'd need to do what Frey said he would do, get professional help - hire a private eye."

Suddenly the undertaking sounded reasonable. A private investigator would be expensive. I began wondering about a second mortgage on my place.

"It's crazy," I said. "But I like the idea."

I had a memory of a party my freshman year at the U. The reviews of the Stones' opening of their Voodoo Lounge Tour at RFK Stadium in Washington were over the top. In a couple of days they would be in Birmingham, Alabama for their final U.S. appearance. Someone got up on a chair and announced that the greatest band of all time was on its last tour and our reputations as rockers depended upon our hearing them. We swore a drunken oath of allegiance to the Stones in particular and Rock and Roll in general and piled into cars, owned and borrowed, and headed south floating on a tide of idealism and beer. I felt the same call to action now and I hadn't had any beer.

"We need to discuss this more at lunch tomorrow. I said. "I'm going to Audrey's now. OK if she comes to lunch with us?"

He thought for a moment. "Since she already knows what Frey is saying . . . Sure, bring her. We need all the discreet help we can get. But you can't leave without telling me about the meeting with your father."

"He is my father. There can be no doubt about that." I proceeded then to relate the whole of my Chicago experience.

When I finished, Derek sat digesting what he'd just heard.

"He said you were his only heir?"

"That's what he said."

"If there is the money there that appearance suggests, it could eliminate or greatly reduce the financial devastation of lawsuits. Had you thought of that?'

"Actually, I hadn't until you said it now. The overwhelming news of discovering I had a father stole my complete attention. You're right about getting unexpected money being a big help, but I'm having a hard time letting myself think of inheriting money. Money muddies the whole event."

"I think I understand. But even if inherited, one doesn't want it to be siphoned into lawsuits. If we have success with our investigation, that won't happen."

"Not to mention protecting my reputation and my medical license.

"Derek, I've got to go; Audrey's expecting me. Thanks a lot for your help."

"De nada."

Audrey leaned over to take the croutons out of the oven causing her spaghetti-strapped dress to fall away, revealing her breasts to their nipples. There I was like an adolescent voyeur, but where else could I look?

I'm sure she knew I'd been looking, but her comment was about what I'd told her of Derek's plan that we become amateur detectives.

"He's right, of course. If Harry is telling the truth, then we three need to get moving. I agree with you that we'd get nowhere with this Lieutenant what's-his-name. And, I totally understand that it would destroy the insanity defense."

117

Her readiness to join the team gave the project more stature. Lost as I was in this pleasant feeling of shared purpose, she had to take the salad bowl out of my hands.

"Derek and I are meeting tomorrow to make a plan of action. Is it possible for you to join us?"

"When and where?"

"Eleven-thirty at Poppycock's."

"Yeah, I can make that. Oh, would you get the wine out of the refrigerator?"

Her request brought me fully back to the current moment and its promise. I was having difficulty eating slowly. She began telling me about how pleased she was with the great local asparagus she'd found at Hansen's Market. Her enthusiasm about the vegetable seemed greater than for her membership on our team. I half jokingly pointed this out.

"Oh Tom, I'm sorry." She sat thinking for a moment. "You're right, but I'm sure I'll get up to speed once we get started."

"Is there a problem with our plan?"

She paused, about to take a bite of bread. She returned the bread to her plate and looked at me frankly. "I'm the one with the problem."

Her expression was of someone who is reluctant to tell another something they won't want to hear. "I'm having a problem believing Harry is telling the truth. You see, according to Marian, he was a pathological liar. In fact, that was probably the main reason she wanted him to be in therapy."

Her statement hit me like a mule kick. If what she said was true about Harry, I'd completely missed it during his therapy sessions. She sensed I was experiencing that awful realization a physician dreads, when it becomes clear that he has missed a clinical sign and made the wrong diagnosis.

She reached out and put her hand on mine. "Hey, you asked

me."

"Why didn't you say something to me before?"

"Because, if you confronted him in therapy it would be obvious your information had come from the outside - from me. I knew that sooner or later there would be evidence of his lying that you could then legitimately deal with."

"Tell me more. Give me an example of his lying."

"Hmm. Marian mentioned his lying all the time. It was a chronic complaint, like a patient repeatedly complaining about his or her teenager. It was such a regular thing that I paid little attention to the details."

I felt depressed. If Harry was a compulsive liar, then it knocked the feet out from under any serious effort to identify another killer.

"It would help me if you could remember at least one concrete example of Harry's lying."

She was lifting her wine glass to her mouth, but put it down again. She thought hard, looking down at her plate.

"This is difficult, because it was told to me in confidence."

"She's dead now."

"Still."

My expression said she was being unrealistic.

"Well, OK. There was this thing with his gambling."

"Gambling?" I wasn't aware of Harry's gambling.

"Yes, Marian said he'd lose large sums and then lie about it - claim he hadn't been gambling. She really felt she couldn't trust anything he said."

It was like she was talking about a stranger. If it were true, then what did it say about his therapy? What did it say about my ability to discern truth from fiction? She must have sensed the pit on the lip of which my self-esteem teetered. She reached over and squeezed my hand again.

"Tom, you asked why I didn't seem to share your enthusiasm and that made me ask myself the same question and what Marian had said about his lying was the answer. I'm sorry. I expect that once we get started I'll feel differently. Let's put further thoughts on this subject on hold until we meet with Derek tomorrow. In the meantime . . ."

14

I awoke the next morning to the sounds of Audrey moving about in her kitchen making breakfast. The night had qualified as a cardinal moment in my life. I thought, as I lay in the bed still redolent with her smell, that our lives were becoming naturally bound together. I was euphoric, expansive. I was desired by one of the most desirable women anywhere and judging from the warm, active lover she'd been during the night, the future held the promise of an endless reservoir of pleasure. My mind, troubled when I'd left the dinner table last night, was now as calm as a Canadian lake at dawn.

I stretched with a sense of youth and power and looked about Audrey's bedroom with complacent possessiveness. The room was small, but its decoration, slick and of the moment, produced the effect of purposeful compactness. The furnishings went with the woman, soft and of high quality. Four pictures hanging on two of the walls immediately put me in mind of New Yorker covers. I'm sure I had seen two of them before. Of course! These had to be the original artwork. Very cool, very Audrey.

I heard her cell phone ring in the distance and her answering it. This broke into my lazy reverie, so I got out of bed. There before me, in a full-length mirror stood man in his prime! I straightened my shoulders, one of which usually sagged below the other, a plague when buying suits, and pushed my chest out. And yes, I made an inflated appraisal of the rest of what I saw, a worthy occupant of any lady's boudoir. I laughed out loud, embarrassed at this spontaneous breakthrough of machismo, and headed toward the bathroom after retrieving my toothbrush from my pants pocket.

I washed my face and dried it on a towel that smelled faintly of Audrey. I'd have to go home to change, so I'd shower there. I looked around for toothpaste, but saw none. The drawer under the sink contained a number of bottles and jars of creams, but no toothpaste. I opened a louvered door in one wall only to find a miniaturized washer and dryer, big enough, I thought for a week's worth of underwear and socks. To the side of the appliances was a stack of narrow drawers. The top one turned out to be Audrey's tool drawer: hammer, two screw drivers, (Phillips and regular), pliers, crescent wrench (medium size), measuring tape, a hacksaw blade held in a small handle, a ball of heavy twine and a box of 1 1/2 inch brads. Robinson Crusoe would have been pleased to have the assortment. No toothpaste.

I combed my hair with my fingers and returned to the bedroom to dress. She heard me and called out that breakfast was nearly ready. The clothes closet had a folding door, which she'd left partly open. I could see tightly packed dresses, and the rack on the floor just as filled with shoes. It came to my mind just how restricted was the space with which she'd had to manage. A partly open sliding door in the hallway revealed shelves stacked with sweaters and blouses.

A shelf near the ceiling ran the length of the hall. Along its length stood at least ten trophies. Several were topped with the small figure depicting the sport involved: woman swinging a racquet, woman swinging a golf club, woman riding a horse, woman schussing a slope. I read the inscription on the tennis trophy. "1984 State of Maryland Sixteen and Under Girl's Champion." I began to read the inscription on another cup when she called out, "On the table and hot. Please come now."

I left off examining the trophy collection. Covering the walls under the trophy shelf were photographs - group pictures mostly of people in various sports attire, in a few of which, I spotted an image of a younger Audrey: at the tennis net, slender and already stunning, or smiling from under a ski helmet, competition number on her tight-fitting jacket. Finally a plaque bearing the familiar interlocking rings. So it was true. I noticed 2002 and something about the U.S. Biathlon Team. I tried to remember what the biathlon consisted of as I walked on into the living room with my previously swollen ego pricked.

Bright morning lit the room, which was commodious compared with the bedroom. The ceiling was somewhat higher than average. Not blinded now by my urgent lust of the night before, I could focus on the details of the room. It was very tastefully decorated like the bedroom. Original drawings and watercolors and in one corner a sculpture most definitely a Croft. No wonder she had seemed to be more interested in his sculpture than in me that first night at my place.

"Nice place you have here, " I commented going into the kitchen.

"It's comfortable but small. The builders took the term, 'Pullman,' too seriously. Since there's only one bedroom, I had to turn the breakfast nook into my computer space," she said, gesturing to the small alcove.

I thought to myself, I know a place you can move into that has plenty of space for two.

"Yeah," I commented, "somehow I thought this apartment would be larger. Maybe you've got storage space in the basement."

"I wish. On the other hand this keeps me from buying too much, since I'd have no place to put it. Anyway, this was only meant as a convenient, temporary roost. It takes only twenty minutes to drive to Laslo Bach's house to work on our book, but it's not close enough for him to make a nuisance of himself. Oh, Laslo called a while ago and in his dictatorial way said I must come to his house at noon—some crisis with the publisher. So, I'm going to have to miss the lunch with Derek. But, I'm on board whatever decision you two make."

"That's too bad—I mean that you're not coming, and, well, the

123

crisis with the publisher too."

She laughed. "It never is a real crisis. I don't know how he'd handle a real one."

Having a woman prepare food for him keys deep, warm feelings of love and gratitude in a man. Certainly all the connections to his caring mother become activated. No doubt a neuronal compliance is already in place to receive those impressions, formed by millions of years of boys watching their mothers cook eggs Benedict at cave entrances, for that was what she had prepared for this cozy domestic moment. She'd made an effort to make something special. I'd have to control my great hunger and eat slowly, appreciatively. Otherwise, I'd wolf down the dish in a couple of swallows.

Breakfast was light-hearted, witty. Lit by the sunlight coming through the east-facing window, her hair radiated a rich chestnut, creating a foil for those chocolate eyes and Raphael skin, so unblemished and clear that her whole face appeared to be in soft focus. Romantic exaggeration? Not a word.

"And now," I said, "for that which is more surprising than Harry Frey's claim of innocence."

"Your father!"

"Yes."

I again related my Chicago visit in detail, interwoven with her many questions, until I had to tear myself away to get home and shower to go to my office for my first appointment.

Away from her, the reality of my legal woes returned, with the added blow of having my belief badly weakened that another person could be found to occupy Harry's jail cell. I was experiencing the ups and downs of those poor heroes of ancient epic tragedies. I've always thought the authors burdened them beyond belief. What was in store for me today changed my mind. The script was following the classic model too closely: hero is introduced boasting about his successes and his grand plans for the future. In other words, hubris, a frailty particularly offensive to the gods, since they believe they should have a corner on it. Hubris must be punished, so a banana peel or its ancient equivalent is introduced, hero slips, finds himself suddenly friendless and the gods lined up to take turns pissing on him. Oh yes, there's the part about a prophecy that predicts his inevitable fall. That, of course, had to be Stanley Kramer's depressing forecast. Today, May seventh, was to be the day the gods got together to relieve themselves upon my head.

At eleven thirty I walked the block and a half to Poppycock and was happy to find the back table under the chalkboard vacant. The table was a good compromise between conversational privacy and public exhibition, since everyone in the back half of the restaurant had to look our way to read the day's specials, but unless they could also read lips, we were safe.

Derek's expression was apprehensive as he walked through the restaurant toward me. He sat down, putting on a smile.

"Is she a good cook?" he asked, while I knew he had another question in mind.

"Cook? Oh, yes, she is a good cook."

"What did she make?"

"Ah." It was during dinner that Audrey had talked about Harry's lying, the subject I was prepared to launch into the moment Derek sat down. My mind tried now to separate that news from what I'd been eating at the time I'd heard it. "Ah yes, fish tacos. Very nice. Really great corn tortillas she'd bought at Oryana."

"A nice evening, then?"

"Yeah . . . why?"

"I'm glad you had a pleasant evening, because it might counterbalance what I heard this morning."

At that moment, Colleen, our waitress, said hello and handing each of us a menu, ran through the specials, an unneeded ritual, for she could have made money betting on what our choices would be, having served us many times before.

When she left I said, "So what dreadful thing did you hear?"

"I was at the hospital this morning to see a patient and I ran into Fred Brazelton. He's on the Ethics Committee you know."

"No, I didn't know. In fact, aside from Gordon Pheney, I don't know who's on the committee."

"Fred told me that ole Gorgon had called a special meeting of the group to deal with—this is a quote—'a high profile case.' He informed the committee that it would be prudent for the Medical Society to have an established position to deal with the media. Actually the way he put it made it clear that there was a need to be ready to disassociate the Medical Society from one of its members. That's you, if you haven't caught on."

Anger swelled in me. This situation with Harry Frey didn't have anything to do with medical ethics. This jerk, Pheney, was either wanting to make himself look important, or me look bad—probably both.

"What have the murders to do with ethics? One could claim I exercised poor judgment, but my decision to not broadcast Harry's threat was not unethical." I was speaking loud enough for people at a nearby table to look over.

"My words exactly."

"What did Brazelton say then?"

"He didn't join me in my attitude of outrage. Said he was keeping an open mind."

"An open mind? Open, that is, to join in when he determines which way the others are leaning."

"Well put."

"Who else is on the committee?"

"I don't know everyone, but I know Spence Phillips and Ron Bostic are. Both tapped by Pheney and both members of his particular subspecies."

Goddamn! I could picture a somber Pheney addressing the committee. "We have a very serious problem to address, gentlemen. The status of the medical society stands to be degraded in the mind of the public by Thomas Morgan's failure to serve his patient's best interest. We must, through our action here, get the message out to the community that Morgan is not representative of the medical society's membership." There would follow a solemn nodding of heads.

"Derek, I've never been on a committee such as this. Do they ask the accused to present his or her side?" My tone had become plaintive.

"Yes, but only after they've already talked it over—and in many cases already made up their minds."

I knew Derek hadn't told me all this to spoil my day. He was worried. "What action can they take?"

"I'd guess they won't want to go so far as to precipitate a lawsuit from you, but like you said, they'll want to go far enough to say to the public, 'See, we're not the bad guys like that rotter Morgan. In other words, they won't recommend rescinding your membership; censuring for unethical conduct is more like it."

I gathered breath to make a resounding argument, but caught myself. He wasn't the one claiming this, only reporting it.

"OK, when is this emergency meeting going to be held?"

"It was," he replied with dramatic brevity.

"Was?"

"They met last night at the Society's office."

I was stunned. It was like receiving news that you had been tried, convicted . . . and hanged.

Derek went on, "Tom, they voted to request a meeting with you right away to hear your story, but as I said, they probably made up their minds at last night's meeting. The impression I got from Brazelton's body language is that unless you can convince them Harry Frey is someone else's patient altogether, and you were out of town doing work for Save the Children, you're going to be censured."

"Son-of-a-bitch." I leaned back and took and let out a deep breath. "Well, thanks for the heads up. Now, to remind you, we were going to meet today to plan how to catch a murderer. Last night Audrey surprised the hell out of me with a piece of news that cuts the legs out from under our project."

"How's that?"

I related how my noticing Audrey's lack of enthusiasm led to her telling me about Harry's compulsive lying, and concluded with the example Audrey was able to remember - Harry's lies about his gambling losses.

"Gambling eh? You know Brian Plante had a reputation for big time gambling. If also true about Frey, this could suggest a link between him and Plante. Could suggest a deliberate and calculated act not arising from insane passion."

Derek thought about what he'd just said, closed his eyes and then opened them with a question. "Do you still think he was telling you the truth at the jail?"

"I did then, but if Marian was right, how sure can I be about knowing when Harry was telling the truth?"

Derek nodded. "Yes, damn troubling." Then he added, "I have an idea; you can visit him in jail again and confront him about the gambling to assess his reaction. You'll be especially alert now to signs pointing to dishonesty."

Yes, I agreed to myself, and I also needed to satisfy myself about who Harry Frey was and if I'd allowed myself to be taken in by a clever liar.

"Good idea. I'll do that this afternoon after I'm finished in the office. I believe I've prepared the ground at the jail so I can see Frey if I need to."

As if she'd been waiting for us to come to this point in our conversation Colleen came and stood at our table, order pad in hand. Her smile was an instant balm, as it must be for all on whom she waited. The smile seemed to originate from an inner glow, always burning. For a moment one basked in it and to some degree nerves, frayed by the day's doings, were healed. I'm a shameless connoisseur of feminine comforting.

After the meal, Derek and I parted. Two months ago, I'd scheduled out the remainder of the week to attend a convention in New Orleans. That whole trip had been erased by the murders. I needed to be here in town to deal with all the shit coming my way. Besides, I'd not be able to give my attention to the scientific papers.

I was in no mood to be in my office, a rare state of mind for me. I like my work. I enjoy working with my patients, whom I see as, like myself, trying to enjoy their lives in the emotional space they can allow themselves. Every enlargement of that space, accomplished through our joint work is what I viewed as the product of my life, like an architect's completed building or a farmer's harvested crop. It's only when the flu bug laid me low that I didn't want to be there . . . and today.

I had witnessed colleagues continue working when a loved one was seriously ill, trying to keep their minds occupied. Others took time off in the same circumstances. I'd thought that the first course would be the one I'd take. Now, I thought differently. I've discovered my work did not banish my worries. It did the reverse. Not being able to concentrate on my work made me feel guilty.

Again, at least part of what was on each patient's mind was my part in the murders. In most cases it was possible to use these thoughts to illuminate an element of their pre-formed attitudes. One man, however, who had felt mentally suffocated by his strict and intrusive mother and who continually demanded reparations from life, occupied himself during the session arguing that he shouldn't have to pay for the hour since all his thoughts had been contaminated by "that damn murder of yours."

There were two messages on my machine when I finished for the day. The first was left by a woman, who needed to maintain the illusion that she was always in control of others and spoke to me as if I were her two-year old son. She said she had to cancel tomorrow's appointment. (One I had already cancelled, because of my trip out of town.)

On the second message, Pat Furst, Judge Hackett's law clerk, sounding not at all upbeat, left the number of her cell phone and asked to be called. I dialed, she answered, asking me to hold on a moment. I guessed she wasn't where she could talk freely.

"Tom," she said quietly, "I wanted to give you a heads up. I heard in a conversation with the prosecutor's secretary that they are preparing criminal charges against you based on the Tarasoff statute." She began to recite as if from a law book - not my favorite literary genre.

"Pat, I know that law. At this point I could ace an exam on it."

"Sorry, I just thought you'd want to know what's happening in the halls of justice."

"I do and I appreciate the call . . . honestly. Oh, and I wanted to tell you that the sheriff made it possible for me to see Harry Frey. He was worried that Frey was depressed and possibly suicidal. You may hear about it from your judge and I wanted you to know."

She laughed. "It will be interesting to see how Hackett handles it."

I thanked her again for the heads up on the prosecutor's plans and we hung up.

I wondered if I should tell Stanley Kramer about Harry's story. I couldn't be sure he wouldn't react in a way that would jeopardize Cutler's defense so I decided against it for the moment. I did want Stanley to know about the Leelanau County Prosecutor's plan to charge me with the Tarasoff violation, so I called.

He reacted to the news as if I'd reported that the price of gasoline had gone up a penny. His sang-froid could be attributed to the fact that he'd thought it was a good possibility all along.

"You'll need a criminal attorney," he said. "Unfortunately, you've already used up our first choice, Holden Cutler, but I'll see what I can do."

"You make it sound like it's my fault, as if I'd used up the last of the cream and I now have only skim milk for my coffee."

He paid no attention to my protest, since he was busy telling Mrs. Booth something.

He began talking to me again. "I was going to call you this afternoon, Tom, because I got a call from an attorney who's representing Brian Plante's ex. The divorce decree reads that alimony is due unless she remarries, he dies or she dies. She's suing you as I'd expected. She claims your negligence has deprived her of her livelihood."

He rolled right along, saying, "Something of interest. I had lunch with a litigator friend, who told me that a client of his, Harry Frey, had come to him the day before the murders wanting to start an action against a guy Frey claimed had embezzled money from him."

"Who was he going to sue?"

"My friend wouldn't say. He was already telling me confidential stuff, but . . . you know how it is."

"No, how is it?"

"You know, you see a guy who is angry and the next day he kills two people. Naturally, you're going to tell a friend about it at lunch."

He was right; it was natural, and yet . . . but I should talk.

"I'll call you, Tom, when I've got someone lined up for the criminal charge."

I had a dead phone in my hand. I hung up, then it rang. It was Derek.

"Say, I remembered after lunch, weren't you going to the convention in New Orleans?"

"Was. I canceled the trip after the murders. Also, I've got to get back to Chicago to see my father. I don't know how much time he has left. My travel agent was able to cancel everything without penalty except the airline ticket. How about writing me a letter, Doctor, saying I suddenly developed a fear of flying."

"No problem, only my letter would say your fear is not of flying, but of landing . . . and having to deal with what's on the ground."

15

What was "on the ground" when I got home was an envelope in my day's mail bearing the medical society's return address. I carried the mail to the kitchen table and tore the envelope open. Its message confirmed Derek's forecast. A meeting of the committee was being held tomorrow at noon at the society's office to discuss a complaint about my failure to comply with the standards of practice. My attendance was requested and I was allowed to bring a lawyer. The letter was signed, Gordon D. Pheney, M.D., Chairman. I was enraged - and embarrassed. Even though I knew from whence this nonsense originated, it felt humiliating to be called to account to my professional society.

I called Pheney at home immediately. His wife answered. I knew her and she seemed like a nice person. I usually felt sympathy for her, but I couldn't keep the anger out of my voice. Her tone said she was in a bind, not wanting to be thought of as taking his side.

"Just a moment, Tom. I'll see if he can come to the phone."

She returned after several minutes. "Tom, Gordon says he is busy and that you can call his office tomorrow."

"Ellen, tell him I won't accept that answer."

She paused, wanting like hell not to be the middleman in this standoff.

"Just a minute."

"What is it?" Pheney said with all the impatience of an emperor being called from a state dinner to take a call from his ne'er-do-well brother-in-law.

"I just wanted you to know that I won't be at your meeting."

I could imagine his joy at being able to report to his gang that

I refused to appear before them.

"That is to say, I can't come tomorrow, since I'll be out of town at that time. I can come next week and would be happy to do so."

I knew he didn't want to wait until next week, but he couldn't say I was uncooperative. I thought I'd made a good move. Not so.

"It makes no difference if you're absent. You were only being given a chance to present your side. Your, ah, issue will be discussed and resolved tomorrow at noon."

"Just a minute, you're not giving me reasonable notice."

"The by-laws do not specify a time, only advance notice must be given, and I believe you are holding that notice in your hand."

"Go f . . ." began to form in my thoughts, and marched right up to my lips and stopped. That would have been a very bad move.

"I'll speak with my lawyer." I hung up.

I sat fuming for several minutes, and then turned my back on further thoughts about Pheney by taking out my cell phone and bringing up the sheriff's number and dialing it. I was going to tell him I had forgotten to say something to Harry Frey when I was there earlier and felt it was important to come back today and see him.

My gaze passed over a pair of long-suffering eyes staring up at me. Kato stood there patiently beside his empty water bowl.

"OK, OK. I know you're thinking you'd be a better caretaker. Maybe we should switch places. You take a turn at juggling my world and I'll stay home here and sleep—and be critical of your every mistake."

His expression said, "Just the water, if you don't mind."

Sheriff Davis came on the line and I told him that it was important that I see Harry Frey again today . . . which was true, though not in the way the sheriff was likely to understand it.

"You know best, Doctor. Please fill out another form about the need for the visit. I'll leave word at the front desk that it's OK for you to visit him.."

Within an hour, I was once again in the room where I'd talked to Harry earlier. He was very surprised to see me so soon. I immediately got to the point of my visit.

"Mr. Frey, today I learned that Brian Plante was known for heavy gambling. Along with that I was told something else I hadn't been aware of which could affect your defense of temporary insanity—that you gambled a lot. It was suggested that there may be a link between you and Brian Plante based on gambling and that this might well be a motive for murder, such as either of you welshing on a bet. In other words a motive based on premeditated revenge rather than on temporary uncontrollable passion."

"Me gamble?" He looked genuinely surprised. "I may bet a friend twenty bucks on the Superbowl or the Derby, but that's not what I'd call gambling.

"Plante?" he went on, "Yeah, I've heard he sat at the high stakes table at casinos, but I've never been there. I've had nothing to do with him and gambling. I know him socially - parties and such, but the gambling story sounds like one of Marian's fantasies."

"What do you mean, Marian's fantasies?"

"Hell, I'd rather not go into that. It was one of those kinds of issues that I'd guess every marriage is plagued with."

He could read my seriousness.

"OK. It goes back actually to her father. He was a gambler, boozer, womanizer, liar and cheat. He created perfect hell for Marian's family and I think she was so injured she has expected a repeat of that behavior in me. And there was this one time; we'd only been married a couple of years. I went to a trade show in Vegas with several guys and I got caught up in the action and lost more money than I could afford and tried desperately to win it back. Ended up losing ten thousand dollars—all the money Marian and I had. She never got over it. She has accused me of gambling and lying to her about it from then on even though, as I said, I never again bet more than twenty bucks a coupla times a year, and I'd do that openly so she'd always know about it."

"I should tell you that the story I'd heard was that you had lost a bundle gambling recently, and you were claiming you'd lost the money by being swindled."

That statement struck a sensitive spot and Harry's reply was intense. "The part about being robbed is the truth. The part about gambling must have come from Marian. When she got worked up, she complained to her friends that I was a compulsive gambler and lied about it. The truth is that I got robbed by Marian's brother in the Petoskey land development I told you about when I started seeing you. He took me for maybe a million on that project. This only came to light a few days ago and I was going to talk about it in an appointment with you, but then I discovered Marian's affair and that pushed everything else aside."

I remembered what Harry had told me about the development. Marian's little brother, Lestor, - little both in terms of age and judgement - was a problem. He'd tried and failed at a number of business ventures. Marian had harangued Harry for years to include her brother in one of his own successful ventures. She thought that a taste of success would do wonders for her brother's battered self-esteem. Harry resisted because he didn't like the guy and thought him shiftless and undeserving of his help. Harry had bought a large and choice piece of land just south of the city of Petoskey on Lake Michigan on which he planned to build a community of luxury estates. Finally, to placate Marian, he agreed to a deal in which, after he made back his investment in the land, he would split the profit with his brother-in-law. In return, Lestor would act as on-site manager of the project. This was not the kind of deal Harry would normally have made. It was way too heavy in Les's column, but he wanted to make Marian happy.

"Anyway," Harry continued, "it seemed that Les ran the project well. We sold all the buildings and retained a profitable service and maintenance contract. It happens that I've got another project out for bids right now and I just happened to recognize that the concrete service bid per cubic yard was substantially lower than it had been for the Petoskey development. I talked to the contractor, whom I knew pretty well. Turns out that he'd charged us the same at Petoskey - much less than our books said we'd paid. I then checked with two other contractors, roofing and plumbing, and discovered the same thing. Out of the total profit, someone had pocketed the difference between what the subcontractors actually charged us and what the books said we were charged—someone meaning my brother-in-law."

"Wasn't there an accoun . . ."

"Accountant? Yeah, only it wasn't my usual guy. Les wanted to use a friend of his - high school friend - who had an office in Petoskey. This guy's got to be part of the scam.

"Where was I ? Oh yeah. When I told Marian what I'd stumbled upon, she went berserk, screaming that I had lost the money gambling and was trying to cover it by accusing Les of embezzling it. When I said my regular accountant would check the books and come up with the truth, she said my accountant would arrive at any conclusion I wished. That's the point we were at the day before I discovered her and Plante together."

Harry's explanation was credible. Marian's perception of reality had been badly warped by her childhood experience and that one big gambling loss of Harry's early in their marriage, so she expected and perceived dishonesty in Harry.

A credible account of Marian's suspicions, or had I heard a clever tale? If Harry had fooled me all along in our treatment sessions, might he not be working his magic once again? I thought of Audrey and what her reaction to Harry's story might be. I could imagine her unfailing rationality pointing out gently that we had no hard evidence to back Harry's story. Evidence!

"Mr. Frey, this rumor about your gambling could hurt you. It suggests a link to Brian Plante, a known gambler, and unless it can be challenged with some hard evidence that you suffered the loss by theft and not through gambling . . ."

The whole implication that a rumor about his gambling would weaken his temporary insanity defense was weak but real. My immediate need, however, was to supply our "team" the proof it needed of Harry's honesty to bolster our resolve to find the real killer—to save Harry jail time and to salvage my good life.

"What kind of hard evidence?" Harry asked.

"The perfect thing would be your brother-in-law's confession."

"That won't happen."

"Then that of his accountant."

"Possible. I met him once. He seemed like a frail person - frail ego. No poker player like Lestor."

"I was just thinking that I have a friend who is an attorney, a clerk for a judge. If she were to appear on that Petoskey accountant's doorstep with your power-of-attorney to examine the books, he just might buckle and give us the confession we need."

"You really think the prosecutor could make a case that I killed Brian because of a gambling squabble?"

"He'll do what he can to discredit the insanity plea. The confession of the accountant would squash the rumor," I said.

Harry nodded. "I can see that working."

I pressed the button calling the guard and asked for a sheet of copy paper and a ballpoint.

Harry wrote the brief note giving Pat the power-of- attorney to examine the books of the Petoskey project, and I witnessed it.

I left Harry and the jail with the document. Now I had to get Pat to join our "team."

16

It crossed my mind to walk from the jail to Hackett's office in the Government Center Building, but figured Pat had probably left for the day. I called her cell and discovered she was still at work putting together a file of material for Hackett to take to a conference in D.C. the next morning.

"He's known about this for two months, but he waited until today to decide to go," she said sotto voce.

"He's there in the office?" I asked.

"Yes, but with no intention to contribute to the preparations for the conference. He's chatting up Washington acquaintances for dinner invitations."

"I'm sure he knew he was placing conference preparations in capable hands."

"As we say in Dallas, 'Shut your mouth.'"

"Speaking of closed mouths, I need to tell you something I want your help with, but which can't be repeated."

"What value is a secret if you can't pass it on?"

I waited.

"OK, since you need my help."

I told her then an encapsulated summary of Harry's claim of innocence and Cutler's defence and of our project to look for the real killer. Also of our need to be sure Harry wasn't the liar his wife claimed by checking out the truth of his story of embezzlement.

"Harry just wrote out a power of attorney to go up to Petoskey and confront the accountant. Now I need an attorney to carry the power of attorney."

"Tell me, has that power of attorney already got my name on it?"

"Ah . . . yes, as a matter of fact."

"That's what I figured. You've figured me as an easy mark for a sad story."

She was silent for a moment letting me wonder what she'd say next.

"OK. I'm not going to ask you to explain all that again, because if you did I'd get dizzy, and fall over. Your proposition does interest me. I'd like to see more of this part of the state. Besides, for a short while when I was in school I'd thought that joining the FBI would be an adventure, so I took some accounting courses. I shelved that idea, but this assignment you're offering sounds like the FBI job I had in mind back then. Those hours squandered on accounting won't entirely be wasted. When do we go?"

"I'd like to go tomorrow, but I have been called before a kangaroo court devised by the Medical Society's Ethics Committee, so the trip will have to wait a day."

"I'm free tomorrow. I'll have Hackett off to D.C., his lunch money pinned onto his lapel. Actually it might be better if I appear at this accountant's door without my psychiatrist. If I appear with the power of attorney without an appointment, his reaction could be a picture worth a thousand numbers."

"I like your thinking."

"What's his name by the way?"

"Lloyd Lambert. Frey wrote it on the back of the power of attorney. You're sure you really don't mind doing this?"

"Like I said, it'll be a diversion and don't forget I'm also a tourist here and I haven't had a chance to see anyplace north of this office yet. Oh, and I also need to know the brother-in-law's name."

I thought for a moment before concluding that I'd never heard more than Lestor.

"Lestor's his first name. I can call a friend and get the last name and call you back."

I dialed Audrey's number.

"After last night," I began when she answered, "everything else I do is just filler until I can see you again."

She laughed. "That's a very nice thing to say, Tom. It borders on poetic, but you'll have to think of another word. 'Filler' makes me think of putty."

Our banter continued in a playful mood, my complimenting her on her salad dressing, saying I'd savored nothing like it before. She countered that no other woman knew the secret ingredient.

I was either going to have to race over to her place immediately, or change the subject. She was at the same place on the page.

"Perhaps we should talk about politics or the stock market," she said.

"Politics it is. There is this political move that Gordon Pheney is trying to make at my expense. You know Pheney of course."

She uttered a short contemptuous snort. "I know Pheney! He interviewed me when I first applied for staff privileges at Munson."

"Pheney interviewed you?"

"Yes. I thought it was someone's idea of a bad joke. He acted like Torquemada deciding if I was to be burned at the stake or flayed alive. It was obvious what kind of creep he was, but I decided I'd better behave, so I endured." She paused, remembering the occasion. "I went home and took a hot bath and shouted curses at the tile work." Then, remembering how this topic started, she asked, "What's he got to do with you, Tom?"

I told her the story and said that I might need character references and asked if I could count on her.

"You are kidding! You need character references? You could

have every member of the psychiatric community there en masse."

Unlikely, but it still soothed my frayed ego. "Thank you. That takes care of that item, but there's something else in the line of business, since we're talking strictly business tonight. I need to know the name of Marian Frey's brother. His first name is Lestor, right?"

"What on earth do you need to know that for?"

I told her about talking to Frey again at the jail and his explanation of Marian's obsession with the idea that he gambled and of his claim that the money he'd lost was because his brother-in-law and his buddy, the accountant, had embezzled it.

"We're left in the same quandary. Is Harry telling the truth here? In other words, can we trust him when he says he's innocent of a gambling addiction? Derek and I decided we had to check it out by confronting this accountant to see if his reaction will give us a clue. Pat Furst, who has some expertise in accounting, will make an unannounced appearance on his doorstep tomorrow."

"Isn't she the woman you mentioned who works for the judge?"

"That's right, Judge Hackett."

"Are you going with her?"

Jealousy, I hoped. "No, she's going alone. I've got this Ethics Committee thing at noon."

A long pause followed. "At first when you told me about making a trip to check out the accountant, I thought it was excessive - not needed. But now I can see it from your perspective. You can't be as sure of Marian's story as I am having heard her talk about it in therapy. I understand that you can't be fully invested in our sleuthing project - and put money into it - unless you're confident about his claim that Marian and Brian Plante were already dead when he found them. Personally, I'm anxious to get started. I made an inquiry about a private detective today and was given a name of someone competent - a former chief of detectives from Milwaukee."

"Wait just one more day and we could all be happier in our work," I said.

"You asked me something. Ah, the name of Marian's brother. Hmm . . . You know, I don't think Marian ever mentioned his last name. She just referred to him as Les or Lestor. But wait; it would be the same as Marian's maiden name."

She was silent for a long moment while trying to remember. "Well, that doesn't help much. I can't think of a time her maiden name ever came up in therapy either."

"It's not critical. Say, that takes care of business and we have the whole evening before us. My place or yours?"

She chuckled. "If you'll settle for meeting for a burger, that would be great, but I'm presenting the discussion of Lionel's paper at the monthly scientific meeting at the hospital and I haven't begun to work on it."

"I should hit the sack early myself to be fully on my toes to face Pheney and his kangaroo court. How about tomorrow night?"

"That's out, sorry. I told Marv Dorman I'd chair his committee meeting tomorrow night. He had a knee replacement, you know."

"What committee is that?"

"Library."

"Ouch, that hurts. The Library Committee comes before me?"

"If the meeting ends early, I'll call you, but don't count on it."

"OK, but night after tomorrow for sure."

"Cross my heart."

As I hung up, it occurred to me that the name of Marian's brother would be included in her obituary in the *Record-Eagle*. I called Pat back and suggested she try to pull it up on her computer.

"I've got it - Lestor Parish."

"Good. I can drop by your office right now with the power of attorney."

"OK. I'll also sign as a witness and have Hackett's secretary notarize my signature with her seal. Makes it look more serious - scare this Lambert guy a little. By the way, make like you're only here on business when you come. I want to send Hackett off to the sleep-over believing that at home here we only think of him."

"Good luck tomorrow, Special Agent Furst."

"Ciao."

Hot and sultry. The humidity blurred the margin where the shade from the limp-leafed maple and the sun-browned grass met. Mr. Naismith, our next door neighbor and I were polishing his Mercury Zephyr Coupe. He told me to call him Chuck, but my mother said I had to say mister. She and Susie Naismith were sitting and talking on the Naismith's porch in the shade of a metal awning. A pitcher of lemonade rested on the upturned end of the orange crate I used in play. Sometimes the crate was the instrument panel of a fighter plane and at other times a pirate's chest.

In Ann Arbor, at least in our neighborhood, polishing your car on Sunday afternoon while listening to Ernie Harwell and Paul Carey broadcast the Tigers' games was the normal thing. Now and then, Mr. Naismith would interrupt his work and come and check on and approve of my work on the hubcaps, my part of the project. Those hubcaps must have hated to see me. I took my job very seriously. Short and strongly built, Naismith had played guard on his high school football team in Detroit. They'd won the city championship his senior year. Mrs. Naismith had shown me a newspaper clipping naming him on the All City second team. All the time he worked on the car, he'd keep up a playful banter with his wife, my mother and me. He spoke to me in a way that said we understood each other being men.

When he kidded my mother, she gave him as good as he dished out. She seemed to get along well with other women's husbands.

Kato jumped on my lap, startling me from this half-dream. I had taken a beer to the harbor-viewing chair when I returned home from the jail and had fallen asleep. Something down there had evoked the dream's content. What was it? Yes, a boy of about ten had been emptying a bucket of water on the ground. My imagination had him helping his father.

Without warning a deep sadness possessed me. With a painful poignancy I'd not remembered feeling before, I longed for the father who had died in a car crash and I started to sob. Just as unbidden, the word, "Daddy," came past my lips.

The flood of sudden sorrow was followed by equally uncontrolled laughter. I laughed deeply and with relief, as if a sure danger had turned out to be a harmless vagary of lighting. The cliché of a heavy burden being lifted is exactly what I felt. In the instant of the weight being lifted, I seemed to realize a profound truth with great certainty, but the content was lost so quickly, that searching my mind as I might, it had slipped beyond recall, like the brief, silver flash of a trout that disappears into deeper water.

Kato sat on the floor looking concerned.

"Hey guy, everything's OK now. Really."

He wasn't convinced, but then he's a chronic skeptic.

A wish to call my father arose within me. I found the paper on which I'd written his number and called. Victoria, the housekeeper, answered. She told me he was napping after having spent a full day talking on the phone with his friends about my situation.

"I'm sorry if my problem has . . ."

"No, no. It has lifted his spirits."

"Good. Please tell him that I called. Thanks Mrs. Morales"

17

"This committee is charged with the responsibility of investigating reports of unethical behavior on the part of any of the society's membership. That membership carries with it a promise to the people of this county that each member is an ethical practitioner of medicine. It is incumbent on this committee to investigate and deal with any such reports as rapidly as possible."

I was inclined to distrust anyone using the word "incumbent." Pheney was making his announcement in a voice that was vaguely familiar. In spite of my swelling anger, I began searching my mind for the reference.

The meeting was held in the Society's small conference room, the seats arranged around a long table so the committee members— already seated when I came into the room—sat on one side, Pheney in the center, and I facing them. They numbered seven—no tie vote possible. In addition to Pheney, Bostic and Phillips, there were two others whom I knew: John Singleton and Ray Janich. Singleton was an orthopedic surgeon and a guy who had no use at all for psychiatry. He believed moral weakness alone caused emotional problems and a heavy dose of reality was the best medicine. His teen-aged son had made an unsuccessful suicide attempt. It came out that earlier the boy had sought treatment through his school councilor, but Singleton had quickly quashed his son's effort. Janich was a nice guy, a team player. Such a good team player in fact, that he'd go along with the team and its leaders without much soul searching. No doubt the SS had been made up of a lot of good guys like Ray.

The Committee members nodded to me as I sat down, then

became engaged in small talk among themselves, while Pheney fussed at arranging documents on the table. I could tell he was chafing at the bit to get going so he could have the pleasure of disemboweling me. He handed out folders to the others. Each looked at the two sheets of paper inside with varying expressions, all the way from Janich's serious concentration to Singleton's bored look that said he had other really serious things to attend to.

"Now." Pheney pushed his half-frames back on the bridge of his nose and consulted a paper he was holding as if he didn't remember my name, "Ah . . . Dr. Morgan, it has come to my attention as Chairman – that is Chairperson - of this committee . . ."

That was it! The son-of-a-bitch was doing the Senate Permanent Investigating Committee's questioning of a cheating corporate CEO. The pretended politeness ironically announced to the Senator's constituents back home watching TV that the Senator knew the witness was a scumbag. Poor Gorgon, I thought, so far from the Senate.

" . . . that through your negligence you . . ."

I interrupted him just to break his rhythm. "Mr. Chairman, that is Chairperson, you say, 'has come to my attention.' Please be more specific about your source of information."

"Dr. Morgan, you will have an opportunity to make comments and ask questions later. At this time we will ask the questions, which by virtue of your having accepted membership in the Medical Society, you have, according to the by-laws, agreed to allow."

He looked to me for a rebuttal, which he would have loved, demonstrating, as he'd claim, my disregard of the rules. I declined to give him that.

He picked up his polemic where he'd left off. "Through negligence, you failed to do what was necessary to prevent a violent act, an act, which tragically, (then with lowered pitch and saddened expression to show sorrow for the dead) resulted in the death of two people—two valued lives."

Again he consulted his paper for the information I was certain he knew by heart. "I am speaking of the deaths by gunshot of Mrs. Marian Frey and Mr. Brian Plante. The man arrested for these slayings is a patient of yours, isn't that so?"

He looked at me over the frame of his glasses, a cross between wise judge and school principal. He was waiting for my confirmation. I looked back at him as if he were giving a boring lecture.

"Did you hear me, Dr. Morgan?"

"Very clearly, Dr. Pheney. This room has remarkable acoustics."

"Would you please answer the question then?"

"I'm sorry, I didn't realize you had asked a question. Would you ask it again?"

He glanced first right and then left at the other members of the committee, as if to say, "Here is the contempt I had predicted."

"Is Harry Frey a patient of yours, Doctor?"

I produced a look of troubled consternation. "I'm surprised at your question, Mr. Chairperson. Surely this committee, above all others, knows that for a psychiatrist to reveal the names of his or her patients is unethical."

It seemed to me that I had just thrown an impromptu monkey wrench into the works.

Pheney reacted vigorously. "This is absurd, Morgan. Everyone knows he's your patient."

"Then, perhaps, you should have invited 'everyone' to answer that question. For my part, I will not talk about who may or may not be my patient."

I tried to remain icy cool, but I could feel burning heat generating inside.

"Dr. Morgan, are you telling this committee that you will not

149

cooperate with these proceedings?"

It occurred to me that I didn't trust people who used "proceedings" either. I managed a laudable attitude of friendly compliance.

"Not at all, Mr. Chairperson, I am only saying that I will not answer a question that I consider to be unethical here at a meeting of the Ethics Committee."

Pheney didn't have a ready reply, but rather than lose his momentum and aura of authority, he pushed ahead. "Let's leave aside for the moment the question of whether Harry Frey is your patient. Everyone in our county, and probably the whole state, knows that this troubled man told his psychiatrist that if he discovered his wife and Brian Plante together he would kill them. Now, I have polled other members of the psychiatric community about the ethical course of action a psychiatrist should take in this circumstance. Each stated that it was obvious that the patient was unstable and should have, for the protection of all involved, been hospitalized. Each believed it was the physician's ethical and legal duty."

He looked at me triumphantly, as Bobby Fisher might have after winning a game from Boris Spassky. I didn't believe him. Those asked might have said the patient should have been hospitalized, but I was sure they'd said nothing about ethics.

Spencer Phillips, sitting next to Pheney, cleared his throat and asked in an impersonal tone, "I'm wondering what your response would have been to that poll, Dr. Morgan, if it were another psychiatrist's patient in question."

Christ! Spence Phillips and I have played tennis together, loaned each other books and now it's "Dr. Morgan." He was practically denying he knew me.

Intuitively, I began speaking to him like an old buddy. "Spence, I would have to know a lot more before answering that question. For instance, Gordie here stated that all the respondents to the question said the patient was obviously unstable. Merely saying that one would like to kill an errant wife and her lover, to my mind, is no proof of instability. Spence, I'd need to have more information about the person's emotional state, his past history and how seriously the man made his declaration of intent. Knowing you as I do, Spence, I'm sure you'd agree that it is easy to make a judgment by hindsight."

Hurriedly, Phillips looked toward Pheney. "I have no more questions."

Pheney looked hopefully at the others for supportive comments. None came.

"Since you will not answer the committee's questions about Mr. Frey, there is no further need for your presence here. That will be all, Dr. Morgan." He put his Montblanc pen back in his monogrammed shirt pocket.

"One moment, Mr. Chairperson," I said. "You said earlier that I would have my chance to ask the committee questions."

He was irritated, but he was stuck. "Very well, what is the question?"

"Has a complaint been made against me by anyone claiming to be my patient?"

"No. By a patient, no."

"Someone claiming to be a relative of a patient of mine?"

"No." He began to busily put his papers together like a news anchor killing time at the end of the show.

"Who, then, brought this complaint to your committee?"

"The Medical Society can . . ."

"Who in the Medical Society?"

"We are not . . ."

"I'm afraid you are. I have a right to know my accusers. Your committee is not the Spanish Inquisition.

"I have another question for the whole committee. Gordon, you claimed to have conducted a poll about a hypothetical question. I have one too, but I hasten to say I'm not going to press you for an answer today. However, I advise you to think about your answer. It is this: a trial has not taken place, no one has been proven guilty. What if it turns out that the accused man did not commit the murders you have in mind. In that case, would you still say the psychiatrist involved was at fault for not hospitalizing him?"

I leaned forward challenging them for an answer.

"If the hypothetical case turns out the way I've just suggested, and the Ethics Committee has already seen fit to censure the psychiatrist, representing him as incompetent, might not that psychiatrist sue the Medical Society and each member of this committee for all he can get?" I paused and brought my voice back to a matter-of-fact level. "I think a good attorney would call that a slam dunk. Being called here to listen to unsubstantiated innuendo and enduring the loss of face that such a summons means to the public, I'd say this same attorney would claim that the psychiatrist has a right to compensation just for your committee's actions so far. Maybe it would be wise for you to write a letter of apology ASAP."

I got up and walked confidently out of the room. I did feel elated, but not confident. It was as if I'd talked a cop out of a ticket by threatening to report that his shirt was unbuttoned. Still, I thought maybe Thomas Christopher Morgan might call my performance a "show of strength."

18

Back at my place, I walked into the kitchen to find Kato standing on the kitchen counter next to my telephone/answering machine. I recognized this as his critical comment on my penchant toward daydreaming instead of being alert to important physical facts like his empty food bowl or a blinking message light. I avoided an impulse to point out some of his shortcomings and simply said, "Thank you."

The message was from Pat, asking for a call.

When she answered, I said, "Hi, how'd it go?"

"It didn't. I called his office last night in order to hear his answering machine tell me the office hours. Nine o'clock. I drove up here to Petoskey this morning so I'd walk through the door after the secretary had had time to start the coffee and check her Facebook page - nine forty-five. The door was locked, so I knocked. This brought the secretary in a civil engineer's office across the hall to her open doorway. She told me she was surprised Lambert's secretary hadn't shown up. I walked around Petoskey for about half an hour - attractive town by the way - bought myself a bagel and coffee and returned to Lambert's office. The door was still locked. I could see that the surprise visit wasn't working, so I called and left a message saying that I requested an appointment and left my cell number.

"The guy's secretary returned my call at three-fifteen. She said Lambert would be happy to talk to me tomorrow morning at nine."

"You didn't say what you wanted, correct?"

"Not what I wanted, but I did say I was an attorney from Traverse City. In my experience getting a letter or a call from a lawyer puts everyone on guard, but there is still an opportunity to read his reaction when he finds out what my client's business is."

"Are you coming back here or staying there?"

"Staying here. I found a B&B called the Bower Inn on the lake front."

"I feel I should come up and lend support."

"That's not necessary, but your company would be welcome."

"I'll come."

"Wait a second." I could hear footsteps, then muffled voices and then she was back. "Mrs. Hooper has another room here."

"Good. Reserve it for me. I'll be there in time for us to have dinner."

The Bower Inn was easy to find with Pat's directions, West Lake Street at the lake front and at the foot of the hill on which the city of Petoskey stood.

I parked in the inn's small lot with three other cars. I didn't know Pat's car, but it was a safe bet it was the yellow Beetle with the bumper sticker, "Lawyers do it if it's billable."

The inn was postcard-perfect, large white frame house with wide wrap-around porch and a picket fence, Lake Michigan in the background—a perfect place to bring Audrey.

Mrs. Hooper went with the place, grandmotherly, steel-framed spectacles and a sweet smile in front of a firm backbone from which any impropriety would rebound to the offender. I introduced myself and was about to ask for Pat, when she walked into the entrance hall from an adjacent room.

She asked, "Mrs. Hooper, since it's such a beautiful evening, can you recommend a restaurant we can walk to?"

"I'm told that The Whitecaps up on Bay Street is good- and there's a view of the bay. When I eat out I only go to the Bayview Inn,

154

but it is probably too far to walk to."

And, I thought to myself, she does that twice a year, on her birthday and Easter.

After completing the registration formality in the tiny entrance alcove and carrying my small bag up to a barely larger room, Pat and I walked up the hill into the city.

We did have a table with a view of the bay, and we were each enjoying our whitefish, when Pat refocused on our purpose for being here.

"Driving up here, I'd rehearsed my dramatic entrance into Lambert's office so many times in my mind that I haven't yet been able to switch my thinking to the best approach needed tomorrow now that the element of surprise is gone."

"He'll be on guard all right. If he's involved in a swindle as Harry claims, he'll be wary of a visit from any lawyer. You won't have the luxury of surprise, but his response to your flashing that power-of-attorney and demanding to see the books should be worth a lot of words."

"OK, Mr. Psychiatrist, what stance do you foresee him taking?"

I did as good an imitation of Johnny Carson's Carnak the Magnificent as I could sans turban, pressing my finger tips to my forehead. "I am seeing him waffle. He won't want to be combative at first. He'll scrutinize the power-of-attorney and Harry's signature. He'll smile showing how cooperative he intends to be and say, 'I see. But the account book isn't here at my office. Sorry.' You'll say, 'I have time to wait for it to be brought here.' And he'll say, "My partner has it and he's out of town." And you'll say, 'I didn't know you had . . .'"

"OK, OK. Thank you. Send the bill, 'Care of the Dead Letter Office.'" She took a sip of wine and added with a note of resignation, "Unfortunately I think you've got it right."

And we left the topic there and I turned the discussion in the direction of her own future and her next clerkship with the federal judge in Ann Arbor.

"I'm glad you reminded me. It happens that my part in this investigation is coming to an abrupt end. I got a call from that judge's office today requesting that I report next Monday. I'm leaving for Ann Arbor day after tomorrow to stay with a friend there while I look for an apartment."

"Ouch. They can't do that! What will Judge Hackett say?"

"What can he say? I was a volunteer with no formal term of employment, and besides, my desk is clean."

"But we need you." I whined pitifully. "I'm going to call my senator."

After the walk back to the inn, brief hugs and pecks on cheeks, we went to our rooms eager for the next morning to come and provide some proof that Harry was not the liar his wife claimed him to be. I brushed my teeth and got into bed with one of the faded Reader's Digests stacked on the night stand. Then I got back out of bed and got my cell phone and dialed Audrey.

She answered in a tone that said a phone call right then was an interruption. "Hello."

"Hi, it's Tom. Catch you at a bad time?"

"Oh, hi. No, it's not a bad time, but hold on a moment, Sue Best is just leaving."

I heard indistinct voices – Audrey saying, "Good night."

She came back. "Sue stopped by to borrow a book after the committee meeting. So, how did it go with the accountant?"

"Pat spun her wheels today. The office was closed. She has an appointment though tomorrow morning."

"Bummer. Did she tell them what her purpose was when she made the appointment?"

"No. Just that she was a lawyer representing a client from Traverse City."

"Ho ho, and don't you just know the guy will be wary if he did have his hand in the till."

"Yeah, not ideal, but we'll play tomorrow as it lies."

"We'll play it? Are you there with her?"

"I came for moral support."

"Where are you staying?"

Now I did hear jealousy for sure. Don't milk it I told myself.

"I have a room at a B&B."

"Tell me it's not the same one she's staying at?" There was teasing in her voice.

"Yeah. We tried to get a double room, but there were only two singles left."

"I've never been to Petoskey."

"I'll reserve a double in the morning."

In the morning Pat and I were preoccupied with the coming meeting with Lloyd Lambert, rendering us less than the sociable breakfast companions expected of B&B guests. I did enjoy the apple waffles that must have constituted the ten-thousandth edition of that dish at Mrs. Hooper's table, but anxious to be paid up and on our way, neither of us demanded the second helpings that the other guests made.

We parked our two cars across the street from Lambert's office, an older, two-story brick building on Mitchell St. It was fifteen minutes to nine. We went into a coffee shop across the street from his office where I planned to wait for Pat while she met with Lambert. I got a cup of coffee and we sat at the window. A fat man wearing a Russian fur hat entered the office building shortly after we sat down.

"There's caution for you," I said. "It must be fifty degrees this morning. Are accountants cautious people?"

"If Harry Frey is right, this particular one wasn't very cautious."

At eight fifty-seven Pat got up. "I can't surprise him, but a lawyer being on time might unnerve him."

Pat crossed the street and got to the door of the building at the same time as another young woman and they momentarily did the "You first" thing.

From an adjacent table I got a copy of the Petoskey News-Review and was looking over the front page items when my cell rang.

It was Pat and her voice was tense. "Tom, get right over here!"

I trotted across the street, glanced at the directory in the small lobby and continued down a first-floor hall to the office and opened the door. The young woman who had entered with Pat was on the phone. Through an open door to an inner office, Pat beckoned to me. I went into the room where I saw a man lying on the floor in the space between an office chair and a desk.

"It's Lambert," Pat said. "I touched him. He's been dead a while."

I couldn't see the man's face; it was turned toward the floor. My gaze went up to the desk surface and a nearly empty bottle of Glenlivet beside a computer monitor. Next to the Scotch was a sandwich-size zip-lock bag inside which I saw a single red capsule. I leaned down and took a closer look. I knew this drug. It was a 100mg capsule of Seconal, an overdose of which had ended many famous lives, like Jimi Hendrix and Judy Garland.

"That pill is Seconal, Pat, a potent barbiturate. I wonder if he . . ."

"Yeah, I had the same idea."

The desk lamp was on. "Looks like he was working late."

"Hmm. Cooking the books do you think? I'd like to hit the space bar and bring the computer out of its slumber - see what he was working on, but it would be obvious to the cops when they arrive that we'd tampered."

I noticed then the old-fashioned glass that stood behind the Scotch bottle.

"Alcohol and Seconal aren't a good mix unless you intend it that way," I commented.

There were voices in the outer room and a man wearing a tie and sport coat came into the office. He took in the general scene, announced that he was Sergeant Laird McCulloch of the Petoskey police and asked who we were.

"I'm Pat Furst. I'm an attorney from Traverse City. I had a nine o'clock appointment with Mr. Lambert, the purpose of which I think you'll find interesting."

"Is that so?" He looked at me. "And you, sir?"

"Dr. Thomas Morgan. It was not my intention to meet Mr. Lambert, but I had an interest in the issue Miss Furst referred to."

He nodded. I could see him file us under, "later." "I'd like both of you to wait in the other room."

We sat in the outer office over an hour, while the lab unit directed by McCulloch went about its business. Finally he came out, pulled up a chair over to the desk where the secretary sat and asked her a few questions, then it was our turn.

Glancing at the notebook he held he said, "Now, Ms. Furst, you said you had business with this man that would interest me."

Pat said she represented Harry Frey, who had been a partner in an enterprise for which Lambert was the accountant. "Mr. Frey believes his partner, Lestor Parish and Lloyd Lambert conspired to embezzle a large sum of money from the company's funds. Yesterday I came here unannounced to confront Lambert, but the office was closed - I don't know why. I called and left a message on their machine saying I was an attorney from Traverse City and requested an appointment. Later in the day, I received a call from a young woman setting up a meeting for this morning - probably the secretary here. We - the secretary and

I - arrived at the same time this morning. The office door was locked. She opened it and together we found him."

McCulloch thought about Pat's neat summary, going over its implications in his mind. He said, "This Harry Frey, is he the same man who was arrested for killing his wife and Brian Plante?"

I wasn't surprised that he knew the name that well. The murders had provided the area media with abundant copy.

"That's right," Pat said.

"And while under arrest for murder, he is concerned about possible embezzlement?"

Pat smiled. "I understand your puzzlement, but you have to understand that Mr. Frey is a businessman. Regardless of the outcome of his trial, money is money. He'd rather his relatives or friends have it than a couple of thieves. The point is, and I hope you'll excuse me for putting in my two cents about Mr. Lambert's - ah, demise, but it looks to me like he worked last night trying to fix the books. If what Mr. Frey suspects is true, he would be afraid to meet any attorney from T.C. with an unspecified client. He worked on the books, drank, despaired and finally threw in the sponge and took a lot of the sleeping pills like the one in the plastic bag on his desk."

"Interesting." Perhaps his faint smile said that he did indeed believe she was a lawyer.

"I'd find it interesting to know what computer file he was working on," Pat hinted.

McCulloch didn't respond to that. He turned and asked the secretary, "Is that right, this office was closed yesterday?"

"Yes. Mr. Lambert said he had some personal business in Alpena and would be gone all day. He said I could take the day off. He suggested it would be an opportunity for me to go to Grayling and see my sister's new baby. He told me to check the answering machine with the remote code throughout the day. He said an attorney from Traverse

City might call to make an appointment and to offer her a nine o'clock time the following morning. He wanted me to call him on his cell if she accepted the appointment time."

"You did that - drive to Grayling?"

"Yes, sir. And I called Mr. Lambert to tell him Ms. Furst made the appointment."

McCulloch considered what he'd just been told. "Was there anything unusual in being given the day off."

She nodded slowly. "Yes, it hadn't happened before."

"May I ask a question?" I said.

McCulloch looked at me and nodded.

"Does Lambert have a family?"

Looking toward the secretary he said, "I already asked Ms. MacFarlane that," nodding to her that she should answer my question.

"Mr. Lambert lived here in the city alone. I gathered from a few remarks that he is divorced and his former wife and two children live in Traverse City."

"Then you don't socialize in any way with him? I asked.

"No. He is - ah, was - a very private person. Aside from office matters, we exchanged remarks about the weather and that's about it."

McCulloch looked at his notes again and then at the secretary. "You told me you didn't know what Mr. Lambert could have been working on, that you knew of no impending deadlines that would have required working into the night?"

"No, I can't think of anything."

McCulloch wrote down Pat's and my addresses and phone numbers and gave us his card. He told us we were free to leave, that he would contact us if needed.

We left the building and sat in Pat's car.

"Wha'dya think, councilor?"

"I think we have the proof you were looking for. Frey told the truth about embezzlement. Lambert realized we were going to uncover the fact and couldn't face his kids."

"You're saying Lambert wasn't a pure scumbag. Pure scumbags, when caught, usually leave town, change identity and set up in business all over again. 'Humiliation' isn't in their vocabulary.

"Thanks for your help, Pat. We've authenticated Harry's story. Now on to the hard work."

"How are you going to proceed?" she asked.

"We're in need of professional help. Hiring a private investigator will be the first step. Audrey has already got a name. It seems the police have no physical evidence that would implicate anyone except Frey, and they did their investigation at the scene immediately after the murders and with tools we don't have, so our task will be that of identifying someone aside from Frey with a motive."

"Well, I wish you luck. Sorry I can't be here for the fun."

19

Leaving Petoskey, I turned onto Spring Street heading south. At the traffic light where U.S. 31 and 131 part company, I got in the right lane to take 31 along the lake south through Charlevoix, but, I didn't turn. The sparse traffic and open countryside of the other highway promised an untrammeled hour of ruminating and brooding. Brooding, because something about Lambert's suicide bothered me. Try as I did, however, I couldn't put my finger on the part that caused the discord. I gave up thinking about it when I got to Kalkaska and just took in the landscape over the remaining distance.

Driving along the stretch of Munson Avenue that skirts the east arm of Grand Traverse Bay, my eye wandered repeatedly to the red neon signs that announced vacancies in the continuous row of large motels, each claiming a sugar sand beachhead on the bay. In another month and until Labor Day, the neon tubing spelling "No", not seen all winter, would again brag full occupancy. T.C. and the villages on the Leelanau Peninsula would come alive with visitors and with a crowded schedule of festivals: cherry, film, wine, art and food. Like most of the year-round folks, I anticipated this period with a mixture of dread and welcome—dread of the traffic and welcome for the tourists' dollars that local businesses depended on to stay in business the rest of the year.

The first thing I yearned to do was call Audrey to tell her about the suicide. I turned off the Grandview Parkway into Hall Street and then into the drive that leads to my office building's parking lot.

The scene a week ago when Harry Frey imagined aloud his gory punishment of Brian Plante starkly broke into my memory as I opened the door to my consulting room and faced the chair he'd sat in.

I paused there for a moment picturing his raised clenched fist, before I closed the door and walked to my desk to dial Audrey.

"Tom," she said in the tone that enters one's voice when awaiting serious news.

"Are you able to talk?"

"Yes, for about five minutes, then I have a patient. What happened at the accountant's?"

"The good and the bad. Good for our purpose and bad for the accountant, Lambert. When we got there at nine this morning, he was dead."

"Dead?" She gasped.

"It looked like he worked on his books trying to make them stand up to scrutiny and then gave up - took an overdose of Seconal."

"You say 'looked like.'"

"Well yeah, that won't be established until there's an autopsy, but that's how Pat and I made it out."

"Jesus."

"Yeah. Driving back here I had a sobering thought: the guy would still be alive if we hadn't gone up there. Our snooping pushed him to seek a way out."

"Now wait a minute. You're not responsible for his death. If he did commit suicide, he's the one responsible. He committed the crime."

"Anyway, onward and upward. You have the name of a detective. Let's meet with him and get his input."

"I'll call him. Hopefully he's got time to see us tomorrow. Tom, I've got to go. How about coming to my place about six. I'll put some food together and we can talk."

"Sounds good. See you at six."

I dialed Derek.

"Tom, you're back. What news do you have?"

"First, where are you?"

"Driving home, why?"

"Give me a call when you get home."

I didn't want to unload what I had to say while he was on the road. I wanted him to stay on the road.

As I sat waiting for Derek's call, the other major concern of mine presented itself, my father, and how long he would live. I had to make a trip back to Chicago in the next few days.

Derek called me back. "Why the mystery?"

"Sorry, but I wanted you to safely be able to give your full attention to what I'm going to tell you."

I then relived every detail since Pat left for Petoskey. When I got to the suicide, I heard his loud groan.

"There's no way to say this without it sounding crass," he said. "I'm not insensitive to the death of a fellow man, but we've got to move ahead. You two found out that Frey can be trusted. His wife was the liar . . . at least she was taken in by her brother's denial of Frey's accusation."

I told him that Audrey had found us an experienced detective and would make an appointment for us to meet with him.

"Good. Better have her make it in the evening, my day is tight tomorrow." In a playful tone he added, "You will be talking to her again tonight, I presume."

"Hey, why not? About tomorrow's get together, it'll have to be in the evening for me too. If the air charter service is able to take me, I'm going to Chicago in the morning to see my father."

"I hope it's a good trip."

Audrey opened her condo door and pulled me into her arms, where she held me in a tight, long embrace, then led me to the couch and asked me to review all that had happened. I knew as I spoke that the story added up to Audrey having been in error in believing Marian's delusion about Harry's compulsive lying. She was now subject to the same disturbing professional doubt I'd experienced when she'd informed me that Frey had taken me in. I became aware that she was no longer paying attention to my report.

"I'm sorry, Tom, but I was thinking how blind I'd been. Marian seemed so sure her brother was telling the truth, and it never occurred to me that she might be trying to protect him. I have to face up to not being any more perceptive than the next guy. Thanks for not rubbing it in." Having said that, she added, "It means I have to question the whole of Marian's claim about Harry's lying and what that might have meant for her." She smiled and lifted her chin as if to say she would work on that issue on her own. "At least now I feel no conflict about devoting myself to our project. Have you talked to Derek?"

"I told him about the private detective you located. He can make a meeting with the guy tomorrow evening. Also, before I came over here, I arranged to fly to Chicago in the morning to see my father. I don't know how much longer he has."

"It's great that you'll be seeing your dad, but it's also my idea of seamless living to be able to call your charter service and fly off to Chicago for lunch. How about including me for dinner some evening in Oaxaca?"

I leaned over, kissing her forehead, her nose and her ripe lips. "Anyone who can afford original New Yorker art for her bedroom walls can afford a charter service."

"It doesn't signify. The pictures were free. The art editor was my college roommate."

"Yeah, but what college?"

"Brown."

"Proves my point."

"I had a scholarship."

"You're wonderful." I kissed her again.

For a long time I've been convinced that a lot of problem solving and mental patching up goes on during sleep. It didn't work this time, at least not right away. Something had bothered me about what I'd seen in Lambert's office the day before, and the feeling of frustrated searching was still alive in my mind when I wakened beside Audrey the next morning. It was later, when I'd left her place and was seated in my Miata, that the answer came to me like a person waiting to tell you a secret just as soon as a third party left the room. In my mind's eye, I saw Lambert's desk and his computer monitor and beside it the nearly empty bottle of Scotch and behind it the glass. That was the piece of the picture that was wrong! If you are drinking, you don't put your glass down behind the bottle. You set it down in front of the bottle - unless you're drinking right out of the bottle, and you don't do that unless you have no glass. I thought about this. I supposed it could happen that a person . . . but no. If you took a drink and put the glass down again on the table, you'd place it in front of the bottle one hundred times out of a hundred, just as one always places a knife down on the same side of the plate - right side if one is right handed, not on the left. So . . . I guess that leaves someone else to have put the glass behind the bottle. Someone drinking with him and perhaps feeding him a fist full of Seconal and then taking the second glass away - but making that one mistake with the glass. Was I blowing a small irregularity way out of proportion? But there was another odd thing. Seconal is not a usual sleeping medication prescribed these days. Is it likely that Lambert would have had a quantity on hand? But who would want . . . ? Of course! It was obvious! If Harry was right about the embezzlement, then the person who'd gain most from Lambert's death would be Harry's brother-in-law, Lestor Parish. He had a lot to lose if Lambert broke down while being questioned and confessed. Neither Pat nor anyone else could question a dead man.

The first thing I did when I got home was take Sergeant

McColloch's card from my wallet. The phone number was the department's number with his extension. All I'd get with a call at this hour was the man on duty, who would never give me McCulloch's home number, but there was also an e-mail address at the police department.

My message described the position of the bottle and the glass and suggested the possibility that Lambert hadn't been alone, that someone may have staged a suicide. I suggested a name. I recommended that he check out the Seconal, see if the drug had been prescribed for either Lambert or Parish.

I was exited when I clicked "send." I felt like progress had been made even though I hadn't the foggiest idea of how it would help our cause except that Harry was telling the truth, a truth potent enough to motivate murder.

Next, I called Chicago. Victoria answered, so I was able to hear her description of his condition. He seemed physically weaker judged by the minute details she was alert to, like letting a teacup slip from his grip. On the other hand, his spirits were high, making many phone calls. She'd heard him laugh more than he had since the diagnosis was made. I'd told her last night that I was flying to Chicago today and I reconfirmed it.

"Glad to hear you're coming here," he said, when he came on the line. "I've been shaking the old grapevine and I've come up with very interesting info for you. What news have you got?"

I told him I had news from a trip to Petoskey that I'd tell him about when I got there.

"Look forward to it," he said pumping a last bit of energy into keeping his voice upbeat.

Before leaving for the airport, I checked my e-mail and saw that I'd gotten a reply from McCulloch. "Thanks for your message. I will be coming to Traverse City Saturday. I would like to talk to you at 10 a.m. at the Leelanau County Sheriff's Office. If there is a problem with that, let me know."

Both Henry, when he picked me up at the airport, and Victoria, when she opened the front door, had that expression that communicates a loved one's end is near. I was afraid as we walked along the hall to the sun porch.

In just three days my father had faded from a man who still showed vestigial evidence of his former strength to becoming a frail invalid. From my clinical experience I knew this kind of rapid deterioration meant he would die within days. In spite of his certain discomfort, he rose to the occasion.

"Couldn't wait for you. Had to dig into this steak."

A nurse had been feeding him clear soup.

"Good thing you went ahead without me," I said joining the joke. "It's not my favorite cut."

"I'll eat the rest later," he told the nurse and she left.

"You said on the phone you'd been in Petoskey. What was that all about?"

I explained the reason for Pat's trip and its tragic outcome and my suspicion about Lambert's death. It wasn't until I'd finished that he spoke.

"Now that you believe your patient, we can get on with our work."

He began scratching his ear. It was ironic to see him pay attention to an itch when his whole body was crumpling.

"Glad to see you're taking action though," he said. "What else are you doing to get yourself out of this mess you're in?"

I told him about the meeting with the Ethics Committee, and he got a big kick out of the finale. I was surprised by how much I enjoyed his approval. I got back to the main problem.

"We're meeting with a private detective."

"We?"

169

"Two friends of mine are working with me to come up with a credible suspect that would force the police to open up the investigation."

He nodded. "Got to approach this with organization. Motive. What have we got by way of motive?" He said this as if he were at a board meeting.

I realized as I began to answer him that I hadn't been at all methodical in my thinking. I felt like I was a student on grand rounds and the professor had just pointed to me and asked for a complete treatment plan for the patient at the foot of whose bed we were standing.

"The motive is unclear," I began. "Either someone wanted to kill Brian Plante and my patient's wife happened to be there, or vice versa. Or, perhaps a killer was hired to kill Harry Frey and killed Plante thinking he was Frey."

It seemed logical as I said it, but at the same time mixed up as hell.

My father's sunken eyes stared at me as if he were deciding whether I was a damn fool or brilliant. He chose a middle path. "Fair enough. Let's take one at a time. The wife was the target and Plante was incidental. In this case, we've got to know all we can about the woman. Did she have a jealous lover?" He pointed to a notebook on the table next to him. "Take that book and write this down, so we don't have to repeat the work."

While I did this, he worked to get into a more comfortable, less painful position. His imperious tone had irked me. I cooled down realizing he wasn't being bossy, only impatient. Wouldn't I be impatient if I had his limited time?

"I don't know anything about her having a lover," I replied. "I didn't know about her and Plante until a patient of mine told me. Frey had never hinted that he thought there was anyone else until the day he saw the two together. I do have another source for that information—

her therapist."

"Well, give it a try. It's important to find out if there was another man. Now let's take the reverse. Plante was the target and the wife got in the way. Who'd want to kill Plante?"

I shook my head.

"It so happens I can help here. Plante, besides being a world-class womanizer, has pulled dirty business deals all over the Midwest. I've been doing some calling around, but the guy I really want to talk to has been in Africa on safari and has switched off his phone. I just had another idea; hand me that phone, Tom."

A process of dialing, shooting the breeze for a short time and segueing into the subject commenced. I got up and went into the kitchen where I knew I'd find Victoria hovering.

"Networking, he calls it," she said, becoming immediately familiar. "He says he's made more money in a golf cart than he ever did at a desk."

"He looks bad," I said.

Tears welled up and she nodded as she grabbed a dish towel. I thought to myself that he was likely doing his last bit of networking. The buddies he was schmoozing with were having their last exchange with him. Many had no idea.

"Do other relatives know of his condition?"

"His sister is too infirm to travel and they seldom talked. The others, nephews and nieces, are only casual relations. No doubt there are those who would still make the trip, but he said he didn't want to spend his last days playing host to strangers."

I walked over and looked out the screen door to the patio. Dusk stood along the eastern sky, while to the west the day retreated slowly, reluctantly—just like my father.

"Tom," he called. His effort was barely audible in the kitchen.

The nurse had returned and was standing over him, watching

him swallow some pills. He did this and then made it clear to her that she wasn't needed.

"What I've got isn't as current and complete as I'd like, but it's something to work on. Goes like this: Plante was a sick asshole when it came to women. Mean. He needed to humiliate them. He'd make a big play for a woman, make her feel special, the top. Wine and dine her, bury her in expensive stuff, plus—he had a knack for the convincing, romantic gesture. Even those who'd been warned swallowed his line. They believed it would be different for them and they'd go ahead and open themselves up to him. Then, wham! He'd drop them, plop, and shift his attention to the next victim, making sure the discarded lady saw him noodling with Miss. or Mrs. "New."

He was smiling as best he could, because of his ability to make a few calls and get this information.

"This, as I'm sure you realize," he continued, "has created some very strong motives for getting even with old Brian, either by the woman herself or her husband or a brother." Sunken, heavy lidded eyes were fixed on me. "I got a woman's name whom he ditched last fall. Probably not current enough. If she's the angry woman Plante replaced with this Frey woman, she's waited a long time to act. The friend in Africa would know more, but in the meantime . . ."

He began to cough. He couldn't hide the pain he felt with each contraction of his diaphragm. The nurse appeared at the door, but he waved her away. The effort he made drained away the last bit of reserve he'd had, but he forced himself to concentrate on what he still wanted to say.

"As I was saying, work can be done in the meantime. The name I got . . . you could check her out."

He collapsed back into the cushions the nurse had put behind him. His face was wet with the cold sweat of the very ill.

"Prudie Goode. Editor of a magazine published right there in

Traverse City, *The Bay and Beyond*." He managed a smile. "Bedtime."

Henry materialized and he, the nurse and I got my father to bed. I wished him good night, but he didn't reply—he was already asleep.

When I came back to the sun porch, Victoria was there with a glass of smoky Scotch.

"What is your impression of his condition?" she asked.

I looked to see if her expression was hopeful; it wasn't.

"Only a few days."

She returned to the kitchen to make me something to eat before Henry took me to the airport. Later, flying home, I reflected on what I'd learned here. In medicine, one is taught to try to account for all the symptoms and laboratory data by one common cause—a variation of Occam's Razor. In the case at hand, I tried, but failed to attribute all three murders to one person, but I experienced a repeated wish to do so. Lestor Parish was my leading candidate for Lambert's murder- if it was murder. He would benefit if his partner in crime weren't around to screw up and say the wrong thing, or worse yet decide to confess. But what motive could he have for killing his sister and her lover? On the other hand, why would any of Plante's former girl friends, or Marian's possible boyfriends care if Parish's fraud became public?

I glanced at my watch as we landed at T.C.'s Cherry Capital Airport. It was an hour later in Michigan and Derek would be home from his office. I called and Donna answered. She asked after my father's condition, then said she'd call Derek, who was out preparing the place in the garden for his annual three basil plants. When he came on line, I told him about my day, first the dirt about Plante that my father had dug up and then about my epiphany regarding Lambert's death.

Derek agreed that if Lambert had been murdered, Parish was the likely killer, but he also didn't see how establishing that would help us.

"I'd say your father's theory about the jealous girlfriend seems psychologically wrong to me. A woman might go to Plante's house to catch the louse with another woman, but she'd be unlikely to go to the woman's house."

"I see your point," I said. "It's more likely that a boyfriend would watch the Frey house to catch Marian bringing another guy home."

"Yeah, but if all we've got is 'likelihood', we've got to admit the jury's choice for watching the Frey house would be Harry Frey himself."

"Hey, that doesn't help."

"I mean that likelihoods won't help us; we need evidence. Anyway, even though neither of us thinks it a promising enquiry, the name your father gave you, Prudie Goode, is a bird in hand."

"Do you think Prudie is short for Prudence," I asked, "or did a randy and rejected high school stud hang it on her?"

"If she's Plante's former playmate, then her name is Prudence. Joking aside, I know a little about her. You've read her magazine, of course."

"I've seen it and thumbed through it, but it's not my kind of thing, a who's doing what with whom and where, wearing what or not."

"That's not entirely fair, but close. A *People* magazine of northwest Michigan is the way it heralds itself. It's published here in town, and very successfully, which makes it unique in today's publishing world. And Prudie as a result is a must inclusion in the T.C. social scene. If you read the *Record-Eagle* instead of relying on the web exclusively, you'd have seen her pictures any number of times: young, stylish, confident. The kind of woman any social climber or politician, male or female, would like to have at his or her side when pictures are being shot."

"Think I should make an appointment to see her?"

"It couldn't hurt, but if you do go, I think you'd better not make an appointment. From that direction, the firewall may be insurmountable."

"You mean just walk in?" I said.

"Some variation on that."

"OK, I'll go, but I think it's hardly worth the effort. If my father's right about the timing, she'd be a jealous killer who'd waited six months to get even. Not exactly a hot-head."

"Maybe she's just been too busy."

I lay in bed thinking of my assignment in the morning. I felt like I did the night before an exam for which I hadn't cracked a book. Why embarrass myself; go jogging instead. Even if I tried the surprise tactic Derek prescribed, I still had to get by secretaries. Considering the issue from Ms. Goode's point of view, why would she agree to talk to me? If she was the woman replaced by Marian, that would make her a prime suspect and whether guilty or not, she'd avoid any contact with a person connected with the case, much like the elected prom queen would avoid a classmate with chicken pox.

"Wait a minute!" I must have said it aloud, because Kato, who had been settled on the foot of the bed, raised his head and was looking at me. The thought I'd just had was this: If she hadn't killed Plante, but could be made to believe she was being considered as a suspect by the police, wouldn't that motivate her to help us identify the real killer?

"Nice thinking," I told myself. As I fell asleep, a plan was forming in my mind, or was I just dreaming?

20

"Yes, Doctor, how can I help you?"

This was a good beginning; he was talking about helping. The first thing I did this morning after feeding Kato and drinking two cups of coffee to clear my mind was to call the Leelanau Sheriff's Headquarters and ask to speak to the head man. The plan that was coming together as I'd fallen asleep was without question totally off the wall, but then maybe no more far-fetched than our whole project of finding a killer to take over Harry's jail cell.

"Sheriff, the other day when you asked me to come to the jail, because you were concerned about your prisoner, Harry Frey, I wondered to myself at that time if your department was actively pursuing the possibility that someone other than Mr. Frey was guilty of the murders."

There was no reply. He was waiting to see if I had more to say. I didn't know if this conversation was being recorded or not, but I decided I needed to proceed as if it was, and take care to phrase ideas in a way that permitted him to help me if he wished to.

Finally he said, "Dr. Morgan, until a case of murder is closed, that is until a person has been convicted of the crime, it remains an open investigation."

"That's what I thought. In other words, individuals who are recognized to have realistic motives for the crime would be subjects of your continued inquiry?"

"That is so." His voice was friendly, comfortable, no hint of a wish to hurry me on my way and get back to the business of the morning.

"In that group would be persons who may have a motive like revenge—jealous or jilted lovers, for instance."

"Anyone with a strong motive is considered. And the type of motive you mentioned can be very strong," he returned.

"Then Prudie Goode, the editor of the magazine, *The Bay and Beyond*, would certainly be one of the people whom you've summoned recently to Sheriff's Headquarters for questioning, since it is widely known that she was recently jilted by Brian Plante."

He laughed. "Surely Doctor you don't expect me to discuss any details concerning the case with anyone not officially part of the investigation."

"No, of course not. It is only that several of Mr. Frey's friends can't believe he is a murderer. They would rest more easily if they could be assured that all with a credible motive, such as Ms. Goode had been called to your office for an interview."

I knew I was pushing. Was he hearing this as offensive interference, or did he hear the request I was making and, if heard, would he entertain for even a moment acting on it?

"I appreciate your interest, Doctor. Now, if there is nothing further I can help you with, I've got a phone call I've got to make." He hung up.

I put the phone down and began to wonder. No, no. I was still dreaming if I dared to think so - if I dared to think Hoss Davis wanted to help me and was going to make the call, and yet he had called me to the jail in order for Harry to tell me he was innocent. He had ignored a court order forbidding Harry visitors in order for that to happen. I didn't believe Sheriff Hoss Davis did that kind of thing without reason.

Forty minutes later, I stood on the sidewalk before the Front Street address of the magazine. A major brokerage firm occupied the first floor of the building. The second floor was claimed by a national internet provider. That left the top layer of this cake of affluence to *The*

Bay and Beyond.

I took the elevator to the third floor and stepped out to face a wall of swirling red marble, a single desk and a receptionist. She was sufficiently preoccupied to be oblivious to my standing before her desk. It seemed to be a troubled preoccupation. It could be a personal matter that troubled her: her teenaged daughter had just called to say she was dropping out of school to run away to Alberta with an oil rigger. Or, maybe - just maybe – it was because her boss had received a call from the sheriff.

"Ahem," I cleared my throat.

She looked up, slowly admitted my presence, and gathered together her usual receptionist persona. "Welcome to *The Bay and Beyond*. How can I help you?"

"I would like to speak to Ms. Goode," I answered, smiling brightly.

"Do you have an appointment?"

"I think so. My name is Doctor Thomas Morgan."

She hit a key on her console and began talking. A concerned look appeared on her attractive face while she glanced toward a hallway to her right.

"Doctor Morgan, I'm afraid Ms. Goode's secretary has no appointment recorded for you this morning. When did . . ."

"I'm sure Ms. Goode will want to see me. I'd better speak with her secretary." I started off in the direction that she had just glanced.

She started to object, but realized she'd have to start shouting, so she turned to alerting the secretary.

Ten yards along the hall, it widened into a space for a desk and a sitting area. The man behind the desk, who was talking into a phone as he looked with irritation in my direction, must be, I figured, Prudie Goode's secretary. I knew he wanted to tell me to go to hell, especially because I sensed he'd been sharing the same concern that I detected in the receptionist's demeanor. Instead, ever mindful of the magazine's image, he managed a half smile.

"I'm Jeff Townsend, Ms. Goode's secretary. I'm sorry, but there is some mistake, since I don't have an appointment down for you this morning, but I'll be happy . . . "

"Actually, I want to talk to her for only five minutes. Right now."

He raised his eyebrows in mock shock as if this was one of the more novel ideas he'd ever heard.

"I am Doctor Thomas Morgan. Get her on the phone and tell her I think we can help one another in the matter of the murder of Brian Plante."

His reaction confirmed that Hoss Davis had made his call, which also confirmed Davis had had his motives for letting me talk to Harry Frey.

The secretary stared at me, not in misunderstanding, but in confusion about his next action. He picked up his phone, said a few words I couldn't hear, and then excused himself, opened the door in the wall behind him enough to slide through and quickly closed it. In only moments he reappeared, leaving the door open.

If I was right and the sheriff had called, I figured Prudie Goode would be wondering right now how each of us had made the connection between her and Brian Plante. It would not help my cause if she concluded the cops had heard of it from me.

"Ms. Goode is able to see you," the secretary, coming back to his desk, said in his practiced manner.

I walked past him and into the impressive office of Prudie Goode. She stood facing me, tall, angular, ash blond, frank blue eyes full of challenge. God had not made an extra effort in Prudie's basic structure, but where the Almighty had failed her she had provided herself with the very best the cosmetic and couturier arts had to offer.

She'd gotten her money's worth. You had to be sharp to see the plain woman behind the superb wrapper. I hoped she hadn't caught me peeping through. I don't think she had; she was too busy sizing me up. I was curious about how she'd proceed.

"You're not what I'd thought you'd be," she flung at me.

Immediately, she had me off balance. How could she have any thoughts about how I'd "be"?

"I don't understand," I said, having completely forgotten my recent fame.

"When I read about it, I pictured a bearded creep with a disdain for his patients and anyone else who might suffer from his bad judgment. I thought you got what you deserved." She sat down behind her desk and motioned for me to take the smaller chair at its side. There was no doubt about who was the intended commander here.

The question came to my mind, "How can you be so sure it isn't true after a brief glance?" I didn't say it, of course, and I also recognized that I couldn't allow her to take command.

"I told your secretary I wanted five minutes and that's all I want of your time. I know you must be wondering how I know about you and Plante. That information is out there. I learned it from someone in Chicago."

She frowned and was framing a question when I hurried on. "I don't know what it is, but the police seem to have made a discovery that makes them doubt that they have arrested the right person. I don't, however, think they want to admit a mistake and let Harry Frey go until they're sure this time that they have the right body to occupy his cell. Friends and I have been working hard to discover who really killed those two—to clear Mr. Frey and . . ."

"Save your own ass."

I smiled. "Ah yes, a valued part of my anatomy."

I continued, "It's a matter of who had a motive. I've learned

Plante had a reputation for romancing a woman and then dropping her hard in a way calculated to make her feel like a used coffee filter—make her want to kill him. My information has you as one of those women. I think he waved Marian Frey in a certain lady's face." I paused and our eyes locked. "I wonder if that lady was you?" I paused again, then added, "Or if she was the one who came after you."

"With this kind of directness, you'll only need two minutes of my time."

I was afraid she meant I was headed for the door and she was already pressing the button for my escort. That wasn't the case.

"I see. If I am the killer that you postulate, you wouldn't expect me to admit it. You're hoping that if I'm not, I'd see the value in helping you—help you name that lady, as you politely put it."

I was nodding my head.

She went on. "In addition, I'd see the value of talking to you instead of the police, who are sure to have among their ranks a person who would see profit in spilling the details of my, er, relationship to Brian Plante to the local press for a little baksheesh."

I said nothing. She was doing fine by herself.

"Brian did just what you described. I'd been warned, but I was foolish to think what every woman thinks—it's different with me. And, indeed it was very different . . . for a while. Then a friend confided to me that she'd been told Brian was seen . . . to be . . . well, overly comfortable with a woman at the Leelanau Hunt Club. The friend didn't have any details, only that the woman was a member and had a horse there. I dismissed it as the creation of some envious female."

She paused, so I prompted, "But it turned out to be true?"

"Brian asked me to meet him at the Hunt Club. I'd never been there before—zero interest in horses. Anyway, his wish to meet there certainly proved there was nothing to this rumor. If he were cheating on me there, he'd never invite me there, right? Wrong!

"When I arrived and asked where I could find him, I was directed to the paddock. I found him there leaning heavily on a redhead, who in turn was leaning against her horse. Brian was stroking the woman's withers – if I've got the right term. Anyway, I turned and left, oozing as much indifference as I could project. I wanted him to know that he and his perverted need to humiliate me came just below Brillo pads in my thoughts."

I blinked at the amount of very private stuff she'd just unloaded. I quietly asked, "What was the woman's name?"

"In order to maintain my myth of indifference, I could never ask the questions I so badly wanted to ask about her."

She noticed my disappointment. "I suppose I could find out."

I liked her gruff way. She was either a very good person to work for or the reverse.

"Can you describe the woman?" I hoped she hadn't done as good a job of burying her interest as she claimed.

She rocked her head from side to side. "OK, let's see. She had auburn hair done up in a single braid—probably because of that helmet they wear. She had the hat in her hand. She was maybe five-five. She had more mammary tissue than was necessary. She was wearing a gold choker—too wide for her—maybe to hide a scar."

I sank back in my chair. There was a scar as a matter of fact. Harry had mentioned Marian's sensitivity about it in one of his treatment sessions, and I'd seen that auburn hair flowing freely across her pillow. I'd seen the gold choker too.

She remarked on the sudden change she discerned in me. "Did I just say the magic word?"

I nodded. "You just described Marian Frey, the woman killed with Brian Plante."

Her feisty manner died as she uttered, "Oh," as if punched in the belly. After some moments she muttered, "I guess that moves me up to number one on the suspect list . . . if your patient didn't do it."

Her fear looked genuine and it came to me then that she now had to see me as a mortal enemy, a person whose priority was to find anyone except Harry Frey to be the killer, a person who had just identified her, Prudie Goode, as the prime suspect. I should have felt a pleasure of victory parallel to her fear. I had a viable alternative to Harry Frey and I had reason to believe Hoss Davis would be receptive to what I'd just learned—hell, he'd participated with me in discovering it. Instead of feeling victorious I felt perplexed. I liked this woman; I didn't want her to be the killer.

Bit by bit, subconsciously, I'd been pulling together an impression of her since I first walked through the door. I didn't think things had come easy for her in life. She hadn't the quick currency of good looks that opens the doors for many. She'd made her way in what was still essentially a man's world—at least it certainly wasn't a woman's world. She'd had to be smart and light on her feet. She'd succeeded, but she hadn't followed the natural inclination to identify with those who had succeeded easily. To me, her manner said anyone who puts in the effort could do what she'd done. She had the aura of a plucky fighter, the kind who refused to go down, but didn't become conceited or bitter because she'd had to absorb much along the way. She'd absorbed pain from Brian Plante, but . . . would she be driven to return it?

"What about an alibi for the time of the murders?" I asked.

She stared into my eyes for a long moment before she answered. I could see that she knew where I stood.

"When I heard about the murders, of course, I knew I had motive enough even if I hadn't identified Marian Frey as the woman I'd seen with Brian. I automatically reviewed what I'd been doing at the time the paper said the killings had taken place. I have a sixteen-foot daysailer I keep at the marina in Greilickville. At times when things get crazy here in the office, I like to take the boat out in the bay alone for an hour or so." She shrugged. "That's where I was."

"Did anyone see you there?"

"I don't know. No one was on the dock when I went out, or when I came back. Did anyone see me? I don't know. I didn't ask. I hoped I wouldn't need to."

My thoughts went elsewhere. "What about the woman Plante was seeing when he met you?" The phrase, "whom you replaced" had crossed my mind, but thank God I didn't say it.

"Yeah, I thought of her too. She married a congressman. I saw her picture in the paper the day after the murders on one of those trips they'd like us to believe is to promote international relations. Bali."

I got up. "My five minutes are up."

My father's effort had produced what I'd hoped for, the person with a motive as strong as Harry Frey's. It was information I would pass on to Hoss Davis, but I wasn't happy about it. I went to the door and had the knob in my hand when I turned and said, "If I were you, I'd go down to the marina and work on that alibi."

She wasn't smiling exactly, but her eyes were friendly. "Thanks."

21

Perhaps not wanting Prudie to be the bad guy caused me to return to that jumbled bit of logic I'd produced in Chicago when my father had asked me about who had a motive for the murder. The angle of looking for Plante's lovers had captured our thinking. Now I considered another approach: maybe Marian had had another lover beside Plante. I knew of her affair with him a good two weeks before Harry did, and it was only his chance spotting her driving in an unexpected place that opened his eyes. I knew from several remarks he'd made in therapy that he never went near the Leelanau Hunt Club, so maybe Marian had made that the locus of more sport than horseback riding. A trip to The Hunt Club became the logical next move.

It occurred to me immediately that accompanied by Audrey, I'd be less conspicuous while nosing around there asking questions. A couple appeared more likely to be going about normal business than a single guy did, and then there was Audrey's looks; I could be opening everyone's locker and rummaging through their stuff and no one would notice with her in the vicinity. Unfortunately, she was presenting a case at the psych department's clinical conference in the afternoon, and I didn't want to wait until tomorrow to see if I could learn anything useful at the Hunt Club.

I needed to call her and explain my absence at her presentation, and I wanted to ask her about Marian—see how far she would go toward enlightening me about Marian's extramarital adventures. I got into my car but before starting it, I dialed her cell. Before I heard Audrey say hello, I heard a woman laughing, then Audrey's voice.

"Hi, Tom," she said, having read my name on her caller I.D.

"Hi. Have you got company?"

"No, I'm at Rhonda's office. We've been going over things we need to do before the Psychiatric Society's annual dinner. What hors d'oeuvres to serve? Can we get a local winery to donate wine? That kind of interesting stuff." Her voice took on a serious tone. "How's your father?"

Her voice had the power to transform my mood. It split the world into two parts, she and I made up one part; the second part was everything else.

"My father's not good, but hanging in there. Thanks for asking. I called because I wanted you to know that I won't be at your presentation this afternoon. My father learned a fact about Brian Plante that has led to an urgent need for me to pay a visit to the Leelanau Hunt Club."

Surprised, she asked, "Why there?"

I wondered if I should go into my reasons. Certainly letting her know what I wanted her to tell me about Marian was now out, with Rhonda in the room. After all, if she said anything on the subject it would technically be a breach of confidence, even with Marian dead.

"It's no big secret, but complicated. I'll call you tonight and tell you all about it."

"OK, mystery man, until this evening."

"I hope all goes well with your presentation."

"Thanks."

I then called Derek at his home to tell him about the interview with Prudie Goode and how I thought the Hunt Club would be worth a visit, and that I wanted him to go with me.

"I see," he responded. "I doubt if . . . well, OK."

"Not quite the enthusiasm of Sherlock Holmes," I said.

"It's just that I hate to miss the clinical conference."

"You can ask Audrey for a copy of her remarks."

"Yeah, but it's not that. I feel I should go to these things to keep up the morale of the group, like the colonial British always dressing for dinner."

"And a lot of good it did them."

I'd never been to the Leelanau Hunt Club. I'd had no reason to; it was basically a stable and I didn't ride. The name gave the place airs. One pictures a pack of hounds yelping after a fox, followed by a score of pink and black clad riders. The Leelanau Hunt Club hunted nothing—unless it was a new, well-heeled member. The story I'd heard was that Granville DeVere, the founder and still the aging president of the club's board, had come here thirty years ago, leaving behind in Connecticut a respected reputation in equestrian circles, to follow his wayward daughter to Leelanau, where she had fled with a young man bent on growing grapes and making wine. Granville began again, and while he couldn't reproduce the "old family" patina of New England, his new enterprise had become recognized as the standard bearer of equestrian tradition in the north half of our state. Each year the club hosted an equestrian competition that drew riders from the whole country and beyond. All the jumping and horsey footwork drew a large crowd. And this crowd spent its dollars at our local restaurants and bars, settled down at night in local lodgings, and bought paperback mysteries from local bookstores. Three cheers for the Hunt Club.

The place is located about three miles south of Suttons Bay off highway M22. One approaches its colonial-style buildings by a half-mile driveway that winds through green pastures bordered by white rail fences where horses looked up from grazing as Derek and I drove by them. I'd swear each made the quick appraisal that we didn't belong there. This paranoia was reinforced by the absence of a visible parking area other than the one just past the front entry that proclaimed, "Members Only." The thought, "What the hell," had me heading toward it anyway, until I reconsidered; wouldn't our mission be better served by being inconspicuous? Since I couldn't identify another place to park—they probably parked spectators' cars in a pasture during the competition—I turned to the services of the young valet, who stood under the entrance awning watching my hesitant approach like a guy waiting for a mosquito to land.

The clubhouse portion of the complex of barns and riding rings conformed to the same functional design. The interior projected another character. If a fencing team should be housed in a Gothic castle decked out with suits of armor and hanging chivalric banners, then a hunt club should be just what we were viewing; deep leather chairs burnished by thousands of applications of jodhpurs to a perfect patina, waxed wood, polished brass, crystal decanters of Port on antique mahogany tables and trophy cases, four in a row along the entrance hall.

We feigned a fascination with the contents of the first case to give us time to settle on what our next move should be. The case was a tribute to DeVere, the club's founder—pictures of DeVere standing next to horses, DeVere holding blue ribbons, DeVere hoisting silver cups and DeVere generally looking satisfied with himself . . . and why not.

"Quite an accomplishment really," Derek said, "building up all this."

The next case astounded us. It featured a large portrait of a man in his mid-thirties. He smiled out at us with confidence, maybe with arrogance. The caption beneath the picture read, "2003 United States National Champion, Lestor Parish."

"I'll be damned," I gasped.

Harry Frey, in his sessions with me, had said that Marian and her brother were "horse nuts", and that the brother spent all the time and money he could mooch from her playing the part of the wealthy

188

sportsman. Harry had said nothing of the caliber of sport his brother-in-law was capable of.

"Well, well, and here he is again," said Derek pointing to another picture.

It was a group picture, everyone in their habits and helmets. Parish was holding a trophy. The caption here read, "United States Equestrian team, 1999 Americas Challenge Cup Champions."

"Son of a . . ."

"Can I help you gentlemen?" said someone behind us in a tone that was a challenge rather than a question. "I am Foster Cockburn, the club manager."

We both turned round to face a man in his mid-forties, a beard trimmed lovingly, well-tailored tweed jacket, silk handkerchief flopping just so out of the breast pocket.

"Oh, hi," I said. "I'm Doctor Thomas Morgan and this is my friend, Doctor Derek Marsh. We have heard so much about this place right in our backyard, but have never been here, and we'd like to look around, if that's all right." I said this just like my mother had taught me to talk to grown ups. I noticed, however, that he winced when I'd said, "right in our backyard."

Cockburn designed his hesitation of speech, as if searching for the right words to let us know that "looking around" the club by the public was just not done.

"We are flattered with your interest, but except during the public events held here, the buildings and grounds are reserved for our members and guests. Perhaps you come as guests of a member?" He knew damn well we weren't guests.

"No, we're not," Derek shot back. I could see that he was pissed with Cockburn's arrogance. "But you've got a neat place here and we just might want to join up."

I almost laughed out loud. Derek was putting membership

here on a plane with the Y.M.C.A.

The man visibly struggled to maintain his composure, as a pope might do if asked by a supplicant to see his appendectomy scar.

"Ah yes, well, a prospective member must—I'm sure you understand—have his or her name put forward by an active member." He moved quickly past this unlikely event of our membership to say, "It is always nice to have contact with those in the local community, but I must excuse myself to attend to other business, so if you don't mind . . ."

The young parking valet appeared suddenly, apparently answering a covert signal. We were being given the bum's rush. A moment later we found ourselves standing under the entrance canopy awaiting my Miata.

"Sorry about that, Tom. My smart aleck remark about membership got us thrown out and we didn't accomplish a thing."

"Nonsense. Old Foster was ready to give us the heave ho when he saw us gawking at the pictures. And we did learn something; we learned what Parish looks like and that he was a helluva horseman as well as being a horse's ass and probable killer."

Derek laughed, saying, "And, we learned we don't want to be members of the Leelanau Hunt Club as long as Cockburn is manager."

We got in the car and I started out the driveway on which we'd entered. On the right, a dirt road angled off toward what looked like a stable. I yanked the steering wheel sharply in that direction.

"I just had an idea," I explained.

"That you want to get us arrested for trespassing,"

"Here it is," I said ignoring his remark. "We go into this stable and tell whomever we meet there that we're interested in buying Marian's horse. I know for a fact that she kept one here at the club. We get him or her talking about horses and then segue into Marian's love life in the saddle."

"Tom, that's a little loose. We've been told . . . "

"I know, I know. But, we've got exactly zilch right now. The prosecutor is preparing to charge me with a criminal offense, I'm being sued for more money than the state deficit and my name will be trash. Do you think I'm overreacting?"

"OK, OK, Donna should have enough in her savings account to pay our bail."

The road got mucky near the stable. I wanted to drive to the backside, where my car wouldn't be visible from the clubhouse and to Foster Cockburn, but I could see the area was so wet there was a risk of becoming stuck. I parked off the dirt track just far enough to permit another vehicle to pass.

A tall man with a weather-beaten face, wearing rubber boots and carrying a saddle over his right forearm, stepped out of a door at the end of the building and gave us a long, suspicious look. He waited until we'd walked up to him before speaking,

"Help ya?"

"We want to look at the horse that belonged to Mrs. Marian Frey. I understand it's for sale."

"Cockburn said nothin' t'me 'bout it bein' fer sale."

"You must be . . ." I hesitated as if searching my mind.

"Fred Tover."

"Right, right, Fred. Foster said for us to come and talk with you. He's tied up right now."

"He wants me t'show her to ya?"

"If you don't mind."

He turned and reentered the stable, putting the saddle on a rack near the door, and walked the length of the long building. As we passed, horses' heads turned to follow us like wedding guests turning to see the approaching bride. Fred stopped in front of a chestnut head. "Odalisque" was on the nameplate fixed to the door of the stall. He took a bridle off a peg and slipped it over the horse's head and led it out into the wide center aisle, talking and stroking all the while.

"Nice animal, Odie. What they askin'?"

"Mr. Frey only wants what he paid for her," I replied, hoping that would suffice.

"What's that?" Fred wouldn't be put off.

In the nick of time from somewhere deep in a memory from one of my sessions with Frey came a number.

"Thirty-five," I said, hoping I hadn't remembered the number of calories in a medium-sized peach.

"Decent."

I could see he now expected me to examine the horse. I'd seen movies where John Wayne or Tommy Lee Jones appraised a horse, and I'd risk faking it if it weren't in front of an expert.

"I don't know much about horses myself. It's for my daughter."

"Most horses are bought fer daughters," Fred said.

"I've been told it's a nice riding horse."

"Depends on who's in the saddle. Mrs. Frey could work 'er good. Damned shame she got killed and all."

Just the opening I was hoping for. "Yes, a shame. You knew her well then?"

"Nice lady. Always had time fer ya. Know what I mean?"

"Indeed. And the man who died with her, Plante, know him too?"

"Nah. He let ya know ya belonged in the stables."

"Ah," I said, nodding knowingly. "But they must have been friends, Plante and Mrs. Frey."

Fred shrugged. I worried that the well had run dry. He pulled Odie aside to make way for another groom, who was putting another horse into the stall across the aisle.

"I mean," I prompted, "being found the way they were."

He picked up one of the horse's front feet, looked at it carefully, and then let go of it. "I wouldn't know 'bout that. She was a nice person. Never should'a got tangled up with his kind." I kept quiet. "Always tomcat'n around."

"Really? Who for instance?"

Fred looked at me but said nothing.

I couldn't push that much farther. "It's odd, as you say, that she would get involved with Brian Plante, when she had another very good friend here already," I bluffed.

"How'd ya know 'bout that?"

I shrugged, as if to say one hears these things.

"Like pick'n 'tween a polecat an' a egg sucking hound."

Picturing this choice that Fred offered diverted me for a moment. "How did he take it? I mean, when she took up with Plante?"

He gave a snort. "Not good."

"Openly angry, huh?" I had no idea whom he was talking about. How far could I stretch this?

"Other ways. Why are ya so interested in Mrs. Frey?"

"The fact that I may buy her horse makes me curious I guess." That was very weak and Fred's not answering said he thought so too.

"You said, 'Other ways.' Funny isn't it how one notices the little things? I'd be interested to know how you knew he was angry."

"More of a bastard than usual. Fired Sam Herman fer nothin' at all."

I tried not to sound too eager. I feigned interest in what the groom was doing in the opposite stall, trimming a hoof with a curved knife, the way one might trim the rind off a Gouda cheese. I was trying to think of a question that might cause Fred to come out with a name, when a voice boomed.

"Put that horse back in its stall, Tover. I told you men only club members are permitted on the grounds. You deliberately ignored me.

You will leave immediately or I'll call the sheriff."

Whatever source of information Fred Tover might have been, it was cut off forever.

"Come on, Derek," I said, "I don't think this is the horse for my daughter anyway."

Cockburn followed us part of the way back to my car, but then returned to give Fred hell for talking to us. I thought Fred could handle himself.

22

We cleared the gates of the Hunt Club and I pulled off the road and onto the shoulder.

"Foster Cockburn," Derek said in wonder. I wouldn't have thought he could get a hard on for anybody or anything except his own reflection."

"If he was the one Fred meant, and I'm sure he was, you can imagine how his blood boiled when Plante came dancing in and took away his candy, while he'd be forced to act the obsequious employee. Humiliating."

"Tom, I think we have a very hot tenant for Harry's jail cell. Let's take what we have to the sheriff."

"I agree that we've identified a credible suspect, but the problem right now is we only have that groom's oblique insinuation that Cockburn and Marian were involved. We need confirmation and I have an idea how to get it. "

"Oh?" He looked worried.

"Lestor Parish. "

Derek did the quizzical frown.

"If Marian and Cockburn were having at it, Parish would be sure to know. It would have been hot news at the Club. Hell, even Tover knew about it. We go to Parish and tell him we'll trade his confirmation of Marian's affair with Cockburn for our silence concerning what we know about the embezzlement. He tells us, or we go to the police. I think he'll agree. What will it cost him to tell us about his sister, when the flip side is possible jail and a loss of face with his pals at the Hunt Club and the National Equestrian whatsit?"

"But Frey has already talked to a lawyer about a lawsuit."

"Who says Parish knows that?"

Derek laughed. "Arguing with you is like trying to get a mattress in a stuff-bag."

"Now just listen. My plan is simple. We pay Parish a visit. Double-team him. Surprise him. Shake him up."

Derek shook his head. "That plan at least boasts spontaneity - the spontaneity of a headlong plunge. As if Parish would even talk to us, let alone submit to your portable lie detector. Tom, think about it; this shooting off in all directions is wild."

I sighed, "I can't argue, except to say that I have to find a quick answer, or I'll be too late to avoid a personal disaster." My tone asked a favor. "C'mon, let's try to shake up Parish."

The beginning of what I hoped was resignation began to replace the troubled disbelief I'd read on his face.

"Do you know where he lives?" he said.

I shook my head and took out my iPhone. "Maybe . . . Hey, we're in luck, got his phone number - a 271 number, a Suttons Bay number, but no street number, just Sutton Heights."

"Suttons Heights; isn't that the new development of huge homes on the hill above Suttons Bay?"

"I've heard about it, but I've never been there."

"Neither have I. Give me your phone." He looked at the displayed number and dialed and it was answered.

"Hi, this is Jerry your Fed Ex man," Derek said matter-of-factly. "I've got an envelope for Lestor Parish, but it must have the wrong address - Flossmore Street. There's no Flossmore that I know of in Suttons Bay."

"What's that? Erinbrook? That's nothing like Flossmore. I know Erinbrook. What's the number there? 44? Good, that's the number on the envelope. And Lestor Parish lives there right? OK. Is he there now? Because he has to sign for the envelope. Terrific. I have to make a delivery here in town and then I'll head up there."

He looked at me. "The maid. She said 'Parish residence.'"

He got a pen from a pocket and wrote the street number on a gasoline receipt he found on the floor of my car. He looked pleased with himself.

"Well done. By the way, how long have you been an imposter?"

"Ha! People who keep their daughter's horse in a glass house shouldn't throw stones."

"So, you know where Erinbrook is?"

"We drive to Suttons Bay and start climbing the hill. There can't be many streets in the subdivision."

"You could have asked for directions."

"Who's going to believe that Jerry, after driving these roads for a quarter of a century, wouldn't know where Erinbrook is, even if it is a new street?"

"A point."

I drove to Suttons Bay, turning left on Adams Street to get to West Street to begin the climb to Suttons Heights. After passing the stone entrance columns bearing the logo and name of the development, the street name changed to Suttons Way, and I saw the first of the mansions, crowding ten thousand square feet and garnished with mature landscaping of fully-grown trees. Erinbrook branched off to the right and I steered up a steep grade, shifting into third. Dense pines and scattered boulders covered the hill on both sides of the road. At the apex a driveway descended off to the right. A plywood signboard displayed the house number and the various permits for a house under construction. At this point Erinbrook ceased to be paved, but continued on down the backside of the hill as a dirt road.

"Here we are," I said turning into the driveway.

In front of us about fifty yards farther along the drive we saw a white frame farmhouse with a decided sag in the roof.

"It's gotta be one hundred years old," said Derek. "Not what I expected."

"The view out over Grand Traverse Bay is awesome though."

I drove up to the house and we got out. From this point we could see around a corner of the house where the skeleton of a huge, new structure came into view.

"There's the reason for the building permits," I commented. "I presume it's going to be a house, but it could also be Google's new world headquarters."

"It's also where the money from the embezzlement went."

We climbed the steps to the porch, where a maid opened the door before we could knock. She had been prepared to open the door to the Fed Ex man and appeared frightened by the two of us.

"We'd like to see Lestor Parish, " I said sweetly.

"Mr. Parish isn't here," she replied in the automatic voice of someone who, like a theater usher, repeats a phrase frequently.

"We know he's here. Tell Mr. Parish we've come to talk about money embezzled from a real estate development in Petoskey. I think he'll want to speak to us."

The woman looked overwhelmed and started to close the door, but when I put my hand on the door, stopping her, she gave up and retreated into the room, no doubt to report to Parish. We waited long enough to begin thinking she had really gone to begin preparing supper before she reappeared and asked us to follow her.

The living room we walked through held only a large armchair and a small table – no rugs. Apparently Parish was holding off the purchase of furniture until the new house was finished. A sun porch had been added at some time since the house had first been built and this was our destination.

Lestor Parish looked older and more dissipated than one would expect in the nine years since his victory photo. He was unshaven with uncombed hair, which enhanced his look of decline. He lounged on a wicker couch, holding a magazine he looked up from only when we were standing before him. He was barefoot. He wore shorts and a T-shirt, which bore the inscription, "Horse (hors), n, 1. A large, solid hoofed, quadruped, Equus cabalus, which lives symbiotically with a parasite, Homo sapiens, which attaches itself to its back."

He looked us over, letting us know he was unimpressed. It also let me know he wasn't going to be thrown off balance easily.

"You are?"

"I'm Tom Morgan and this is Derek Marsh; we're friends of Pat Furst. She, as you know, went to Petoskey and discovered evidence, which we now possess, that you and Lambert stole money from your brother-in-law."

He stood up in a sudden rage. "Get the hell out of my house! You're the ones who got that Petoskey cop to call and ask a lot of questions. I didn't know what the fuck the guy was talking about and I still don't. Get out!" he demanded, pointing toward the front door. "This is pure bullshit."

"If it's bullshit, why did you let us in?" I shouted back.

"I let you in, because I thought you were implying someone had stolen money from us."

"Harry Frey will testify you did it," I shot back.

"Harry Frey? Who is Harry Frey? If they don't put him away for killing my sister, they'll send him to a nut house. Who gives a shit what Harry Frey says?"

He went to a coffee table, picked up a portable phone and jabbed in three numbers.

"This is Lestor Parish, 44 Erinbrook. There are intruders in my house. I need the police."

"Let them come," I said. "I'd like to tell them the story." It was all I could think of. I really didn't want to be standing here trying to explain about embezzlement in Petoskey to a Leelanau sheriff's deputy.

His expression changed from outrage to suspicion. "Wait a minute; why are you really here? You guys want something. I know who you are now. You're Harry's psychiatrist. The one who's in deep shit for not warning people that Harry was dangerous."

I wondered if the sheriff was, indeed, at this minute sending a car or two up here, since Parish had seemed to go off the line. All I needed right now was to be arrested for trespassing. The maid could say I pushed the door open.

"What we want," Derek said stepping in, "is to know anyone beside Brian Plante with whom your sister was involved."

"What? Are both of you nuts?"

"We're willing to forget about the embezzlement, if you tell us what we want to know," I said.

He became much calmer. "I'm curious. What makes you think Marian had another boyfriend?"

"We don't just think, we know it was Foster Cockburn; we just want you to confirm it," I replied.

Everything I'd learned about reading people's emotions told me his were acknowledging that Cockburn was our man.

"Wha . . . Oh, I get it. You're trying to hang the murders on someone else to save your ass. It's true, all you shrinks are nuts."

Derek tried for more leverage. "We also have information that points to Lambert being murdered."

I could see this knocked him off balance for a moment, but he recovered.

"I'm not saying another word to you fuckers. I'm waiting for the police to get here." He laid the phone back on the table.

It occurred to me that he might have faked the call, but on the other hand . . . I took out one of my cards and laid it next to the phone.

"We are still waiting to trade confirmation about Cockburn for our silence. If I don't hear from you by the morning, we're going to the sheriff. Let's go, Derek."

As we walked back through the living room, Derek said under his breath, "Who shook up who back there?"

On the wall near the front door hung a copy of the equestrian team photo we'd seen at the Hunt Club. I stopped to look at it.

Derek, already on the porch, said, "Tom, come on. If a patrol car is on the way, we don't want to be here to greet it."

"Just . . ."

"Now!"

23

At the end of Parish's driveway I stopped the car. Which road to take, the paved road we'd come on, or the dirt road to the right that descended the other side of the hill?

"The way we came," Derek said urgently. "We can't be sure the dirt road isn't a dead end."

"But if the cops are coming, they're probably taking the paved road."

I concluded Derek was right. We couldn't take the chance the dirt road didn't end at some old sugar shack. I sped down Erinbrook, then on to Suttons Way, then West Street and back into downtown Suttons Bay. We were clear. If Parish had called the cops and not faked the call, I was sure he would cover his call with a lie when they arrived. He was not about to complicate his very precarious position.

I was lost in thought during the return drive to Derek's. I could sense that he was on the point of saying something several times, but didn't. I thought I knew what he would say—Parish had bested us. We had been surprised by his stonewall response and had resorted to pretty foolish comebacks. Parish's anger had me doubting my certainty of his guilt. I reminded myself that it had taken nerve to pull off the embezzlement scam and that ability could account for his performance with us. He was a consummate con man. Apart from these thoughts another impression or memory hovered just beyond my conscious awareness, but like a pesky fly, it wouldn't light long enough for me to catch it.

I dropped Derek off and drove home. At the top of the stairs, in front of the door to my loft I found a paper bag with a bottle of wine inside. With a marker, Tony had written on the bag, "Try this over ice. I stole it from Mt. Olympus." It was from Longview Winery, a good local vineyard. The label read "Sweet Winter Ice." I was touched by his gesture, but it would have taken more than this to relieve my angry frustration.

I sank into the harbor chair. A man and a teenager out on the dock were engaged in some kind of misunderstanding. The man waved his arms and the boy affected an attitude of grand indifference. The man, who bore a facial likeness to the boy, was chewing him out for some infraction or error. They could have been enjoying their work together; instead they shared misery.

Kato stood at the window watching the same scene of conflict. He turned and looked me in the eye. I knew what he was thinking, "And you people think you're at the top of the animal kingdom."

He was wrong. I didn't feel myself to be at the top of anything at the moment. This coming Monday I'd probably be arrested and charged with violation of the Tarasoff law, following which, I'd become a true pariah to my colleagues. A court date may already have been set in the suit brought against me by the former Mrs. Plante, and the damned Ethics Committee might still censure me in spite of my defense three days ago.

And taken altogether, what had I discovered so far? Only two things: maybe Marion had been screwing Foster Cockburn, and Harry Frey wasn't a liar, but I already knew that. And then, the pesky fly alighted for a moment and I saw in my mind's eye the picture of the equestrian team. The phone rang. Approaching it I noticed that the message light was blinking. I ignored it for the moment and answered.

I didn't recognize Victoria's voice for a moment, because it was husky from crying.

"Doctor Morgan, your father died an hour ago."

My chest felt suddenly crushed by the news and I was gripped by anger that surprised me. I had known that his death must come, but suddenly it seemed so unfair . . . before I'd had a chance to know him.

"I'm sorry," I said at last. "How are you, Victoria?"

"I'm alright." Just answering the question seemed to help her pull herself together. "Do you have any special wishes regarding the funeral? Your father made all the arrangements with the funeral home."

My mind was blank on the subject. "Whatever he planned is fine with me."

"The . . . the funeral will be Monday. He didn't like funeral homes and said he didn't want to 'stick around in one for long.'"

It sounded like the man I'd met.

"He left some papers and a notebook that he wanted you to read. The last . . ." She was silent for a moment while she composed herself. "His last words were about you, how I should be sure you got the notebook and to tell you . . ." Again the pause. "Tell you he was sorry he let so many years pass and that . . . he loved you." I could hear her crying.

Tomorrow was Saturday. I felt the need to go to Chicago and read through the notebook—to know him better before I buried him.

"If it's alright, Victoria, I'd like to come there tonight and read through the things he left for me."

"Of course it's alright, Tom. It's your home."

I hung up still surprised by what she'd said, "It's your home." I was resisting thinking of myself as his heir. I needed to call Audrey and tell her about his death. I also had to change my plans to meet her this evening. I figured she'd be home from the conference by now and she was.

"Audrey, I had some bad news just now, my father died a little while ago."

"Oh Tom! Tom, I'm so sorry."

"His death shouldn't have surprised me, I knew it was a matter of days, but it did just the same. Listen, the funeral is going to be Monday. Because I need to fly to Chicago this evening to take care of some details, I can't see you tonight."

"Of course, I understand completely."

Her voice was soothing. Nothing could have equaled its effect on me at that moment. Then I had a thought.

"I'd like you to go with me if you would and can." I anticipated her to beg off. She seemed to have need for tight control over her life and more time to plan.

"Ah . . . Would we be coming back Monday or Tuesday?"

"I'm thinking Tuesday morning."

"Hmm . . . I'd have to cancel patients tomorrow morning, Monday, and Tuesday morning . . . But I very much want to be there with you. Yes, yes I can. I'll start calling my patients."

"Wonderful. We'll be flying with the charter service, Air Services. I'll call you back with our departure time."

I went to my computer and sent an email to Sergeant McCulloch in Petoskey to inform him that my plans had changed for the next day and I couldn't meet with him.

The air charter service could arrange a flight at 7:15 that evening. I called Audrey and let her know, and then I began to walk aimlessly around the loft inundated with a mix of emotions: sadness caused by my father's death and pleasure at the thought of Audrey being at my side.

Again, I became aware of Kato standing and studying me like a clinician trying to arrive at a diagnosis for an insurance form.

Going into the kitchen to pour myself a glass of wine, I again noticed the message light still blinking on my answering machine.

"This is Les Parish, I've given further thought to our conversation. I'm sorry I flew into you the way I did. I had problems on my mind. Anyway, we might be able to do business after all. Meet me at my house at five o'clock."

I checked my watch. It was 4:25. The drive to his place would take twenty minutes. I could make it, but I didn't want to drive back up there when this could be handled on the phone. All he had to do is confirm Cockburn's relationship with Marion and I'd go to Sheriff Davis. I looked up his number and called it. The machine came on. Damn!

My business with him shouldn't take more than fifteen minutes. That would be enough time to see if he was cooperating or trying to jerk me round. It would take another twenty minutes to drive back here, another forty-five to pack some clothes, pick up Audrey and drive to the airport for the 7:15 flight. It could be done.

For the first ten minutes of the drive up to Suttons Bay I was totally occupied with passing slower cars on the winding road along Grand Traverse Bay. Finally at Shady Lane I had a clear stretch of road ahead of me, and I began to think of the encounter with Parish that lay ahead. But instead of imagining his possible evasions, my thoughts were drawn to the photograph of the equestrian team I'd seen on his wall, a copy of the one that hung in the Hunt Club. There was something familiar about it, a disturbing feeling of déjà vu. I was on the point of dragging the memory up to daylight, when I rounded a curve by Northern Lumber to find a flagman waving an orange flag at me. Driving way too fast and preoccupied to boot, I had to slam on my brakes, causing the guy to jump back with his pole and stop sign and shout some expletives I couldn't hear.

Almost immediately he spun the sign to "go", and I moved on again slowly along only half a lane of pavement.

Once past the roadwork, the memory connected to the picture hung tantalizingly just beyond my grasp. I was entering Suttons Bay now and had to make a left turn at the 45th Parallel Café onto Broadway Street. A car leisurely backing out onto the street from the post office parking lot forced me to stop. I got going again, turning onto Lincoln and began the climb out of the village and up toward Parish's house. After the entrance columns to the Suttons Heights subdivision came Erinbrook and the steep, curving stretch of road up the pine-covered hillside. I slid the shift forward into third gear and gunned the engine, and as I did, the memory appeared like turning a page in a book. I knew where I had seen that picture before - before Derek and I saw it at the Hunt Club!

I climbed around a sharp turn to find the afternoon sun directly in my eyes. That instant my windshield exploded! I was thrown back against the seat. My hands left the steering wheel and the car veered toward the side of the road. A loud whack slammed the windshield post next to my head and I heard the whine of a ricocheting bullet. Someone was shooting at me! Hell, I was shot! I grabbed the wheel and aimed the car toward the center of the road and jammed the gas pedal to the floor. I was covered with crumbled glass and my left shoulder burned deeply.

I managed to steer around another bend, while trying to stay low. There were no more shots. I was probably out of the line of fire.

Crazy! Parish must be fucking psychotic!

I accelerated ahead until I got to the crown of the hill where the pavement ended and the dirt road descended into the valley. I stopped for a moment to assess my injury. The front of my shirt was wet with blood. Was I bleeding to death? Blood was flowing freely, but not pumping. I told myself to be calm; remember my months in the ER! The wound was at the very top of my shoulder. I reached as far as I could over my left shoulder with my right hand expecting a large exit hole, but found none. I drew back and looked at my bloody hand. Above my hand, I caught movement in my rearview mirror and saw a figure carrying a rifle and wearing a khaki coat and hat come out of the woods, running toward the road. I jammed the shifter into first and pressed the gas pedal to the floor and shot down the hill swerving to avoid the bullet I expected. None came. He must not have had a clear shot. I had bent far forward intent on dodging a bullet and accidentally solved a problem; how to drive and keep pressure on the wound. My leaning forward suddenly had locked the seat belt and the wound was now directly below the strap. The pressure, however, caused me to cry out from a sharp pain in the area of my clavicle. I'd have to accept the pain in order to stop the bleeding. My breathing was fast from fear, but free. It was unlikely that the bullet penetrated the pleural cavity. I was out of danger—if the road didn't turn out to be the dead end Derek thought it might be.

To my profound relief, the road came out onto a highway. I recognized where I was, highway 204 across from Scott Hill. Suttons Bay's main street was a quarter of a mile away. I paused from my panicked flight for a moment before continuing on. At that moment, a totally bizarre impression hit me. The face of the rifle-toting person wearing the khaki coat had been . . . Audrey's.

24

It had to be an illusion – a trick of light – an apparition produced by an adrenalin-soaked brain, an apparition of a wished for face to substitute for a frightening reality. I'd think about it later. Right now I needed medical help. I knew a physician who had an urgent care clinic in the village. I also knew a surgeon, who, as a member of a group practice, worked a couple of afternoons a week in Suttons Bay— my ex-wife, Cora. I'd try the other guy first.

What the hell had just happened? I had to call the police. No, that could wait. First came medical treatment.

I managed to turn from highway 204 onto Suttons Bay's main street. The urgent care clinic was less than a mile away. Now, free from the terror of immediate death, the memory of where I had seen the group photo of the equestrian team stepped front and center. Its significance hit me and nearly paralyzed me. I eased the car to the curb in front of Martha's Café and shifted to neutral. Yes, I had seen the photograph on the hallway wall at Audrey's apartment! At the time, I hadn't recognized her in the photo, but its pattern - the guy with the silver cup standing in the middle, grandstand in the background - had left an impression. There was no doubt it was the same picture. Would Audrey have had it on her wall with all her other awards if she hadn't been in the group? It was the significance of her being in that picture that had me sitting helplessly at the curb. It meant Audrey had lied to me. I had asked her if she knew Marian's brother's name when Pat was about to make the drive to Petoskey. She'd said she didn't know it: she'd never heard it. She had to know Lester Parish's name—she was on the same team with him, for Christ's sake! Why had she lied? Did she have some connection with Parish and this whole embezzlement thing? No, it was too absurd. There had to be a simple explanation.

To be able to think logically was perhaps man's greatest asset. With me, however, logic was a stubborn master. It would never let me accept a perfectly usable and desperately desired rationalization for long before holding it up for logical review. Right now I wanted to put my confusion out of mind. Audrey could have no part in the shooting. I intended to marry her. But my mind stubbornly insisted that I had one fact; she'd lied, and one very strong impression; that of her face on the person carrying the gun. My logical mind became compliant suddenly and suggested a compromise. I could very easily run a simple test to clear up my absurd mental crisis. I'd call her. If she was home packing for our trip to Chicago, then she couldn't have been taking pot shots at me. She'd still have to explain the lie, but I was sure there was a simple explanation. Maybe she was jealous of Pat's helping me and hadn't wanted her to succeed with her mission.

I was still bleeding and needed to quickly get more definitive treatment than my seat belt provided, but I was also compelled to carrying out my test of logic. I dug my phone out of my pocket and rang Audrey's number.

"Hi Tom," she said, surprise in her voice. "I haven't finished packing yet."

"Hi. I'll explain everything when I see you later, but I just want you to know there will be a change in plans. Lestor Parish took a shot at me; in fact he got a little piece of me. It's not serious, but -"

"What? He shot you?"

I had to wait through her expression of disbelief before I could continue. As I listened, it crossed my mind that there was something odd about her speech. It was as if she were walking, more than a little out of breath.

My delay in responding caused her to say, "Tom, are you there?

210

Are you all right?"

"Yes, just a second . . . "

"Are you being honest about your injury not being serious? Where are you?"

"It's not serious, just a shoulder wound, but I'm on my way to Traverse City to the ER at Munson Hospital. When I'm patched up, I want to come to your place for some TLC. That OK?"

"Of course, but what do you mean he shot -"

"Sorry, sweetheart, but I've gotta go."

I hung up and called information and now got the number of Cora's clinic. When Zeus had gone too far in bedeviling some poor mortal, he tended to lean over backwards to give the guy a break. He did it now; Cora was working at the clinic that afternoon and came on the line. I told her about my condition, where I was going and what I wanted her to do for me. She didn't question me. She digested what I'd just told her for a brief moment and said, "Right."

I then slipped the gearshift into first and got back on the road for the short four block drive to Audrey's apartment.

The apartment's parking area had four cars in it. It came to me that I didn't know what car she drove. I'd seen her twice in a Lexus, but she'd said it was a loaner. Anyway, there was no Lexus in the lot. My plan was to get first aid from Cora and then go and ring Audrey's doorbell and see if she was packing as I hoped. It was essential for my test, however, if she had been the one with the gun, that I'd get to her place before she could drive down from Parish's place, so she couldn't claim she'd been home all along. I'd told her I was going to T.C. for treatment, so she'd think she'd easily have time to get back to her apartment before me – if it had in fact been her on the hill with the gun.

I desperately hoped I'd look back on my test maneuver as paranoia brought on by all that had emotionally happened to me: the double murder, my father's death, and having been shot and wounded. For sure, if it turned out I was wrong, I'd never say a word about this test of mine to Audrey.

Cora arrived a few minutes after I did. I got out of my car, holding onto the roof while I steadied myself. Dizziness and a dry mouth told me I'd lost more blood than I'd thought. The seat of my car was now as scarlet as the exterior paint. I waved to Cora to park her bulky Range Rover in the space next to my car where it would shield my small roadster from the view of any other car entering the parking area.

Cora got out and I told her to get my keys out of the ignition and open the trunk where she'd find my tennis bag. Inside were a clean shirt, a pair of warm up pants and a towel that I wanted her to use to cover her passenger seat, because of my bloody pants. She brushed the towel idea aside saying she'd need it elsewhere. Climbing inside her car, we looked at each other.

"Long time no see," I quipped.

She ignored my attempt at humor and went to work with scissors cutting off my shirt, and then kneeling on the seat, she examined me soberly, first the tear in my shoulder, and then my back for an exit wound. She listened to my lungs with a stethoscope. She cleaned the wound with alcohol sponges then put thick pads of sterile gauze over it and applied a wide adhesive tape over the pack and around my chest to maintain pressure on the pack.

She worked with rapid efficiency. Unerring, competent efficiency was one of the first things a person noticed about Cora. I had been amused watching people become aware of this trait when they'd first met her. Never a doubt what action was to follow, never a wasted move. I had been struck first—as was everyone—with how crackling smart she was, upstaging her fetching blond beauty. She seemed to be so unaware of these assets—her attention always being focused on other, to her, more interesting matters—that one questioned whether she ever bothered with a mirror.

She retrieved a sling appliance from her medical bag and with it immobilized my left arm. This immediately relieved much of the pain. Two shots followed: antibiotic and Demerol. Too late, I thought I should forgo the narcotic, since I'd need command of my wits for what I planned.

"How's your tetanus?"

"Up to date."

"You'll live. Looks like the bullet caught the acromial branch of the clavicular artery. It missed the clavicle, but the compression probably caused a linear fracture. You're lucky. The bleeding has stopped as long as you don't move around too much, but you've lost a fair amount of blood."

"I'd say about a pint."

"I'd say more. You should be in the hospital," she said as she began wiping the blood off my upper body with alcohol sponges and the towel from my tennis bag.

"Pull my tennis shirt on, please."

"It would be better to leave it off until I get you to our office where I can stitch this up."

"That will have to wait a while, there's something I have to do first."

Without further argument she pulled the shirt on over my trussed-up arm.

"There's a pair of warm-up pants in the bag; I need those too."

No argument this time. "OK, but it would be easier if you got out of the car."

"I don't want to be seen by a certain person who may be about to drive into the parking lot."

There followed a struggle like changing into a bathing suit in a car.

"Thanks. You wouldn't happen to have something to drink in that medical bag of yours?"

"Sorry, no. It's the loss of blood. Now tell me what this is all about."

I gave her an outline of what Derek and I had been up to. How coherent an outline I'm not sure given my physical state, but she nodded as I went along. Finally I told her why I'd wanted her to meet me like this.

"Shouldn't you call the sheriff instead of doing this?"

"Don't you see that I need proof?"

"Still, I -"

"Wait," I interrupted and ducked down as low as I could.

A silver Lexus coupe had entered the parking lot and parked near the back entrance of the building.

I started to get out of the car, but Cora grabbed my neck, forcing me to look at her. "Be careful."

I experienced a fleeting awareness of liking Cora's touch and concern, but I turned to the object of my plan. I got out of the car and quietly closed the door. Staying close to the back bumpers of the parked cars and bending low, I moved quickly now, forgetting my injury. From this low position I could only see the top of the entrance door swing open.

I sprinted forward as the door swung to close, catching it just before it engaged the catch. I slipped through the doorway and stood trying to catch my breath, trying to be quiet. I heard steps ascending the carpeted stairs to the second floor. I climbed part way up and stopped, again catching my breath and listening for the insertion of a key in a door lock.

Hearing the sound, I moved quickly the rest of the way up the stairs and along the hallway until I stood beside her. She looked around - shocked.

"Hi, beautiful," I said.

.

25

"Tom, you startled me. Oh, my God, I can't believe Lestor Parish shot you. I thought you said you were going to Traverse City to Munson Hospital. How could you get treated so quickly?"

"As in everything, it's who you know," I quipped. "Where were you just now? You were here at your apartment just a few minutes ago."

"Where was I?"

"That is the question."

"The moment you hung up, I went to the pharmacy to pick up a prescription. I thought there'd be plenty of time before you drove to the hospital and back."

Her quick reply surprised me. "A prescription for what?"

She gave her head a little shake, as if puzzled by my questions. "Come on in," she said entering her apartment.

Inside, she hung up her windbreaker and placed her purse on a table by the door and turned to me. "A prescription for Celebrex; I've got a mild tennis elbow. Why do you ask?"

I reached out and took a pine needle from her hair. "Is there a pine tree in the pharmacy?"

She looked baffled.

"Tom darling, you're not well." She put a cool hand on my forehead, feeling for a fever.

I had a problem here. The idea that had exploded in my mind like a firework, causing me to pull over to the curb was a mental image of Audrey with a rifle, and the bizarre idea that she had been the shooter. It had two roots, the realization that she'd lied to me about knowing Parish, and that impression of seeing her face. Plus, I had knowledge of her skill with a rifle—a biathlete no less.

The idea was crazy—an assault upon what I most wanted to believe, and one I strongly wanted to disprove. I'd called her and she'd said she was packing. I'd come to see if that was true. It wasn't! I'd caught her in another lie, a lie that supported the idea that she'd tried to shoot me.

But now she claimed she'd stepped out to get a prescription.

I became aware then that my thinking was a little wobbly-- the loss of blood and the Demerol. Wait a minute! If she'd picked up a prescription, it would be in her purse. I was afraid to challenge her to prove her claim by producing the drug. If she was telling the truth, I'd already done enough damage to our relationship. I needed a sneak peak into that purse.

"I'm incredibly thirsty – blood loss I think. Could you get me something, water, juice?"

"Of course." She pointed to a chair, saying, "Sit down before you fall down."

Over her shoulder she said, "My God, start at the beginning and tell me everything that happened."

The table where she'd laid the purse was in view from the kitchen where she now stood with her back to me. I picked the purse up and carried it farther into the living room. I couldn't open it with one hand and was forced to kneel down and put my knee on the bag to open the catch.

"Beer OK?" she called out.

"Yes, I'd love a beer." I managed to answer as I searched wildly, digging deep and turning the contents over as if I were mixing dough. No container containing Celebrex!

I became aware of her standing in the kitchen doorway, two glasses of beer in her hands.

"What the hell are you doing?" she gasped.

"No Celebrex," I challenged.

"No Celebrex? I don't understand." There was hurt and bewilderment in her eyes.

"You said you went to pick up a prescription, but it isn't in your purse."

She stared at me a moment. "Who ever treated you should have hospitalized you."

She set one glass down on the table and walked to where her windbreaker hung and reached into a pocket and brought out a small, paper bag. Out of this she withdrew a plastic vial used by pharmacies to dispense prescription drugs.

"See, Celebrex. Is this what you were looking for?" she asked.

I could see her wrestle with her feelings, anger on the one hand and sympathetic understanding on the other. I stood up and held out the purse, which she took from me.

She took a deep breath and let it out saying "Forgive me darling, I let my feelings get hurt, when I should have realized all this is a reaction to the double blow of your father's death and then this awful attack. It's OK. It's only natural to strike out at the world."

She held out a glass of beer and I took it eagerly and downed half the glass in one long swallow.

I met her eyes. "You lied to me, " I said. "I'm sure one of those pictures hanging in the hall there is of the U.S. Equestrian Team. You wouldn't have hung it unless you were in it. Lestor Parish is in that picture. He was the team captain. Therefore you must have known him, but you told me you didn't know his name."

She stood contemplating me as if trying to understand unnatural behavior.

I plunged ahead. "While I was sitting in your parking lot just now, I asked myself why you'd want to conceal the fact that you knew Parish. Were you involved in that scheme to defraud Harry Frey?"

She shook her head vigorously. "Stop. Stop a moment, Tom. I never told you I didn't know Les. Of course I know him. As you said, we were on the same team."

"But, I asked you specifically if you knew his name, and you said you didn't recall ever hearing Marian mentioned her brother's name."

"You must have misunderstood me. Tom, you're delusional from dehydration. Have you told Derek any of this?"

"No."

She took her cell phone out of her purse and asked, "What is Derek's number? I think we need him here."

"No, don't do that," I said. I was fast becoming sure I was making a complete ass of myself.

"OK, but you need that liquid," she said, pointing to the glass of beer in my hand.

I nodded and drained my glass. "I'm still thirsty, may I have some of yours?"

"I have the beginning of a cold. I'll get you another," she said.

She left me feeling confused. I thought I had caught her in a lie, but she had seamlessly turned it around into a matter of my misunderstanding. Could that be? I felt very tired, very tired.

She returned with another beer. "Take it easy, don't swallow it all at once."

I drank deeply nevertheless. Then I remembered something. "You were the one who claimed Harry was a compulsive liar, which he isn't. You told me that, so I wouldn't trust him when he said he was innocent. You wanted me to think he was guilty—you wanted everyone including the sheriff to continue to think so."

I'd stood up and shouted the last part. But why would she want everyone to think Harry was guilty? Did she kill Marian and Plante? No, no, that's impossible. I was talking to her on the phone at the time of the murders. I attempted to go back to the idea of her being the shooter on the hillside.

"Why did you . . . lie . . . about . . . what was it you told . . ."

"What?" She shook her head in apparent loss of patience with me. "You need more liquid."

She righted the glass, which was tipping in my hand and guided it to my lips. I drank the rest of the beer, but lost my balance and staggered a bit as I finished it.

"Here." She took the glass and supported me toward the couch.

I didn't feel well. I wanted to say something important, but I couldn't remember what it was. I had trouble bringing Audrey's face into sharp focus. She was smiling . . . not a friendly smile. I tried to get up, but couldn't. Someone was pushing me down. I lay in a long corridor. I could hear the other kids slamming their locker doors, - running - yelling. A teacher started shouting—telling everyone to stand still.

Laughing women. Laughing, talking together. A man said something and the laughter became flushed with sexual innuendo. Somehow I was aware of these subtleties but I could make no sense of it all. One voice was right above me speaking as a mother would speak to an infant while expecting no reply. My nose hurt –something in my nose, pulling. I made an effort to protest.

"He's waking up," the voice said. "Thomas! Thomas! Open your eyes. That's good. You've had a long sleep. Thomas!" The voice was friendly. I wanted to respond.

"Gumpt," I managed.

"You don't mean it! Tracy, he just said, 'gumpt' to me."

I knew I'd made a great joke. I just needed to go back to sleep.

Then, I awoke on my own. There were people around me going about their business. I was in a bed with side rails. A curtain hung around the bed. It was an emergency room . . . or a recovery room. There was a tube in my nose that bothered me. A figure approached rapidly.

Cora leaned her elbows on the side rails and looked down at me.

"Welcome to planet earth."

"Cora," I croaked.

"Everything's OK. You're in good condition." She poked at the dressing on my shoulder.

"What do you remember?" she asked.

I had the odd sensation of struggling to remember what remember meant. It meant something earlier - dialog from the first act poorly remembered at intermission. A name broke through.

"Audrey," I said with wonder.

"Audrey indeed! I know you used to take a sedative for trans-Atlantic flights, Tom, but she slipped enough zolpidem into your beer for a flight around the world."

I didn't know what beer Cora was talking about. I remember Audrey had a bottle of Celebrex.

"How did I get here?"

"When you left me and followed her into the apartment, I realized how stupid it was for me to have gone along with your "plan." Why I did is too complicated to go into, but I became afraid that what you were planning could only end badly, so I called Sheriff's Headquarters. I told the person who answered that you had been shot and you were in the act of confronting the person you thought had shot you. They came immediately, first a detective, who went straight in and broke down the door and right after him a deputy arrived."

"Where is she? Where is Audrey?"

"In custody." Cora laughed. "She was indignant at first – indignant that the cop had busted her door."

I thought of all this as best I could. "I don't remember any beer."

"Maybe you will eventually, maybe not, but she had laced a glass of beer with zolpidem. I'm surprised you didn't notice the beer had an odd taste. Maybe you didn't want to hurt your hostess's feelings."

I simply didn't remember. She could have been talking about another person. I wanted to drift back asleep. She saw this and squeezed my arm.

"Do you remember my telling you to be careful when you left my car?"

I did remember sitting in her car while she worked on me. I remembered her hand on my neck. "Yes, I remember."

"I said that because I care about you . . . very much."

26

Monday night, the day of my father's funeral was very dark and very still as if every animate creature was holding still to listen. Only occasional sounds disturbed the silence, a car horn, a jet climbing out of O'Hare, miles to the southwest. No stars, no moon. The blackness seemed to immediately absorb the light from the living room behind us before it reached the edge of the patio. The stillness was also in me, the deep dulling stillness that comes from exhaustion of body and mind. The others felt it too. Cora, who had asked to come with me for the funeral, sat pensively. Derek, mixing drinks from bottles brought outside from the den, moved carefully, as if not wanting to disturb anyone's thoughts. Donna and I stood looking out into the dark garden like ocean-going passengers at the rail.

A few dozen of his friends, including Henry and Victoria, and we four, had buried Thomas Christopher Morgan in the afternoon. All had returned to the house afterward for food and the ritual of moving from consolation for a loss to planning for tomorrow. I met all of his friends and talked with as many as I could. My left arm in a sling was, of course, inquired about first. I managed to dismiss it as an accident and redirect the focus onto themselves and their relationships with my father. Their stories were similar, best times of their lives at this place or that, or of a void that could never be filled. Several of the men spoke to me as if I were a young man who would now need help and guidance and offered their help if and whenever I should need it – in loco parentis.

When all except our group had departed, we'd strolled outside onto the grounds, Cora and Donna examining the beds of spring bulbs, Derek puffing on one of my father's cigars, and I lost in thought. Suddenly I was aware of being very tired, but also very hungry. I announced that my life depended upon eating the thickest, juiciest, most tender steak in all of Chicago and the others joined in, grateful for the change of pace.

Those two hours together at the restaurant became one of those occasions never to be reproduced. Derek, in an imperceptible way, made up with Cora. They had been friends at one time back in Detroit, but when the breakup came, Derek chose to remain loyal to me. Donna and Cora discovered a strong affinity. As for me, I basked in that bittersweet knowledge that life is short, and while someone dear has departed the scene, we were still to be counted among the living. That feeling merged with my great relief from the strain and worry of recent days. The pleasure we experienced in one another's company lifted each of us to that self-centered belief that all that was important in the world was happening at our table. At one point, however, this bacchanal of shared love was interrupted in my mind by the thought that we were dancing on my father's grave. But, just as quickly, as if he had smiled across the table at me, I felt he had joined the party.

We were drained when we got back to the house where we were staying the night. One by one we drifted out onto the dark patio.

Having supplied each of us with drinks, Derek said, "Tom has something I'm sure he wants to share with us."

Donna, standing next to me, joined in, "Yes, Audrey Shaw. Tell us about her, Tom."

Cora and Derek moved closer.

I had told Cora the background of all the events on the flight to Chicago, but once we'd landed, the subject had been ushered off stage, while the drama of the funeral took its place.

"It's been on my mind too," I said. "As you might imagine, every moment the funeral wasn't demanding my attention, my thoughts reflexively returned to puzzle over Audrey. What Derek is referring to is the conversation I had yesterday with Sheriff Davis."

"Yeah," Derek said. "Tom thought my life was lacking in suspense. He wanted me to re-experience a kid's Christmas Eve anxiety. He called me and said he'd had a long talk with Hoss and what he'd been told was incredible. But, he claimed he was too tired to do the story justice and would fill us in today."

"Sorry about that. So, apparently Hoss didn't brief you on the story, Donna?"

"I was away from headquarters all day, but I feel left out anyway."

"Maybe it's a man thing, Donna."

She made a fist and I shouted, "Don't hit me," pointing to my sling. "I'm a sick man."

Derek pulled the patio chairs together and we sat down.

"First off," I said, "I'm not sure how much of this Hoss wants to get around. He didn't tell me in so many words to keep it to myself—he must have known there was no way I wasn't going to share this with you, but his manner told me the information shouldn't go beyond the department. Perhaps he told me all of this, because he thought he owed it to Derek and me."

"Owed it to you?" Donna said.

"My hunch is that Hoss believed Harry's claim of innocence. The DA was happy with Harry's plan to plea guilty, and your department hadn't been able to come up with evidence to the contrary, so I think he subtly pointed me in the direction of looking for another killer. And, that looking almost got me killed."

I glanced at Cora and saw the doubt I expected.

"Anyway," I went on, "it goes like this. You all know why Pat Furst and I went to Petoskey and what we found there. After I came home I got to thinking there was something wrong about the position

225

of the bottle and the drinking glass on Lambert's desk. The glass was behind the bottle and that wasn't natural. I sent Sergeant McCulloch an e-mail pointing this out. It turns out he had already noticed the same thing and examined the fingerprints on the bottle. There was one very clear set of Lambert's prints. It looked like he only handled the bottle once. Impossible, because of the amount he'd drunk. McCulloch became suspicious that the suicide was a set up to cover murder. The obvious suspect was Lestor Parish, so McCulloch called Hoss Davis, since Parish lived in Leelanau County. Hoss suggested they double-team Parish, threatening him with arrest for murdering Lambert. They did that the evening I was shot. It turned out that Parish is one of those types who would squeal on his mother if it would spare him any pain at all. Embezzlement was one thing, but facing a murder charge was an entirely different matter. He crumpled and told McCulloch and Hoss more than they could have imagined. He told all he knew—about anything."

"As they used to say in the old "noirs," he sang like a canary." Derek said.

"Exactly. Anyway," I continued, "McCulloch had already initiated a review of Parish's phone records and by the time he and Hoss paid their call on Parish, he'd discovered that the night before Pat Furst drove up to Petoskey, Parish had made a call from his home phone to Lambert's home. Parish emphatically denied any part in Lambert's death, but when McCulloch said he knew Parish had made the call, the dam broke.

"He admitted making the call, but said Audrey Shaw had come to his house that evening and demanded that he make it."

"Audrey?" Derek gasped out.

"It turns out that they have known each other since they were on the U.S. Equestrian Team in 1999. Parish admitted to Hoss and McCulloch that he had embezzled the money from the Frey building project and had bought a parcel of land for his own development venture with the money, but he needed more money in order to get a construction loan. He'd heard from his sister, Harry's wife, that Audrey had moved to the area, in fact that she was now his sister's therapist. So he approached Audrey for a loan, telling her that while it was his own undertaking, Harry, whose success Audrey would have heard about from her patient, would be guiding him. Audrey was interested, but she wanted a part of the action, a partnership."

"So, Audrey was a partner in a building venture that had used embezzled money to buy its land," Donna summed up.

I nodded. "Parish freely admitted all this to the two cops. It was like, `See Mr. Sheriff, I'm coming clean, I admit to being a swindler, but I'm not a murderer.' He said Audrey was unaware of the fraud when she became a partner, but later began to get wise to it, but was taking the course of not asking questions while looking forward to her share of the profit. Later, when she heard from Marian Frey that Harry was claiming he'd been swindled, she confronted Parish and he admitted what he'd done. She told him she would forego any profit from the deal. She'd settle for getting her money back immediately and having any mention of her name removed from the records. Parish instructed Lambert, his friend and a party to the embezzlement, to begin doing what Audrey wanted. Lambert had barely started, when Derek and I decided Harry's truthfulness had to be checked out and I told Audrey that Pat Furst was going unannounced to Petoskey to confront Lambert.

"That's when Audrey drove to Parish's house and demanded that he call Lambert. My thinking is she wanted the record to show that the call originated at his house. When Lambert came on the line, Audrey took the phone from him and told Lambert of Pat's planned surprise visit. She told Lambert that the best way to foil the plan was to close the office the next day. Lambert agreed and that was the end of the call and Audrey left."

I paused and asked if everyone was with me.

"Sort of," "Cora said. "You've left me up in the air about this suicide being murder. You seem to be saying that Audrey got him to ingest both the Seconal and the whiskey."

"It's pure speculation. So far there's no proof. McColloch found no Petoskey pharmacy that had filled a prescription for Seconal for Lambert."

"Seconal is a controlled substance," Donna said. "Which means that a record is kept of every prescription written for it. The Petoskey police are checking to see if Audrey has written a script."

"The DEA, the Drug Enforcement Administration, doesn't approve of physicians writing barbiturate prescriptions for themselves," Derek said, "So I doubt that they'll find one that she'd written. If she had some Seconal - and I believe she did - it would be more probable that she'd had trouble sleeping on a vacation in some place like Mexico and bought some without difficulty at a local drugstore."

"There's another, although subtle, link between Audrey and Lambert," I said. "I called Pat Furst in Ann Arbor after I'd recovered from the overdose. She reminded me that Lambert's secretary gave her an appointment knowing she was an attorney, but not her intended business with Lambert. The usual sequence goes, 'I'd like to make an appointment with Mr. X.', and the secretary's response is 'May I tell Mr. X what you want to see him about?' This didn't happen, Pat speculated, because Audrey had already told the accountant why Pat was coming and told him to make an appointment with Pat for the next morning. Something else struck Pat as odd, although she didn't consider the full significance until later. When McCulloch was questioning the secretary there in Lambert's office, she told him her boss had instructed, 'If a Traverse City attorney calls, offer *her* an appointment at nine.' Only Audrey knew that a *woman* attorney from Traverse City was travelling

228

to Petoskey.

"My construction of what happened in Petoskey is this. After getting Lambert to close the office, Audrey must have driven to Petoskey telling him they were going to work on the books together and be ready for his meeting with Pat the following morning. Her plan, however, didn't really include a meeting between Lambert and Pat, because Lambert would be dead by then."

"But, wasn't murder an unrealistically extreme reaction to prevent the exposure of fraud? She could truthfully claim she hadn't knowingly been party to the scheme," Cora argued.

"You're right. The only reason I can think of—remember she was a legal partner—is if Pat reported finding evidence of embezzlement, it would become known that she, Audrey Shaw, was a partner in a company begun with stolen money. Even if she claimed ignorance of wrong doing, an unsavory residue would remain. Plus she had entered into what promised to be a lucrative venture by using information she'd learned from a patient – in psychiatric circles a no-no almost as forbidden as having sex with a patient. She'd no doubt be able to get past any criminal prosecution for the theft itself, but her name would be muddied and her national, professional ambitions would take a big hit."

"And," Derek stated emphatically, "She did have those ambitions!"

That was said with feeling. My friend clearly had his own opinion of Audrey, one he hadn't revealed to me before.

"Has Hoss questioned her?" Cora asked.

"Yes, " Donna interjected. "I heard that he had."

"Yes, and her story was part of what Hoss told me yesterday," I said. "He claimed Audrey denied everything. She never went to Parish's house the day he called Lambert. Knows nothing about Pat other than what I'd mentioned briefly on the phone. She'd never been to Petoskey in her life. She did loan Parish money; they were old acquaintances, but she never signed a partnership agreement. She knew of no fraud. In other words she claimed to be exactly what I would have told you she was, a person who was simply very helpful to her old friend Les.

"Here's another little wrinkle. I called her from the B&B where I was staying in Petoskey the night Lambert was killed. She said she had just returned from a committee meeting and a friend of ours, Sue Best, was there at her place having stopped by to borrow a book. I heard what I took to be their saying good night to each other. This, of course, extinguished any later thought I might have had about her being in Petoskey, until it occurred to me a little while ago that she could have answered my call on her cell phone, the only phone she uses, while being only a few blocks away in Lambert's office, faking all the parting conversation with Sue Best."

"I take it you haven't talked to Sue about this?" Derek said.

"No, I'll do it as soon as we get back." I thought about this for a moment. "Also, how likely is it that Sue, who lives in Traverse City, would have driven fifteen miles to Suttons Bay to borrow a book?" I laughed. "Duh!"

Everyone was silent, digesting the information I'd passed on.

"OK, next stunner," I announced, trying to keep emotion out of my voice. "Parish told the two sheriffs Audrey had had a hot sexual thing going with . . . Brian Plante."

"What?" Derek's exclamation was almost a scream.

Hearing this from Sheriff Davis had depressed me even more than thinking she'd tried to kill me. Talking about this without betraying how much this revelation had hurt was hard.

"Yes, Parish said he'd happened upon them in flagrante at the Hunt Club – in the tack room no less. She warned him to keep his mouth shut."

"She warned him?" said Cora. "What gave her leverage to

'warn' him?"

"Nothing that I know of - except her personality. Hoss said that after hearing Parish talk for a while, you recognized that Audrey was definitely the alpha partner. He said, 'Parish may have been captain of the riding team in the past, but she has him saddled today.'"

Donna laughed. "That's the Hoss we all know and love."

Cora wasn't aware of just how much this news of Audrey's affair with Plante affected me. Derek and Donna were, and in their body language I detected a withdrawal from this sensitive issue.

I went ahead while trying to be the neutral reporter. "Hoss said that Parish had no idea of how long they'd been involved. Then Hoss asked me, 'Doctor, since Marian Frey was in treatment with Audrey Shaw, what would be the likelihood for Marian to mention her affair with Plante in a treatment session?'

"I couldn't answer him right away, because I was so stunned by the implication. Audrey had told me on our first date that she knew Marian had become involved with Plante, but when Hoss asked me that question it occurred to me for the first time that Audrey had a strong motive for killing both of them, Marian because she had beat her out with her lover, and Plante because of his betrayal. I told the sheriff I knew that Marian had told Audrey."

"Did Hoss ask Audrey about this?" asked Donna.

"Yes. He checked each and every one of Parish's allegations with Audrey. Regarding his claim about her affair with Plante, Hoss said she shook her head in disbelief and said she hardly knew Plante, having only spoken to him once at the time they were introduced at the club. Hoss commented to me that her attitude implied it was obvious that Parish was inventing a tale to deflect his guilt. However, Hoss said she never accused Parish angrily or insisted on her opinion. Hoss said that was unusual in his experience with those who were guilty. Judged by his experience, she sounded and behaved more like an innocent

231

person who'd been falsely accused. At no point did she hesitate, or refuse to answer his questions, or demand to have her lawyer present. Hoss said he found this unusual for a sophisticated person who was familiar with legal representation. He speculated that she didn't want a lawyer there who'd interfere with her performance—the perfect, simple, straightforward and confidant testimony of a woman with nothing to hide."

"She's a piece of work," said Derek.

"Are you saying the sheriff believes her or not?" Cora asked.

"Belief would be characterizing his position too strongly," I answered. "He said Parish's story had 'the ring of truth.' It's more like Hoss is in awe of her sang-froid, her cool confidence in simply denying all incriminating action with a story that can't be disproved – so far. Although Hoss is inclined to believe Parish, at the moment it comes down to his word against hers."

I didn't say it, but I'd had from time to time during the day experienced a wave of doubt about Audrey's guilt on all scores. I'd think: She was very sympathetic and understanding, when I was accusing her of having shot me, not at all defensive—and she'd claimed to Hoss that she'd given me the drug, because she was afraid that in my delirium I'd hurt myself. My friends apparently didn't experience this same doubt, but then they didn't have the same reason to want to believe her.

"Oh, and another thing. I'd told Lieutenant Panetta when I was in the hospital about the plan I'd had to catch her returning from the hillside rather than being home as she pretended to be, and about how she'd brushed that aside by claiming to have been at a pharmacy, producing the bottle of pills from her coat pocket. Hoss questioned her about this. What do you think she said?"

"Who me? – What pharmacy?" Donna said.

"Exactly. According to her, she'd never said anything about a pharmacy. She'd just returned from the post office where she'd mailed back a Netflix envelope. Panetta did find an empty medicine container in her kitchen. It was for the zolpidem they pumped out of my stomach. She had picked up thirty pills from the pharmacy the day before—prescribed by another physician. She must have bluffed me by pulling that vial out of her jacket pocket and saying, 'Celebrex!' Apparently she managed to dissolve all thirty in my beer. But it proves nothing. She denied telling me she'd just come from the drugstore and never mentioned Celebrex. According to her, all of my nonsense about the pharmacy and Celebrex was a product of my delusional state, which in turn derived from my loss of blood.

"I know that there is little besides a motive to connect her to the double murder, but I'll bet Hoss asked her where she was at the time of the murders," Donna said.

"Yes, and she said she was home talking to me on the phone. Her alibi is nearly airtight. The police forensic unit fixed the time of death to be within half-an-hour of the time the post-mortem temperatures were taken. Harry Frey called me within a few minutes of discovering the bodies, and I hung up the phone after talking to Audrey at her apartment only a minute before he called me. You can figure the shots were fired within five minutes of my calling her."

"You said, 'nearly airtight', Tom," Cora said.

"If she'd had her car there at the Frey's house to drive to her apartment and dash inside, she might have gotten there in time to answer my phone call."

"Well, what about that?"

"She couldn't have done that. Harry told me he'd had to wait on M22 for a few minutes before South Shore Drive was opened and he was able to drive home. It had been closed for an annual 10K run. His house is off that road, which means no cars had been on the road for at least an hour or more, and he met no car on the drive to his house after the road was opened."

"Tom, you said you called her at her apartment, how do you know she was there? It's the cell phone thing again," Cora said.

I had no immediate answer. It was as if she'd asked, "How do you know the hospital gave your mother the right baby?" One doesn't know for sure; one has a strong assumption based on circumstance.

"I see what you mean," I said. "I'm not sure why, but I had a very strong impression she was at home."

The impression had something to do with what I'd just said, "drive to her apartment and dash inside."

"You seem lost in thought, Tom," Donna said.

"Oh, it's nothing. There was . . . but I can't remember now."

"She's in police custody, right?" Cora asked, moving along.

"She is," Donna answered. "She's being held as a suspect in an attempted homicide—Tom. It's tenuous, because an overdose of zolpidem is not usually lethal and as a physician it's fair to say she knew that. But I'm getting ahead of Tom's story."

The three looked at me.

"Ah yes. The next chapter in that story is Parish's rendition of the shooting on the hillside."

"Before you begin, Tom, could we go inside," Cora said. "I'm feeling chilly in this thin blouse." She crossed her arms over her chest with a shudder.

Victoria, hearing us come inside, came to the living room door. "Can I get anyone something from the kitchen?"

After hearing our negative answers, she said, "In that case, I'll be going to bed. Good night."

When she had gone, Donna said, "I was talking to her earlier. She has worked for your father twenty-four years. It will be a hard adjustment for her. What are your plans, Tom?"

"You mean where she's concerned?"

"Yes, and Henry Thorp."

"I haven't any plans. It has never entered my mind until today that I'd need to have any. It will have to be status quo, I guess, until I have time to discuss it with them."

"It's a shame," she said. "This place is their home."

I had nothing to add. I'd have to talk to them.

Derek made his rounds with the drinks. "We're waiting to hear Parish's version, my friend."

"Yes, well, he said he'd called Audrey and told her about Derek's and my visit. He said her voice became very determined and tough. She said he needed to call me and tell me he'd changed his mind and was ready to cut a deal, and would meet me at his place at five o'clock. He was to insist we not talk about the details on the phone. 'Morgan must drive to your house!' she'd demanded.

"Audrey arrived at his house fifteen minutes later. She told him that both copies of the partnership agreement had to be destroyed. She placed her copy on the desk in his den and sent him off to get his copy from a safe in his bedroom. When he returned, she wasn't there. He wandered outside, looking for her. He went over to the building site of his new home, thinking she might have gone there to view the progress. While there, he heard two shots and then saw her running up his driveway carrying a rifle that looked like one of his and wearing a coat and hat that she hadn't had on when she'd first come there. He thought it could have been his hunting jacket as well. He didn't like the looks of things, so he hid behind some rolls of insulation. He was terrified when, after looking for him in the house, she came toward the new building still carrying the gun. She was very near to him when she got a call on her cell phone. That had to be my call to her as I sat wounded in my car in front of Martha's Cafe. She immediately broke off the search for Parish, returned to his house where she returned the gun to the rack and left, taking his copy of the partnership agreement with her. Parish didn't know, of course, that her hurry was to get back to her apartment before I did."

Cora looked bothered. "Tom, what doesn't ring true for me again is the extreme action you're claiming she took just because she was afraid she'd be found out for having used information she'd heard from her patient to make an investment." She was shaking her head.

"I understand," I said. "Even though I now see her as needing to kill Lambert in order to preserve her reputation, murdering me for the same reason is nuts. She would have to have considered the possibility that I'd told others. But she may have had another motive for killing me. She knew that Harry was going to plead guilty by reason of temporary insanity. If nothing rocked the boat, no one else would be considered as the killer. Now if she was the real killer, my trying to prove that Harry was innocent was something she'd desperately want to stop."

"Hmm, " Cora allowed reluctantly.

"I know how you feel. One has to keep in mind that she was a very competent competitor. She'd brazenly gone for the first prize time and time again in sports and I imagine in her life in general. She'd always won."

"Now, let me speculate on how Audrey had planned for events to go. She was going to shoot me, return to Parish's house and shoot him in the head with his rifle – his thumbprint on the trigger. It was to look like a murder/suicide. He'd murdered me in a wild attempt to stop me from revealing his embezzlement of Harry's money, and then, realizing Derek also knew and had probably already told others, he gave up and shot himself. Her plan suffered a setback when she couldn't find Parish and I also wouldn't cooperate by being properly shot—her failure to kill me, given her proven skill with a scope-equipped rifle, really puzzles me. Puzzles me perhaps more than anything else. Anyway, she must have still thought she could make it work by first putting the gun, coat and hat back in his house – fingerprints wiped clean - then killing me in her apartment, and later doubling back to have another go at killing Parish."

"Not quite," Derek laughed. "She'd need him to help bury you first."

"Why the hell not?' Cora said, laughing with him.

"So, what did Hoss tell you Audrey said about that afternoon?" Donna asked.

"Exactly what you'd expect. She told him she was home packing to fly to Chicago with me, when she got this frightening call from me, saying I'd been shot and was on the way to T.C. for emergency repair and would then come to her place afterward. Knowing my drive from Suttons Bay to T.C. and back plus ER treatment was a two-hour undertaking at a minimum, she went to the post office to mail back a Netflix envelope. When she returned to her apartment, I came up beside her shouting, "Where have you been?" I was out of control she claimed. She told me about going to the post office, but I paid no attention. She said she then took off her jacket and began to hang it up, when she discovered a bottle of sleeping medication, zolpidem, she'd picked up at the pharmacy the day before. She transferred the bottle to the pocket of her jeans to put it later with her toiletries for the trip to Chicago. I was so out of control, she said, that she decided I needed immediate sedation for my own safety, so when I asked for something to drink, she dissolved a couple of the sedatives in a glass of beer. I continued to scream and act wildly, so she gave me more. The moment I became subdued, she intended to call the paramedics. She attributed my behavior to loss of blood and the news of my father's death. She, of course, was deeply sorry if she miscalculated the amount of sedative she'd given me."

"Three cheers for improvisation," Derek said.

"It's very canny improvisation. There's not a single element that can be disproved," I said soberly.

"If she did the shooting," Cora objected, "there must be some evidence of her being at Parish's house. As I understand it, the place is a building site. That means loose dirt where tires leave tracks, and what about gun powder residue from firing the rifle?"

"Good questions. I don't know about the residue. Sheriff Davis didn't say anything about that when I talked to him, but I have an answer about the tire tracks."

"I know about the residue," Donna said. "It wasn't considered until after Hoss questioned Parish. The issue on the front burner when Audrey was booked was your condition, Tom, and what the circumstances were when the zolpidem was administered. It was on the strength of Cora's description of you before Audrey slipped you the "mickey" that led Hoss to hold her on suspicion to commit murder. The first thing she requested of the deputy upon being jailed was a long, hot shower. We are a friendly, obliging department, so she got what she'd asked for. Whether she had any traces of residue before the shower, they were long gone when we got around to test her the next day. There was residue on Parish's hunting jacket and hat, but he admitted to some target practice just a few days before, so the residue proves nothing."

"Tom, you said you had information about tire tracks," Cora said.

"That takes us back to Audrey's version of the afternoon. After she got the call from me asking her to go to Chicago for the funeral, she got her carry-on bag from her closet and began to make selections of the clothes she would take. Parish then called asking her to return a pasta machine she'd borrowed from him—that would be the call, according to Parish that he made telling her that Derek and I had been to his house. She told Hoss she'd decided to attend to the return of the pasta machine right away and then return to her apartment to continue packing. She drove to Parish's place, but he didn't come to the door. She figured the maid had left for the day, and he was probably at the construction site. Since she didn't have time to go there and didn't really want to spend time talking, and finding the front door open, she went in and left the machine on the counter in his kitchen and left.

"Before you ask, I'll confirm that her tire tracks were in front of his house, her open, partially filled suitcase was on her bed and the pasta machine was in his kitchen when the sheriff went there to check out her story."

An incredulous Derek gasped, "You mean she went off to Parish's house on her mission to kill both you and him carrying a pasta machine?"

"Nothing like being thorough," Donna quipped.

"Yes," I said, "She knew her tires would leave tracks and she'd provided herself with an answer. But that was only for backup. Keep in mind that although she'd taken some precaution relating to gunpowder residue – coat, hat and probably gloves – she wouldn't think that precaution was really necessary; I'd be dead and Parish, a suicide, would be accepted as my killer."

The others were silent as, I'm sure, they reviewed Audrey's story for flaws.

"Well," I said with a tone that announced the tale was at an end, "I think I've summed it up the best I can. Audrey's story as Hoss related it to me is all we'll hear from her camp from now on. The only difference, it will now be argued in the confident bass-baritone of her lawyer, Roscoe MacGruder. We all remember him from the TV interviews when he defended the Virginia Governor's daughter. Hearing his telling of Audrey's story, the listener will swear that it's the only sensible explanation of events, entirely rational, one that any normal adult will recognize as solid fact. It will come our way modulated on his velvet inflections, accompanied with his patented intimacy, which winks and suggests to a jury member, 'You and I, friend, know a bull's-eye from bullshit.'"

Cora said laughing, "In a way, I prefer her story. It's much less loony than the notion she'd try to cover her participation in a scam with murder, and further murdering her lover and her patient, when she'd discovered she was being sexually upstaged. I don't know her, but from the bit I've picked up, she sounds like a much more intelligent and calculatingly goal-directed person than this impulsive behavior would imply."

There was silence in the room for perhaps half a minute. I knew I couldn't argue with her feelings. Then Derek spoke.

"I think I can convince you that she really wasn't impulsive, but first one has to understand the Audrey Shaw psyche."

Derek's statement surprised me. Just minutes ago he'd emphatically declared that Audrey was ambitious. It was certain that my friend had feelings about her that he hadn't shared with me.

He looked my way, as if he'd read my mind. The look contained apology and seemed to say, "I hope at this time it's OK for me to speak my mind."

He began, "From the moment of her first arriving here, I witnessed a heightened reaction among those who met her, both male and female – though of a different sort for each sex. All the men instantly fell in love and at the same time were overawed. Our friend, Tom, was one of the few to get the courage to ask her out." He smiled at me. "And even he was slow about it."

Derek continued, "I sensed that my reaction to her stood apart from that of most of my friends. I was like one of Ulysses's sailors, my ears plugged with wax, immune to the siren's song. In other words, I was very happily married.

"The male side was easy enough for me to understand. The reaction of the women was more diverse, but on the whole positive. The common reaction one might expect when such a devastating femme fatale drops anchor in a woman's territorial waters is latent hostility. Audrey, however, had a way of enlisting women on her side, as if she were their representative in a world still favoring men. At the same time, she saw to it that men never experienced her as a soldier in the feminist cause. A very neat trick!

"Many in the psychiatric field would label her a narcissistic personality, a person whose every thought makes his or her own interest the sole motive for action. I don't think that describes Audrey and I don't believe most men, Tom included, would have been attracted if that were the case."

His eyes flicked in Cora's direction, reading her reaction. "I think Audrey's actions represent the extreme steps a woman will take to please the man she loves."

Both women looked at me.

"No, old Tom here wasn't that guy. He could never have been. That position had been occupied long ago. Audrey's heart belonged to Daddy. I found her to be a fascinating study and collected my data bits and pieces at a time. An unwitting and substantial source was Tom. I believe Audrey Shaw represents a simple case of, to use an unfashionable term, the unresolved negative Oedipus or Electra complex – run amok. Everything she did, every accomplishment, every accolade was to be laid at the feet of her idealized, deceased father."

For sure this subject absorbed Derek. Although he proclaimed his immunity from her charms, his interest in her was loaded.

He went on. "She's identified with the values of a dedicated, career army officer – analyze the situation, define your options, choose a course of action and act! She constantly had her eye on the high ground to take in the name of her father, while defeating every other rival along the way. There were intermediate hills on which to plant her flag, but the ultimate peak was to become recognized as the leader in her field.

"Her goal was to be recognized as leader, not to be the best physician and therapist she could be. A personal ethical standard for doing the best for each of her patients never signified. It would have been a sidetrack, taking time and energy away from the objective. This permitted her, as Tom just told us, to use what she'd learned in her sessions with Marian Frey to make a quick buck in Parish's deal. After all, money was needed for the look of success and that appearance was essential to her purpose. She needed money without devoting time to its making. Such time was needed for politics. The time she spent "collaborating" with Laslo Bach on his book was pure and simply a political move. Her personal dynamics are simple, but very energetically driven."

Derek smiled mockingly at his dissertation. "An instant portrait by that wizard of caricature, Professor Derek Marsh."

Donna said in comic exaggerated adoration, "That's my man."

"So, if I understand your argument, " Cora said, "her behavior was not impulsive, but instead good, rapid-acting, military damage control."

"Exactly."

"I can spot one situation in which she didn't act with deliberate wisdom," Cora said. "Her getting involved with Brian Plante. How do you explain that lapse, Professor?"

"Well, he did have an heroic image similar to her father's, but I'd never try to explain the chemistry of sexual attraction. It will be the very last thing science will unravel. The discovery of the fate of the universe easily comes before that. BUT, can you imagine the fury when her huge ego was wounded. To be put aside in favor of her own patient for God's sake! As I said, I'm daunted by the puzzle of why a particular person can arouse strong sexual attraction in another, but I have no problem with understanding her need to salve the double wound she'd suffered by killing them both. And the detail of how she shot Plante originates from the same primal source as Harry Frey's fantasy of how he would kill Plante. Her emotional reaction was explosive, but the execution of her plan was in her usual carefully thought out style. I can't explain how she got to and from the Frey's house, but I'm certain she was there and did the deed."

We sat silently, thinking about Derek's words.

He got up abruptly and announced it was not only past his bedtime, but was fast approaching his getting up time. A gross exaggeration, but a comfortable way to exit the discussion of Audrey Shaw. We broke up with hugs and kisses, going our separate ways to rooms Victoria had prepared. Cora's kiss told me there could be more to the evening if I desired it. I did.

27

I got back to my house at eleven Tuesday morning. I had canceled my morning appointments since we were spending the night in Chicago. For a while there, I had felt tranquil thinking Harry Frey's and my worries were over. That is, until I reminded myself that Audrey was only being held on suspicion of attempted murder - filling me with sleeping medication. She had not been charged with the murder of Marian and Plante - there was no evidence. The same went for Lloyd Lambert's murder. Harry was still in jail pending his trial. So all my potential problems were ripening nicely. A tight feeling in my chest let me know just how non-tranquil I was.

I parked in back of my building and opened the door to the back stairwell. A doorway there communicates with the rear of Tony's wine warehouse. The door was open and immediately, the doorway was filled with Tony himself.

"Tom, I left the door open so's I could hear you come in. Sorry about your old man. Com'n in, Primo Panetta is here pickin' up some stuff. Say, how's your shoulder?"

"It's coming along; thanks for asking."

A bottle of red wine stood open on Tony's office desk. He got a glass out of a cupboard, filled it and handed it to me.

Tony raised his glass. "To your father, Doc."

We drank. I was touched.

"Primo's been tellin' me the details of this thing with your girlfriend. It's outta sight. And after you'd given her that great Alsatian Riesling."

I laughed at his priorities. "She never had any, Tony. She's a vodka drinker."

"Explains a lot. But no kiddin', she was your woman, so how could she try to kill ya?"

"It's simple. She was never 'my woman.' I can see now she only pretended to be close after the murders. I have a friend whose wife is a sheriff's deputy. I realize looking back that Audrey had wanted to stay close to hear any news of the investigation. I couldn't see the truth at the time."

"Yeah, but . . . "

"Oh there were signs, if I'd let myself see. For instance there was a time I asked her to be a character witness for me. She sidestepped. She said I'd have no trouble finding plenty of people who'd vouch for me. She didn't say right out that she'd be there for me. Also, she never allowed herself to be seen with me in public after the murders. She also urged me to tell you, Lieutenant, the details of Harry Frey's threat. I was to be the incompetent psychiatrist whose bad judgment led to the death of two people. She was happy, of course, that Harry was arrested, but the negative attention I was getting came as a bonus." I smiled to myself looking back and said, "I didn't realize it until this moment, but at our first date she encouraged me to be on a professional committee with her, but after the murders, she never mentioned it again."

Tony had been watching my face, nodding. "Primo tells me she's one cool babe. He thinks they got zero chance gettin' a conviction."

I looked at the lieutenant.

"Thing is Hoss has got to charge her or let her go. The attempted murder charge is weak. We all know she's guilty, but her claim of error is hard to refute and besides no doctor would choose the drug she gave you to kill someone."

"That's right," I said. "I think her goal was to kill me, but the drug, zolpidem, was only a way to knock me out. Suffication most probably would have followed."

Panetta nodded. "Anyway, her hot shot lawyer will probably get her freed today. Hoss would like to charge her with the murder of the two lovers. She had as good a motive as Harry Frey and a character to go along with the motive. Trouble is this MacGruder would have a jury falling outa the jury box with laughter at the evidence we've got. The prosecutor is afraid that if she's charged with murder without adequate evidence to get by the arraignment, MacGruder will sue for false arrest and the county ends up with no funds to cover his paycheck. "

I couldn't help laughing, even though it was gallows humor for me.

"We haven't made a helluva lot of progress," he continued. "We got three issues: the attempted murder, the double murder, and the murder of the accountant. The Petoskey police have been looking over the books from the Frey/Parish Petoskey deal and so far they've not found her name in the books once. The embezzlement that Frey claimed, however, looks to be right, but indications are that it was entirely the accountant's doing. So I'd say she put in a successful session of midnight book cooking.

"Where the double murder is concerned, phone records show that immediately after her therapy session with Marian Frey on the day before the murders, the Shaw dame called and cancelled her office appointments for the next day. We figure the Frey woman told her in that session that she was meeting Plante at the Frey house the next day and Shaw was clearing the deck for action. Again, so what? She'll claim she thought she was coming down with a bug and suspected she wouldn't feel well the next morning.

"Also we found the partnership agreements she'd signed with this Parish guy in her car's glove box in an envelope with the car's warranty papers. When Hoss first questioned her she'd said there was no such agreement. So he confronted her with the evidence and she said –"

"Wait don't tell me, let me guess," I said. "Hoss must have misheard her."

"Yeah, she never said there was no partnership, only that she hadn't taken the papers from Parish's house, because they'd been in her glove box all along, ever since they were first signed. So she's retrenching, giving a bit of ground, willing to risk the fallout over embezzlement - backed by her knowledge that the books now make it look like the dead accountant - who can't defend himself - was solely responsible."

Panetta's frustration was palpable. He drained his glass. "I'd give my *coglioni* for one scrap of hard evidence that places that broad at the double murder scene."

I went upstairs and put my overnight bag on the bed. I felt bad. I owed Panetta. He'd come barging through Audrey's door and helped save my life. He had struck to the heart of the matter—phone calls, partnership papers didn't mean a thing— he needed to place her at the scene. I stood in my kitchen staring out the window. I was remembering "the scene" as described by Harry when I first got to his house. He'd said he'd heard a noise in the direction of his kitchen and had thought Marian was there. He'd gone there but didn't find her. It was then that he'd first become aware of the gunpowder odor.

Wait! "Scrap!" That's what Panetta had said, "one scrap of evidence." Harry said he'd bent over to pick up "scraps of paper" from the floor. That's when he smelled the gunpowder!

I flew to the back stair well and raced down the stairs and into Tony's office. They were both startled to see me come charging at them.

"You still have Harry's personal property, the stuff he had with him when he was arrested?" I barked.

"Well, yeah. You mean his watch and wallet, that kind of thing?" Panetta answered

"And whatever may have been in his pockets."

"Yeah, sure."

"Have you looked at it?"

"Not myself, but I was told there was nothing to do with the murder."

"Nothing to do with the murder?" I asked.

"I took it to mean nothing incriminating," He shrugged, not understanding my puzzled look.

"Harry Frey told me he'd gone to his kitchen thinking he'd heard his wife there. She wasn't there, but he saw scraps of paper on the floor and he bent down to pick them up, noting that one was a grocery receipt. Being nearer the floor, where the odor was strongest, he recognized the smell of burnt gunpowder and began following it to his bedroom. Don't you see? His mind was on the smell and not on the paper scraps he'd picked up. Isn't it possible that he stuffed something small like a grocery receipt into his pocket, rather than taking the trouble to throw it in the waste basket?"

"A grocery receipt?" Now it was Panetta who was puzzled.

"I think he said one was a grocery receipt, but it's the other piece of paper I'm talking about. Might it have been Audrey that Harry had heard in the kitchen - on her way out the back door?"

"You mean she could have dropped a piece of paper?" His voice said he thought my reasoning was pretty thin.

I shrugged a "worth a shot, what else have we got?"

"What the hell. I'll check it out Doc."

I went to my office and my afternoon appointments wondering if Harry had, as I speculated, put the two pieces of paper in his pocket. I'd asked Panetta to call me, but I hadn't thought to specify my office number. Maybe he called my home number.

Before I left the office, I called Sue Best and received the answer I now expected; she had not gone to Audrey's place after the Library Committee meeting. In fact she had chaired the meeting, because Audrey had called asking her to, saying she didn't feel well. So, Audrey had lied. She'd faked those parting words with Sue I'd heard on the phone. Why lie if she hadn't been covering up the fact that she was sitting in Lloyd Lambert's office, assisting him on his trip to see his maker?

I climbed the stairs to my loft and walked into the kitchen. Kato was standing by the answering machine looking up at the blinking light with a worried expression as if it meant trouble for both of us.

Panetta's excited voice said, "Doc, you hit a home run. I'm happy to be able to say I wasn't the one to go over what Frey had in his pockets when he was booked. There was the grocery receipt you'd mentioned, but there was also a gift from heaven. It was the bottom part—the receipt—that's torn off a registration form for the 10K run that was held in Suttons Bay the day of the murders. It's dated that day. Guess who filled it out? She must have figured that being one of the runners was a good way to get to and away from the Frey house without attracting attention. Somehow she managed to drop the receipt in Frey's kitchen. Anyway, the only way it could have gotten there is if she carried it in. We got her, Doc!"

I hung up in a daze. So, it really was true. My bizarre idea that Audrey had shot at me had come full circle to include the murders. No longer was this speculation; it now had a concrete base. I could picture her running – probably pacing herself near the rear, where she wouldn't be noticed. At the Frey driveway, she'd stop to tie her shoe, waiting for the right moment when she could run unnoticed to the house. The few runners who might have been within sight would be so involved with their own laboring lungs and burning muscles they'd not notice her. Labored breathing brought a memory of Audrey answering the phone that day, seemingly out of breath. I'd commented and she'd told me she'd been on her treadmill.

That was it! That's what I was trying to remember that made

me so sure she was at her apartment. But, wait a minute . . . There'd been no treadmill! I'd seen and practically cataloged everything in her place the morning after I'd slept there. I'd felt something was missing. She'd been out of breath, because she'd just run 10K and committed a double murder. Then my brain was illuminated with another thought. It was my phone call to her as she was passing through the kitchen to the back door of the Frey house that had caused her to reach into a pocket - probably a warm up jacket pocket, it was cold that day - to take out her phone and by accident pull out and drop the registration receipt.

The receipt was hard evidence. Everything else the prosecutor had to work with had been putty-soft, easily wiped aside by MacGruder using Audrey's denials—she didn't say this and she didn't go there. Panetta had crowed that we had her. If it was so, it hadn't come about because of our brilliance. She had outwitted us all along the way. The fatal flaw in her plan lay in shoving the receipt into the same pocket as her cell phone.

28

In the first two therapy sessions after Harry Frey was released from jail, he talked mostly about his feelings for Marian, of both love and betrayal.

Near the end of the third session, he said, "I guess I never told you about the nightmares I had as a kid. But then I'd forgotten about them until they came back when I was in jail. Every night, every fucking night. The last couple of nights I tried to stay awake just so I wouldn't have one."

"No, you never told me. What were they like?"

"It starts out that I'm outdoors someplace. It's dark and cold. There seems to be something I'm supposed to do, but I don't know what it is and I can't find the person who could tell me, and there's a time limit—I've got to find out quickly or it will be too late. I wake up with my heart racing."

Even the telling of this brief fragment had caused him to breathe hard.

"Always the same dream?"

"Exactly, every night . . . or it seemed like every night for a good long time when I was a kid."

"About how old do you think you were?"

"Around the time we moved. I was twelve."

I already knew much about that time period in his life from our previous sessions. His father's real estate business had failed, forcing the sale of their home and a move from a middle-class Lincoln Park neighborhood to a flat in Chicago's Pilsen area, a tough, dirty place as Harry remembered it.

His father, in Harry's memory of that time, was a bitter, angry man, who was quick to find fault with his wife and three children—especially Harry, the oldest. The notion that he was at fault was already well established at the time his father's business failed, so to Harry it followed naturally that in some way he was at fault for that too. Harry's mother became depressed after the move to Pilsen and apparently never recovered. Harry had added this to the list of his crimes.

Harry hated his father and dreamed of defeating him, destroying him even.

"What comes to mind about that time?" I asked.

"My Mom and Dad were always fighting after we moved."

"About what?"

'Well, you see my old man had always wanted to be an engineer, but he couldn't finish school, because my Mom got pregnant with me. He never got over being mad about that."

Shades of my own father's story, I thought. I wonder – yes, I'm sure I also thought he would have become an engineer if I hadn't been born. That had never come up in just that way in my own analysis. I preferred to focus on my anger at having been abandoned by his death.

"In other words," I said, "your being born caused all of the trouble."

"Yeah, putting it that way – yeah. But I didn't know what I could do to change things."

"Sounds like your dream."

He looked puzzled for a moment. "Oh yeah, in the dream, I didn't know what I was supposed to do." He was silent again, this time for a longer interval. "I felt bad and wanted to make it right by finding some way to change things--make my mother happy--my father too."

"When you were in jail, what was it you had done that was similar to ruining your father's life?"

"What I had done? In jail? Hell, I hadn't done anything."

"The nightmare you were having there says otherwise. When you were twelve you thought you had been the cause of your father's failure and unhappiness. What could be the parallel when you were in jail?"

He appeared to mull my question over and threw in as in passing, "I sure caused you a lot of trouble . . . I'll always be sorry for that."

"In what way did you cause me trouble?"

His tone said it was obvious. "Well, there were all those accusations that you had been wrong not to warn - Hell! You would have had to warn Marian that Dr. Shaw was going to kill her!" He laughed out loud. "And you sure as hell didn't know that."

"So what did you do to cause me trouble?"

"Uh . . . Nothing really, I guess. But my lawyer didn't help your situation any. I could have refused to go along with him."

"And almost certainly get a life sentence in the process. Could you really have refused to go along with his plan? Could you any more than you could have refused to be born? Were you really at fault in either case?"

He was silent for a full minute before muttering, "I'll be damned."

I told him our time was up for the day. It had been a productive session. The therapy didn't seem to have been damaged by all that had happened.

Near the end of the session, I'd heard the mailman open the outer door. When Harry left I went out to the waiting room and retrieved the mail. Walking back into my office I shuffled through the usual bills and promotions, and then came to a large manila envelope and two envelopes with the logo and return address of the Grand Traverse County Medical Society. I tore open the manila envelope. Inside was a copy of the magazine, *The Bay and Beyond*. On the cover was a Stickup with a hand-written note, "Dear Dr. Morgan, May I draw your attention to page twelve." It was signed, "Prudie."

Page twelve began a section called, "Living Up Here." The first item read, "Recently one of our fine physicians, Dr. Thomas Morgan, was put through hell, because many people jumped to conclusions without possessing the facts. It's a failing to which many of us (yours truly included) tend to succumb. Now, he is due many apologies. We offer a *Bay and Beyond* toast to Dr. Morgan, who stuck by what he thought to be best for his patient."

I felt uncomfortable reading this. Even though she'd said good things - perhaps too good - I'd already had more than enough notoriety.

One of the Medical Society envelopes bore the inscription, Office of the President. I opened it next.

"Dear Tom,

It has come to my attention that you were made to appear before the Ethics Committee to explain your action in a recent tragic event. The Committee acted on its own in this regard, and, in my opinion, improperly. I have instructed the Chairman, Dr. Gordon Pheney to extend an apology to you.

Assuring you that your membership in the Society has always been valued by its members and by me personally, I am.

Yours truly,

John"

I looked at the other envelope. Did I want to witness old Gorgon eating humble pie? I decided not and threw it in the wastebasket.

I stood at my desk and looked at the chair Harry Frey had been sitting in and remembered how the unforgettable events of the past days had begun with Harry's threatening words reverberating in the room. So much had happened since then: the excitement of new love then a confrontation with grizzly death, the surprising discovery of my father and his loss, meeting Pat and making a good friend, my near death, then numbing disillusionment as Audrey's character unfolded, the like of which I'd never known existed. Finally there was Cora and the promise of a new beginning.

Although Audrey would probably never be tried for the Petoskey murder, the case against her for the double murder had gathered solid strength with the discovery of the 10K receipt. Roscoe MacGruder, who'd planned to demand the dismissal of the case for lack of evidence, would now have to work for his fee.

I had to get on home to straighten up the place, because Cora was coming over. This morning I'd told Tony Salpino about the date and he immediately went back into his stacks and returned with a bottle of Chateau d'Yquem. He handed it to me as if he were handling the Holy Grail.

"Doc, I gotta feeling *this* is the night we wanna make our best impression. This stuff is guaranteed!"

I left my office and locked the door anticipating the night ahead.

Epilogue

After three days of deliberation, a jury found Audrey guilty on two counts of first-degree murder. She was given two life sentences. Roscoe MacGruder appealed, of course, but lost. Just four days later, I received a short, printed and unsigned letter bearing the postmark of the Women's Huron Valley Correctional Facility.

"The sun reflecting off the windshield blinded me."